THE CLASSIC CAR KILLER

The members of the New California Smart Set love to dress in the fashions of the 1920s and dance to the music of that bygone era. They even bring out a magnificent vintage limousine for display at their annual gala — which is promptly stolen. Insurance investigator Hobart Lindsey is called upon to unravel an intricate puzzle that soon leads to brutal murder and an attempt on his own life. Aided by his streetwise police officer girlfriend Marvia Plum, the unlikely partners are off on another hazardous adventure!

RICHARD A. LUPOFF

THE CLASSIC CAR KILLER

Complete and Unabridged

LINFORD
Leicester

First published in Great Britain

First Linford Edition
published 2016

A catalogue record for this book is available
from the British Library.

ISBN 978–1–4448–2772–9

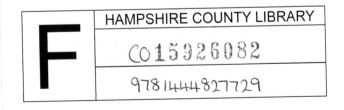

This book is printed on acid-free paper

1

Somebody had gone to a lot of trouble and money to colorize *Casablanca*. But Hobart Lindsey's mother insisted on watching it with the TV controls set to turn everything back into shades of gray.

Lindsey had sat through the picture many, many times. He recognized the greatness of the film, but it was Mother who insisted on watching it every time they showed it on cable, and if it didn't turn up for a few weeks she would make him rent it on tape for her.

Mother was happier living in the past; she was better able to handle her widowhood that way. She thought that Dwight Eisenhower was just starting his presidency and Josef Stalin was menacing the free world and that her husband — Lindsey's father — was alive and was serving on the destroyer *Lewiston* off the coast of North Korea and was going to come back to her someday.

The telephone's insistent ringing brought Lindsey back into the present. He left his mother sitting on the sofa and hurried to answer it.

The voice on the line was unpleasantly familiar. 'Lindsey, I'm glad you're home. You'd better hustle down to Oakland and handle this. Now!'

Lindsey moaned inwardly. Harden at Regional. His phoning Lindsey at home on a Saturday night was unprecedented.

'What happened in Oakland, Mr. Harden?'

'You'd know if you put in a few more hours, Lindsey. I don't suppose you've checked the incoming claims tape lately, have you?'

'I check it every morning, Mr. Harden. Ms. Wilbur or I take every call that comes in during business hours, personally.'

'You understand the International Surety KlameNet Program, don't you?'

'Yes, sir.'

Every International Surety office in the world was hooked into a regional computer center, and those were all linked to the company's worldwide data-exchange system. KlameNet logged every incoming claim, whether it came though the branches' own computers or off the overnight message tapes that the smaller offices used.

'You can access your office from your home, Lindsey. Why haven't you done anything about this claim? It came in more than an hour ago!'

'It's Saturday night, for heaven's sake. I'm at home. I would have got the claim off the tape first thing Monday morning. In the meantime, I'm sure the proper authorities know about it. What is it, a life claim? An auto accident?' Lindsey wiped his brow with a handkerchief. It was a chilly night, but talking with Harden made him perspire.

'Look, Lindsey, I'm telling you to get yourself in gear. Grab a pen and write these details down. This is a motor vehicle theft claim.'

Lindsey wrote, trying to keep up with Harden's dictation. Why all the fuss over a stolen car?

Harden was saying, 'The amount is $425,000, Lindsey. That's four, two, five, comma, zero, zero, zero dollars, Lindsey.

Did you get that?'

'But — what kind of car could that be? Even a Rolls — '

'It was a 1928 SJ Duesenberg Convertible Phaeton, Lindsey. Stolen from in front of something called the Kleiner Mansion in Oakland. You know it?'

Lindsey searched for an errant memory. 'Yes! They used it on the cover of the Oakland phone book a few years ago. I must have seen it at the office.'

'Yeah. Well, you hightail it out there, cowboy, and see what the hell is going on.'

'It's my weekend, Mr. Harden.'

'It's $425,000, Lindsey. And we don't pay you to be a clock-watcher.' His tone was ominous.

'I — I'll get right out there, Mr. Harden. Er — who's the owner?'

'This is another one of those fruit-and-nut cases you seem to specialize in, Lindsey. The car is owned by something called the New California Smart Set, whatever the hell that means. Probably a nancy social club. They were having some kind of shindig at this Kleiner Mansion.

4

They only roll the Dusie a couple of times a year, for super-special occasions. And now it's gone!'

'Okay, Mr. Harden. I'm on my way.' He started to lower the receiver, then stopped. 'Uh — who phoned in the report?'

'The claim came in from the president of the outfit. Guy named Oliver van Arndt. He's waiting at the mansion.'

Harden hung up without another word. Lindsey knew that Harden was both feared and disliked throughout International Surety. But he seemed to take special pleasure in harassing Hobart Lindsey, especially since the incident of the quarter-million dollars' worth of comic books. They'd been burgled from a shop in Berkeley, and Lindsey had recovered them for the company, saving International Surety a bundle. And then he'd persisted further, and with the help of Berkeley Police Officer Marvia Plum had not only regained all the stolen goods, but solved three bizarrely interconnected murders.

All now in the past. Lindsey had

enjoyed his proverbial fifteen minutes of fame. He'd enjoyed a brief, intense relationship with Marvia, and that alone had been a miracle in his drab life.

But it had ended. He'd won the praise of his employer's national office and the seething jealousy of his immediate superior, Harden at Regional. He'd gone back to his routine life of processing claims by day, and keeping an eye on his mentally unstable mother by night.

* * *

Lindsey got Mother off to bed, then jumped into his Hyundai and headed for the freeway. He found Lake Merritt easily enough and drove around it until the Kleiner Mansion loomed up. It looked like something out of a Charles Addams cartoon. The Alameda County Courthouse rose nearby, and East Fourteenth Street, the main arterial that ran all the way from mostly black west Oakland through the city's struggling downtown and out to suburban San Leandro, carried light traffic past the lake.

Could be he was getting another chance of excitement. A sixty-year-old Duesenberg worth nearly half a million dollars was far from routine.

A white Oakland police cruiser stood in front of the Kleiner Mansion, its roof lights flashing.

Lindsey parked beside the cruiser and scampered up the front steps of the mansion, patting his pockets to check he had his notebook and pencil.

A uniformed Oakland police officer was questioning a man and two women, and jotting down their responses. He turned as Lindsey approached. 'Who are you?'

Lindsey introduced himself and handed each of the others his business card.

The cop studied the card, then Lindsey. He hadn't changed before leaving Walnut Creek, but it was too late to do anything about that now.

'Okay, Mr. Lindsey. Your company carries the policy on the Duesenberg?'

Lindsey nodded. The cop had a tan Hispanic face with high cheekbones, and a thick handlebar moustache. His speech was unaccented.

'You can get a copy of the police report sometime Monday, but I don't suppose you want to wait that long to get involved, do you?'

Lindsey shook his head.

'Okay. This is Ms. Smith, the resident manager of the Kleiner Mansion. And Mr. and Mrs. van Arndt, of the New California Smart Set. I'm headed out of here. And you might as well have one of mine.' He handed Lindsey a business card. It read, 'Oscar Gutierrez, Oakland Police Department', and it had a phone number on it.

Lindsey slid the card into his pocket organizer and watched the police cruiser pull away. 'Mr. van Arndt, Mrs. van Arndt, Ms. Smith — maybe we should step inside and you can give me some facts.'

'Don't you want to look at the scene first?' Mr. van Arndt spoke. He was a tall man, wearing an old-fashioned tuxedo with silken lapels. His hair was slicked back with a glossy substance that shimmered in the lights that surrounded Lake Merritt. His upper lip bore a pencil-thin moustache. He looked a little bit like Mandrake the Magician.

Lindsey was taken aback. 'Was it your car that was stolen?'

'Not exactly. I drive a 1946 Ford Sportsman. But yes, the Dusie was stolen from right there. Wasn't it, Wally m'dear?' He pointed to a spot near Lindsey's Hyundai, managing to turn his head simultaneously toward the woman who stood beside him. She wore her light brown hair short, a band circling her forehead and a feather rising from behind her head. Her dress was clasped at both shoulders and was draped in champagne-colored folds.

'We've been over the ground, Ollie darling.'

Lindsey noticed that she was swaying slightly, with a half-empty martini glass in one hand. She wore expensive rings on several fingers.

Still, it might be a good idea, and it couldn't hurt. 'Would you show me, Mrs. van Arndt?'

The woman giggled and took Lindsey's hand. She led him to a spot on the gravelled driveway. It swung in a U-shaped loop off Lakeside Drive. There wasn't much traffic on the drive this time of night. The air was chilly and moist. And beyond the mansion, a low bank of fog hung just above the surface of the lake.

Lindsey peered at the thick gravel driveway. It would show tire tracks, to a certain extent, but it would hold little if any detail. 'Not much to see here. Let's go back.'

She took his hand and pulled him along toward the mansion. 'Ollie isn't really so jealous, he just likes to keep an eye on me. We have the same birthday, you know. That's how we met. I mean, we met at Antibes. Have you ever been to Antibes?'

Lindsey hadn't.

'Well, don't bother, it's ruined now. But it used to be wonderful. Ollie and I were both there on vacation and we discovered that we had the same birthday, even the same year. Our parents even named us for famous people. He's named for Oliver Wendell Holmes. My name was Wallis Warfield Simpson Stanley. Now we're

10

Ollie and Wally van Arndt.'

She swayed up the steps, still dragging Lindsey by the hand. He was happy to transfer custody back to her husband. They went inside the mansion. The entrance featured a cloak room the size of Lindsey's house. They passed through it into a huge, high-ceilinged room lighted by electrified chandeliers. The furnishings looked more Victorian than Art Deco.

A handful of men and women stood around in period costumes, looking like refugees from a stage production of *The Great Gatsby*. One exception to the tuxedo-and-gown set was a black man in a World War II-era uniform. He sat slouched in a period chair, the sleeves of his olive drab Ike jacket marked with a tech sergeant's chevrons. A row of service ribbons was pinned above the jacket pocket. He appeared to be dozing. A white-covered table bearing the decimated remains of a buffet meal stood at one end of the room, a deserted bandstand at the other.

'This was our annual 1929 gala,' Mr. van Arndt said.

'Where did everybody go?'

'When the Dusie was stolen — well, a few wanted to keep the party rolling, but it just put such a damper on, it fizzled.'

'Did anyone see the car taken?'

'Joe Roberts did, but he was too upset to stay. He's our youngest member, thirty-three years old. Some of the members didn't want to let him join, but he convinced them. He's a scholar and researcher. In fact, that's why he joined the Smart Set.'

Lindsey had his pocket organizer in his left hand, his gold-plated International Surety pencil in the right. Only top performers got the gold-plated models.

'Did you want to talk to Joe?' Mr. van Arndt asked.

'He actually saw the car stolen? How did the thief start the car? Were the keys left in it? Or did he tow it away?'

'I didn't see. Wally and I were dancing. Roberts must have gone outside for a breath of air. I'm afraid he'd had a few sips more than he should have.'

'And?' Lindsey kept his patience.

'Well, you tell it, Wally, m'dear.'

'He came in waving his arms and shouting, 'It's gone, they stole the Dusie!'' Wallis furnished. 'And then he fell down on the dance floor.'

Mr. van Arndt said, 'Poor chap passed out. He'd had a bit too much — I mentioned that, didn't I? I'm afraid the excitement and the sudden change did it.'

'And you say he left? He took a cab? I hope he didn't try to drive.'

'No. He gave his statement to Officer Gutierrez before leaving, and Dr. Bernstein took him home.'

'Dr. Bernstein?'

'Martha Bernstein, Ph.D. She's in the Sociology Department at Cal.'

'Is she a member of the club? Or was she here as a guest?'

'Oh, she's a member all right. I was against her, too. Like young Roberts. But she insisted on joining. The Kleiner Mansion is municipal property. We have to let anyone join who wants, if we want to meet here. I'd be all for moving to private property, myself. But the board of directors voted to stay, so we have to deal with these bureaucrats.'

13

Lindsey noticed Mrs. van Arndt's sour face. 'You don't like her either?'

'Don't like her looks, manners, clothes, or her attitude.'

'Did she do or say something in particular?'

'I don't think she loves 1929.'

Lindsey sighed. Wasn't anyone willing to cope with the present? In his mother's case there was an excuse. She'd been a pregnant young wife when Lindsey's father was killed aboard ship in the Korean War, and had never got over the shock. Her doctors had urged Lindsey to institution-alize her, but he'd never been able to bring himself to do it.

But now this — what kind of craziness was this about 1929?

Mrs. van Arndt was swaying slightly and rubbing her cheek against her husband's tuxedo shoulder. 'I mean, we all formed our Smart Set club because we all love Art Deco and the era it symbolizes. We all know that things used to be better than they are now. Some of our older members actually lived through the crash of '29.'

'We almost called it the HarCooHoo Club,' Mr. van Arndt interrupted. 'In honor of Harding, Coolidge and Hoover. Those were the days, Mr. Lindsey.'

Mrs. van Arndt said, 'After the crash, everything went to hell in a handbasket, Mr. Lindsey.'

'But not Dr. Bernstein?'

'Tweedy mannish woman.' Her eyes flashed. 'She *studies* us, can you imagine that? Like specimens under her microscope.'

The van Arndts had sat down facing Lindsey. Mr. van Arndt took his wife's free hand between his two and massaged it. To Lindsey he said, 'She gets agitated now and then. But it has become a sordid, ugly world, Lindsey. Dr. Bernstein wants to publish a paper about us. She comes to meetings and sits and watches and writes.'

Lindsey looked at his own hands, holding his golden pencil and pocket organizer.

'That's all right, old man,' Mr. van Arndt said generously. 'You're here on business. Dr. Bernstein even told me the name of the paper she's planning: 'Anachronistic Mimesis and Temporal Alienation, Violent and Nonviolent Acting-Out Strategies of Compensation'. What do you think of that?'

'I don't even know what it means,' Lindsey said. 'I'm afraid I'm losing the thread here. You told me this fellow Joseph Roberts actually saw the Duesenberg stolen, and gave a statement to Officer Gutierrez. And then Dr. Bernstein did — what?'

'She loaded him into her Land Rover and took him home.'

'Yes, but where did they go home to? His home or hers?'

'Please, Mr. Lindsey,' Wally van Arndt said, 'that is not a polite question at all.' She plucked the olive from her glass. 'Besides, they didn't say.'

2

In the morning Lindsey phoned Oakland Police Headquarters and asked for Officer Gutierrez. Gutierrez wasn't in so Lindsey asked if he could get a copy of the theft report on the Duesenberg. Gutierrez had said Monday, but it couldn't hurt to try. The operator said she'd transfer the call, but after a dozen rings Lindsey decided that nobody worked at headquarters on Sunday.

He didn't like working on weekends himself, but Harden had really come down on him about this claim. International Surety could stall for a while, hoping that the Duesenberg would be recovered. But eventually, they'd have to pay. Unless they could prove contributory negligence. Leaving a car like this one out-of-doors and unguarded, especially in a city with a crime rate like that of Oakland . . .

Any Duesenberg, especially a 1928

Phaeton, must be a prize plum for collectors — and consequently for thieves. And if they'd left the keys in the ignition, the company could make a strong case against the owners.

Whoever had parked the car and left it standing in the driveway . . . Lindsey suddenly realized that he didn't know who had driven the car last night, who had left it parked in front of the mansion. Ms. Smith had disappeared somewhere in the mansion while he was talking with the van Arndts, and that couple had practically drowned him in their own boozy bonhomie, though they hadn't given him nearly the amount of information he needed.

But he was going to recover that Duesenberg, or give it a hell of a shot, anyway. It was his chance to be alive again!

Mother was settled contentedly in front of the TV, and he phoned their neighbor Joanie Schorr and asked her to come over for a few hours.

Leaving his mother in Joanie's care, Lindsey drove to his office. He called up the New California Smart Set's policy on the computer and studied it. Who had sold the policy? A broker located in Oakland. East Bay Quality Insurance Limited. He'd dealt with them before, with a stuffy individual named Elmer Mueller. Not much chance they'd be open on Sunday either, but it was worth a phone call. No luck, but they had an answer machine, so he left his name and a request to call back.

He slipped his pocket organizer out of his jacket and studied the notes he'd made in Oakland the previous night. Mr. and Mrs. van Arndt looked like a pair of lightweights, although they might still be helpful in tracking the stolen Phaeton. But Joe Roberts was the one he needed to talk to first.

There were half a dozen Joseph Robertses in the Oakland directory. Three were at home when he rang. None of them had ever heard of the New California Smart Set. Two of the numbers rang fruitlessly. He got one answering machine, left his name and number, and asked that Joseph Roberts to call him back.

There was an M.R. Bernstein, Ph.D., in the book. He dialled the number.

'Dr. Bernstein here.'

'Martha Bernstein?'

'Yes.'

He told her who he was and asked if Joseph Roberts was at her house.

She said he was. She said she'd summon him, sounding gleeful at the prospect.

Roberts sounded hung over. Lindsey said, 'I represent the International Surety Corporation, and I'm processing the insurance claim on the Duesenberg Phaeton that was stolen last night. I'd like to come out there and have a chat with you, Mr. Roberts.'

'I don't know . . . ' Lindsey could hear the sound of an off-phone conversation. Then: 'Ah, I don't think that would be such a good idea, Mr. Lindsey.'

'You want to collect on this claim, don't you?'

'It's not my claim. It wasn't my car.'

'You're a member of the New California Smart Set, aren't you? It's registered in the name of the society.'

'Look, I don't know who took the damned car. I told that cop everything I saw. Actually I don't remember too much about last night. So why don't you just get the police report?'

'I intend to, Mr. Roberts. But I'd still like to talk with you. You might have seen something useful.'

'You're not a cop, are you?'

'I'm an insurance adjuster.'

'Then do your job. Get out of my face. I'm hung over, pal.'

Lindsey heard the phone slam down.

He mulled things over. Maybe the theft of the Duesenberg had been an inside job. Some member of the Smart Set who coveted the club's collective property for his personal use. Or who thought he might be able to sell the Dusie for a sweet price.

Or maybe the theft had been engineered for the specific purpose of collecting on the insurance claim. What would happen to the $425,000 if and when International Surety paid off? Would the club use it to buy another classic car? Or would it go into the

21

general fund? Or would an officer of the club find a way to convert the payment for his personal use?

Lindsey jotted a note to pursue that line. Was there a member of the club in financial hot water? The New California Smart Set had all the earmarks of a cozy bunch of millionaires, but there might be a scattering of ordinary citizens in the club as well.

For instance: was Dr. Bernstein independently wealthy, or did she have to work for a living? The van Arndts had said that she was on the faculty at the University of California. If she had to live on a professor's salary, well, Lindsey knew that academics nowadays earned a living wage, but they were hardly up there with movie stars or professional athletes. Dr. Bernstein might be happy to get her mitts on half a million dollars. Who wouldn't?

Wait a minute! Van Arndt had said that the club was forced to take in members it didn't really want, because the Kleiner Mansion was a public facility. Ollie had spoken of moving the society to a clubhouse of its own, so it could become the kind of snooty, exclusive outfit he apparently preferred. They could buy a very nice clubhouse for just under half a million smackers!

Joseph Roberts's voice on the phone had sounded a lot like the voice on the message tape at one of the Joseph Robertses' homes. Lindsey found a map of Oakland, searched for Roberts's street in the index, and found it near the Oakland Estuary. He made up his mind.

He dialled home. Joanie Schorr assured him that Mother was all right and that she was willing to stay for the rest of the day.

He drove to Oakland and found the Embarcadero. Roberts's address was in a block of modernistic condos opposite a railroad track and an industrial slum. But the condos themselves looked expensive, and with the estuary on the other side, it seemed a safe bet that the occupants wiped the sight of the factories and warehouses from their minds when they got home at night.

He parked and found Roberts's apartment, and settled in to wait for the man to come home. Better to beard the lion in his den.

The bright gray afternoon was deepening into the charcoal sky of dusk and Lindsey had turned on the Hyundai's engine and heater to fight off the chill that crept palpably out of the estuary.

A silver-gray Porsche pulled into Roberts's parking space. Lindsey could see that Roberts was returning alone. Dr. Bernstein must have dropped him off where he'd left his car. Lindsey jotted down the Porsche's license: JAZZ BBZ.

Roberts climbed out of the car, armed its alarm system, and headed for his apartment. Something else for Lindsey to check on — had the Duesenberg been equipped with an alarm? Had the thief known enough to disable it? Was there more evidence here of contributory negligence, or of an inside job?

Lindsey followed Roberts to his front door and tapped him on the shoulder as he extended his key.

Roberts turned. His eyes looked red and he had clearly not shaved that day.

'I'm Hobart Lindsey. International

Surety Corporation. We chatted earlier today.'

'I thought I told you I didn't want to talk to you.'

'You said not to come to Dr. Bernstein's house. I didn't. Thought you'd be more comfortable talking in your own home.'

'You guys work on Sundays?' Roberts turned and inserted his key in the lock.

'There's a lot of money at stake, Mr. Roberts. I'll only take a few minutes. Please.'

Roberts shoved the door open and gestured Lindsey inside.

'Thanks.' Lindsey preceded Roberts into the apartment and waited while he pulled the door shut. He stood uncomfortably while Roberts deliberately hung his overcoat and cap on a brass tree.

Making no attempt to take Lindsey's coat or offer him a seat, Roberts headed for the small bar at the end of the room. He proceeded to make himself an oversized martini. He turned around and lifted the glass to his lips, his eyes on Lindsey.

Lindsey noticed that Roberts's hand shook slightly as he raised the glass.

Lindsey lowered himself to the sofa and laid his pocket organizer on a blondwood coffee table. 'Now, Mr. Roberts, the van Arndts tell me that you actually witnessed the theft of the Duesenberg.'

'I was pretty blotto at the time and I wasn't seeing much of anything.' Roberts lowered himself into a chair near the coffee table. 'I think I'd made a little pass at Jayjay and she got pretty mad at me. Stupid hag, I was doing her a favor. I went outside. I figured fresh air would do me some good.'

Lindsey said, 'Who's Jayjay?'

'Jeanette James Smith. You know, the gal who runs the mansion for the City of Oakland.'

'Sorry I interrupted. You got outside . . .' Lindsey nodded his head encouragingly.

'Look, here's what I saw. I was standing on the edge of the lawn, looking toward the lake. You know, they fixed up the old necklace of lights surrounding the lake, and I was looking at reflections. Well, then I heard the car door slam and I heard the motor start up. But that was behind me, you see.'

'Yes. Do Duesenbergs have self-starters? Or did somebody have to crank it?'

'Good question. Yeah, it has a self-starter. I was checking on that a few weeks ago. They came in on the 1911 Caddie. Sure, all the Dusies had 'em.'

'Did you see how many people were in the car?'

'Not really.'

'How many door slams did you hear?'

Roberts closed his eyes. 'Look, you want a drink, Lindsey? Or maybe coffee? I can put on the Melitta.'

'Oh, coffee, please. But — the number of slams.'

Roberts stood up. 'Yeah. I was trying to remember. Now that I think about it, there might have been two. Is it important?'

'If there was only one slam, there was probably only one thief. If there were two slams, there were probably two thieves. Maybe more. The Duesenberg is a convertible?'

'Four-door convertible.'

'All right. How certain are you that you heard two slams? Not one, not three or four.'

Roberts walked out of the room. Lindsey heard him moving around in the kitchen. He came back and settled into his chair. 'That'll take a few minutes. Maybe I should have some with you instead of this stuff.'

'Think hard,' Lindsey persisted. 'How many slams?'

'Two.' Roberts disappeared the last of his martini and set the empty glass on an ebony coaster. 'Definitely two.'

'Did you tell Gutierrez that?'

'I think I just told him I heard somebody slam the car door. He didn't ask me how many slams.'

Lindsey jotted a note. He looked up. 'Then what?'

'Two slams, starter noise, lights went on, car pulled out of the driveway into Lakeside Drive. For a couple of seconds I just watched the car pull away. Then it dawned on me, nobody should be driving the car then. Not the Duesenberg. It was supposed to stay there until the party ended, then the chauffeur was supposed to take the officers to their homes. That's a perk. Then he'd bring the car back to the garage.'

Lindsey was jotting as fast as he could.

'Then I ran into the mansion to tell everybody, and I guess I must have blacked out. They got some coffee into me and I was able to talk to Gutierrez a little, then Dr. Bernstein took me back to her place and got me to bed on the couch.'

Lindsey frowned. 'On the couch?'

Roberts looked sour. 'What business is it of yours? You're an insurance adjuster, not the morals squad.'

Lindsey hastily held up his hand. 'I'm not judging you. Or her.'

'Besides, Mason would have killed me.'

'Mason?'

'Ed Mason. Used to play line for the Raiders. He and Martha have lived together for years, ever since the Raiders were in Oakland.' The odor of coffee was wafting into the room.

Roberts went out to the kitchen and brought back a loaded tray. 'Look,

Lindsey, what's going on here? Why don't you just pay off the claim?'

Lindsey filled his cup and tasted the coffee. He had to admit that it was better than the Mr. Coffee product that he and Ms. Wilbur drank at International Surety. 'Right, we could just pay the insurance after a while if the Oakland police couldn't track the Duesenberg down. But we don't want to rely on anybody else. If we can find that car, we can save a fat wad of money.'

Roberts ran his hands through his thinning hair. He really did look dreadful. 'Maybe we can talk some more, but not now. I've got to get into bed.'

'You have an office? Somewhere you'll be tomorrow?'

'Yeah. I have a little cubbyhole downtown. In the Clorox Building. Just phone first. Not too early, say after two p.m. One benefit of being your own boss is you can set your own hours.'

Lindsey nodded. 'Okay.' At the doorway, he said, 'When you check your machine, you'll find a call from me. Ignore it.'

He let himself out.

3

There wasn't much Lindsey could do on a Sunday night. Mother was able to cook dinner for them before turning on *Murder She Wrote* and watching it in black and white. They could have saved money by buying a black and white TV, but usually Mother went to bed early and Lindsey was able to reset the controls and watch the late news in color.

Lindsey wondered if Mother was slipping ever farther into the past. For a while she had been fixated on 1953, the year Lindsey's father had died and he was born. But now she seemed to wander the corridors of time, from the Truman era to the roaring twenties, without rhyme or reason.

Lindsey sat with his pocket organizer in his lap, jotting notes and trying to figure out a way to get the Duesenberg back. Before he pushed them too far he wanted some more info, and somebody to talk the case over with.

★ ★ ★

On Monday morning he arrived at his office in Walnut Creek. For once Ms. Wilbur had got there ahead of him. She greeted him with a smile and a message. 'Call Mr. Harden.'

Lindsey pointedly took his coffee and sipped before he hit the speed dialer for Regional.

'What about that Duesenberg?' Harden snapped without preliminary.

'I'm working on it.'

'"Working on" doesn't tell me squat, man! What have you accomplished?'

'Ah — I scrutinized the scene of the crime. In Oakland. The Kleiner Mansion. And I established contact with the police investigator. Officer Gutierrez. And I talked with Ollie and Wally and they put me in touch with — '

'Ollie and Wally? What the hell is this, Lindsey, some kind of comedy act?'

'I was starting to tell you that they put

me in touch with an eye witness to the theft. A man named Joseph Roberts. I interviewed him yesterday, at his home, and will follow up. I also spoke with the resident manager of the Kleiner Mansion and with several other members of the Smart Set. Ollie and Wally are Oliver Wendell Holmes van Arndt and Wallis Warfield Simpson Stanley van Arndt, and they run the society. Thank you, Mr. Harden.'

As he hung up Ms. Wilbur said, 'You've come a long way, Hobart.'

Lindsey said, 'You think I'll get fired, Ms. Wilbur?'

'I don't think so. He has a boss, too. He cans you, he's got to justify it to Johanssen. She's a fan of yours, ever since you got back those comic books for us.'

Lindsey smiled. He phoned Oakland and reached Officer Gutierrez. 'Yeah,' Gutierrez said, 'we work crazy shifts. I'm in here all morning doing paperwork. You want to talk about that Dusie, this is a good time.'

Lindsey drove into Oakland and left the Hyundai in a lot under the freeway.

He found a receptionist who actually knew who Officer Gutierrez was and phoned through to him. Gutierrez came out and told the receptionist that Lindsey was okay, he could have a visitor's badge. They wound up at Gutierrez's desk in the middle of a noisy bullpen.

Lindsey asked Gutierrez, 'You assigned to auto theft full time?'

'For the past two years.'

'What do you think of this case, Officer Gutierrez?'

'You can call me Oscar. Can I call you Ho — '

'Just Bart, please.'

'You know, auto theft is a very high-volume operation. We get thousands of these every year. Most of them solve themselves. Car's abandoned, or gets stopped for some routine matter. But this is such a peculiar case. I mean — a Duesenberg, for heaven's sake! They haven't built those things in thirty years. They're scarce as hens' teeth. How could anybody hope to get away with it? You can't drive a Duesenberg anywhere without gathering a crowd.'

'Actually they haven't built Duesenbergs for *fifty* years, perhaps more. Company almost weathered the Depression, but didn't quite make it. They were built from 1920 to 1937. Outfit down in southern California started building seven-eighth scale replicas in the late seventies but they're not true Dusies. Nice cars, though. I wouldn't mind owning one.'

'But they're scarce, right?'

'Not really. They turn up at collectors' meets and concourses all the time. Must be over a thousand Dusies left. They managed to round up thirty or forty Tuckers for that movie they made here in Oakland. Now that's a scarce car. And there are scarcer, believe me!'

Lindsey studied a blank sheet in his notebook, then looked at Gutierrez again. 'What would be a really scarce car? What would be a really top price?'

Gutierrez grinned, his teeth brilliant against his black moustache and dark complexion. 'Scarcity alone doesn't make a car valuable. It's supply and demand. Then there are unique items — one-of-a kind experimental vehicles, custom models. And cars with association value. The Beatles' Rolls. Hitler's Mercedes. They could be worth millions!'

'I guess that makes my Duesenberg small potatoes.'

'Not really. We're paying attention, believe me.'

Lindsey nodded. 'Good. You have the report ready, then?'

Gutierrez opened a manila folder, pulled out a flimsy sheet and handed it to Lindsey. It was the standard auto theft report; all that made it remarkable was the auto involved. 'You think you can get it back?'

Gutierrez shrugged. 'I don't see how an SJ can slip between the cracks.'

'Any idea where the car is now? I don't suppose you made any progress over the weekend.'

'No, but we know all the classic car collectors in the state. We get good co-operation from the car museums. The Behring people out at Blackhawk and the Harrah's collection in Reno. And the parts and service garages that specialize in classics.' Gutierrez looked Lindsey in the eye. 'What's your company's policy on buy-backs?'

'We don't like to do it. It's too much like blackmail and it just encourages more of the same. But we still do it if we have to. If we could buy back the Dusie for, say, ten percent of the insured value, we'd be fools not to. But then we'd still want to see the thief caught. And we'd want our money back, too, if there was any way we could get it.' Lindsey paused, then added: 'Oscar, do you think they'll try and sell it back?'

Gutierrez shrugged. 'They'd more likely contact you than us, Bart.'

'Not a peep so far. I'd have known if they'd contacted the company.'

'Well, it's only thirty-six hours. You might hear yet.'

'In the meanwhile, I'd hoped for some police action,' Lindsey said frankly.

'We can't send a SWAT team out to recover a stolen car, Bart. Too many cars get stolen. And we've got too many other problems. We can't compete for man-power with crack houses springing up and gang wars breaking out all over Oakland. And meanwhile we're in a budget crunch and we can't hire the cops we need. Jesus, man, we can't pull officers from other jobs to look for your stolen car.'

'I want that car back.' Lindsey slipped the auto theft report into his pocket organizer and stood up. 'Stay in touch, will you?'

Gutierrez said, 'So long. Don't forget to turn in your visitor's badge.'

Lindsey found a phone booth in the lobby and dialled the University of California in Berkeley. Maybe Martha Rachel Bernstein, Ph.D., could tell him something useful. He reached the Sociology department secretary and learned that Bernstein had finished teaching her morning class and was in her office. Lindsey got through and introduced himself.

'You're the man who called yesterday. You still trying to pester Joe Roberts?'

'I'd like to talk with you now, Dr. Bernstein. I'm investigating the theft of the Duesenberg from the Kleiner Mansion Saturday night.'

'I didn't take it.' She laughed unpleasantly.

Lindsey sighed. 'I'm just gathering

information at this point. I have no idea who took the car. May I come up and talk with you?'

'I was going to work here for the rest of the morning, but if you want to come over I suppose it will be all right.'

He got his Hyundai back and started for Berkeley. As he headed up Broadway toward College Avenue, he reflected on the Gutierrez meeting. The only worthwhile item had been Gutierrez's comment on buy-backs. Maybe Gutierrez was tied in with an auto ring? If he was, he could set up a buy-back, rake off part of the ransom, and quash the police investigation at the same time.

It was all very neat!

Perhaps *too* neat. But it was just something to bear in mind. Lindsey wondered if there had been many buy-backs of stolen cars in Oakland. Probably better to follow up through the industry than through the Oakland Police Department. If Gutierrez was part of a ring, better not to make him nervous at this point.

Lindsey managed to get into a campus

parking lot at Cal, and threaded through a mixture of young clean-looking students and crazed street people to Dr. Bernstein's office. What kind of woman would he find? A doctor of philosophy who lived with a former Oakland Raiders lineman . . .

'Dr. Bernstein?'

She stood up and smiled faintly. She was a stocky, tweedy woman with short brown hair. She shook his hand vigorously. He handed her a card and she dropped it onto the top of a desk cluttered with papers, journals, and notebooks. To one side a computer monitor glowed, a pie-chart in three colors filling the screen. At the other end of the desk Lindsey saw a huge cut-glass ashtray holding down a stack of photocopied forms. A brown-wrapped package of Philip Morris cigarettes and a monogrammed book of matches lay in the ashtray.

'I didn't think they made those any more,' Lindsey said.

'Don't think they do. I keep 'em there as a reminder. I'm supposed to be a smart woman. I got hooked on tobacco when I was twelve years old. Kept smoking when my father died of heart disease thanks to butts. Kept smoking when my mother died of lung cancer thanks to butts.'

'What made you stop?'

'My friend Ed Mason. Said he'd move out if I didn't quit. I believed him. I'm strong and independent too, not just smart.' She turned to her computer and clicked at the keyboard until the screen went dark. 'Okay, Lindsey, what can I do for you?'

There seemed little point in asking directly about the Duesenberg. Instead, Lindsey asked, 'Why did you join the Smart Set?'

'What a nifty question! What's it to you?'

'I want that car. My company will save a fortune if I get it, and that means a lot to me. To my career.'

'An honest man.' She grinned. 'Well, I joined the club to study the freaks. Pardon me, the members. To study the members.'

'And you're an honest woman. I heard about the paper you're writing. 'Anachronistic Mimesis' — whatever that means.'

'Should be an easy journal placement. Maybe do a popular version for *Psychology Today*, then tuck it away as a chapter for my next book.' Her eyes flickered for a moment. There was a cork bulletin board covered with scraps of notepaper and news clippings, all held in place by colored push-pins. Beside the bulletin board, in a glass-fronted case, she kept four or five copies of each of her books. She caught him following her own glance. 'My brag shelf.'

'Very impressive. This paper you're working on — the one about the Smart Set.'

'Yes. Anachronistic mimesis — imitation of other eras. It's about people who don't fit in. Lots of different ways of not fitting into society, and lots of ways of compensating for that. I mean, there are plenty of standard roles available to us in our society. Businessperson, homemaker, academic, factory worker, soldier, cop, and so on. Notice how we define ourselves by our work. Not all societies do that, but ours certainly does.'

She spun in her chair and slapped a fat

leather-spined book on the shelf behind her. 'Dictionary of occupational terms. Fifty thousand entries, and they keep issuing supplements. But a career isn't an identity, is it? How do you define yourself, Lindsey? That's my field.'

She was one hell of a lecturer, Lindsey thought.

She leaned forward. 'Those people at the Smart Set, they can't live in the present. So they live in the past. What is it about this year that they can't take? The political scene? Ecological disasters?'

When he didn't answer she resumed. 'When I was in grad school, kids ran off to join communes. And some who weren't kids at all. Beat the daylights out of blowing up buildings and killing people. Now these Smart Set people are living in the 1920s.'

'Sounds harmless to me.'

'Probably is — relatively speaking, anyhow. I studied another group, calling themselves Creative Anachronists, who live in the twelfth century. They hold courts and tournaments and bop each other over the head with rubber lances. A

43

lot of violent acting-out in that bunch. The Art Deco people are nonviolent, but it's the same syndrome.' She slid some papers around on her desk. 'People can't stand it here, they go there. You see what I mean?'

Lindsey didn't get time to answer.

'So these Creative Anachronists go to live eight hundred years ago. I've looked at some science fiction fans — they do the same thing, they go to live in the future. What's funny, some of them are the same people. I've studied some Sherlock Holmes people. They have a slogan: 'It's always London, and always 1895.' I kind of like that.'

'And these Smart Set people live in 1929. Very, very interesting.'

Lindsey jumped in as she paused for breath. 'So you're not really interested in Art Deco yourself?'

'Vargas, silver fox furs and cloche hats? I know the buzzwords. It's as interesting an era as any, I suppose. If I were a historian. I'm not. I'm a sociologist. Let me put it this way, Lindsey. I'm interested in the people who are interested in Art Deco.'

'Can you give me any clue about anybody in the club who would steal the Duesenberg?'

'I thought it was a passer-by. Somebody who saw the car and jumped in and drove away. Were the keys in it?'

'Apparently.' Lindsey unfolded the report he'd got from Gutierrez at Oakland police headquarters. 'They're not certain, but nobody could turn up the keys at the mansion, so they figure they must have been in the car.'

'That isn't conclusive — they don't really know whether it was an inside job or an outside job.'

'That's right. I'm leaving the possibility of an outside job to the police; they're better equipped to handle that. But if it was inside, I think I might do better than they can.'

'They don't mind your getting into the case?'

'I'm not a private eye, Dr. Bernstein. I'm just an insurance adjuster.'

'That's very interesting.' She picked up a pencil and jotted something on a yellow pad. *I'm making notes about her*, Lindsey thought, *and she's making notes about me.*

'Well, do you think somebody in the Smart Set might be responsible?'

'Someone might. Let me think about this. I've got your number.' She scrabbled on her desk until she found his card. She levered herself out of her chair and pinned his card to her cork bulletin board.

4

After lunch at a student facility, Lindsey phoned Joseph Roberts at his office. Roberts said he could come right ahead.

Lindsey drove back to Oakland. The Clorox building was a huge marble-walled slab, part of downtown Oakland's sometimes sputtering renaissance. Roberts's office was at the top of the building on the twenty-fifth floor. A plain door was marked J. Roberts Enterprises. Lindsey knocked. Roberts's voice invited him in.

The room was modern, its furnishings minimalist. Roberts sat behind a metallic contraption. Atop the gadget, on a thick slab of glass, stood a computer. The walls were lined with framed movie posters.

'What do you think? Not bad, eh?'

'You look a lot better than you did yesterday.'

'Feel it, too. Wow, for a while there I figured I'd have to look for work as a George Romero zombie extra!'

'Are you an actor, Joe?'

Roberts laughed. 'Hardly! Hitchcock was right. Actors are cattle. That ain't me, babe!'

'Then what do you do?'

'I write the scripts. Did my first script when I was a sophomore at Hollywood High. Later on I was a mail boy at Paradox; made a friend in the script department and got 'em to look at my work. Couldn't sell to Paradox, but they passed it along to a smaller outfit. They bought the script, made the picture. They got some Hong Kong money. *Swinging Schoolmarms*. See that poster, right behind you?'

Lindsey turned and looked at the poster. It listed Joseph Roberts as screenwriter.

'I'd appreciate your help in this matter of the auto theft. I realize that you weren't quite up to par yesterday.'

'Yep, *Swinging Schoolmarms*. Maybe it wasn't exactly *Fatal Attraction*, but they brought it in under budget. Can you imagine making a feature film for one million eight fifty anymore? Of course that was in '83. I was just twenty-seven years old — a lot of guys don't get to do a feature till they're thirty, thirty-five years old. Or never.'

'That's wonderful, Joe.'

'I've done erotics, slashers, westerns, thrillers. Want to do a real, classic-style noir PI flick next. Got a brilliant idea for casting, too. Sean Penn and Madonna. Nothing like a good, juicy divorce to energize a relationship — generate electricity on the set. I'd want to direct it myself. Go right up there with the greats.'

'If you're so interested in Hollywood, why are you working here?'

'Hah! Good question.' Roberts jumped from his seat and stood with his back to Lindsey, peering out the window. 'I hate LA, that's why.' Roberts turned. 'But that's where the industry is. So I commute as often as I have to. Anybody who can help it lives someplace else. LA is one miserable town.'

'You mean you commute between Oakland and Los Angeles?'

Roberts smiled. 'Well, I keep a little place down there. My little cottage in the valley, you know.'

Lindsey said, 'I see. And you're working on your next film now?'

'TV series. I'm thirty-three years old and I've got my own series. My concept, I pick the scripts, I write the ones I like. Already did a pilot. Network loved it. We'll be on next season.'

'You're switching from motion pictures to TV?'

'Done both all along. You ought to see my episodic credits. You ever watch *Kelly Scalese*, cop show? *Galaxy Force*, sci-fi? Did scripts for 'em all. Almost got nominated for an Emmy. There are so many bums peddling their scripts down there, anybody has a shred of talent can't help succeeding.'

Lindsey had the feeling that this conversation was slipping away from him. He'd meant to ask a few polite questions about Roberts's work, get him talking freely, then switch the subject to the Duesenberg and the New California Smart Set.

'I don't want to take up your time,' Lindsey interrupted. 'It's just that, as the only eye witness to the theft of the Duesenberg, I was hoping you might be able to give me some help.'

'Didn't we go over this yesterday? I don't see what I can do to help you. I'm awfully busy, you know. I have to start stockpiling scripts for *Jazz Babies*. You know who this is for? I don't even want to say it. Look at this.' He picked up a matte-finish Cross pencil and sketched a network logo.

'Is that the name of the show? *Jazz Babies*? Oh, that must be what your license plate means. Very clever. Mother wanted to watch that film on movie of the week.'

'That's what they do with pilots nowadays. They put 'em on as movie of the week. If they fly, the pilot pre-sells the show to the public, and you get a ready-made audience from day one. If they crash, at least the net makes some money off the pilot so it isn't a total loss. Did she like it?'

'Well, she wasn't feeling very well . . . She has these spells when she has to lie down, so she missed the movie. But she wanted to see it.'

Roberts turned to his computer and entered a few words from the keyboard. 'There, that should remind me to give you a tape for her. She'll love it a lot.'

'Is that why you joined the Smart Set? Are you doing research for your TV show?'

'Nobody down there knows that.'

'I won't tell.'

'Sure. Bunch of old geezers. You get some of those old-timers off in a corner, get a couple of drinks inside 'em, they won't turn it off about the old days. They love to talk about it.'

'And you listen.'

'Sure. Have to do research. They all know what I do for a living; they've all figured it out by now, why I'm there.'

'You just said nobody knows.'

'Well, not *officially*. Unofficially, some of them know. They get a thrill out of thinking they're the only one who's caught on.'

'Your license plate is a clue, isn't it? And I imagine most of them would have seen your *Jazz Babies*.'

'*Jazz Babies — The Movie*. I like to call it that to distinguish it from *Jazz Babies — The Series*.'

Lindsey grunted.

'Once we're on the network, I'll be made,' Roberts said. 'There will be no stopping me then!'

'Who do you think stole the Duesenberg? Surely you have a theory?' Lindsey pressed. 'Let your creative imagination roam.'

'I can think of a lot of people who'd love to own a Dusie — even me. But not to steal one. It's too hard to hide.'

There was an uncomfortable silence, then Lindsey said, 'Well, I'll be on my way. Thanks for your time, Joe.'

Roberts swung toward the door. 'Think I'll ride down in the elevator with you. Take a little walk, get out of this air conditioning.'

On the way to the lobby, Roberts said, 'Where you headed now?'

'I don't know.' Lindsey frowned. 'I think I'd better get back to the Kleiner Mansion while it's still daylight. Walk around the scene, maybe talk to Ms. Smith.'

'Like some company? I wasn't getting

much done today on *Jazz Babies*. Maybe this'll clear my head for me.'

Lindsey shrugged. 'Sure.' Maybe, away from his office with its posters and publicity stills, Roberts would talk about something besides making movies.

They crossed Broadway, heading toward the mansion. When they got there, Lindsey noticed a discreetly lettered sign giving days and hours that the mansion was open to the public. It normally closed at three p.m., and it was now almost four. He rang the doorbell anyway.

The door opened. Ms. Smith said, 'I'm sorry but we're — Oh, you're — '

'Hobart Lindsey, right. We met briefly.'

Roberts said, 'Hello, Jayjay.' She ignored him. 'Did you want to come in, Mr. Lindsey?'

Lindsey said, 'If you don't mind.' He wondered why she'd snubbed Roberts.

As Lindsey stepped inside he heard Roberts say, 'Come to think of it, I've got to get some work out today. So long, Lindsey. Nice seeing you, Jayjay.'

Jayjay Smith locked the door behind Lindsey, pulling down a translucent shade. No fancy party togs today: she was wearing a pale blouse and a pair of old jeans.

'You actually live here, Ms. Smith?'

'It's convenient for me. I could never rent anyplace liveable on my salary. And if I didn't live here they'd have to hire a watchman. So — I get a free home, Oakland gets a free watchwoman.'

She had led him into a parlor he hadn't seen on Saturday night. On the way, he saw that the evidence of the Smart Set's gala had been cleaned up.

Lindsey said, 'I wonder why Joe Roberts left in a hurry?'

She gave him a slightly rueful look. She was fortyish, with a slightly fleshy look to her. Hair in a natural arrangement, cut to the length of her jaw. Some light makeup. Well-preserved, as they said in some of the old novels his mother had got interested in lately.

Lindsey shrugged. 'Perhaps he was embarrassed because of the other night. Getting sick and all.'

'You don't know what else happened?'

Lindsey felt uncomfortable. 'Well, he did mention, ah . . . he'd made a pass at you. But I wouldn't think that would be so terrible.'

She laughed harshly. 'He didn't tell you how *many* passes he's made at me. But surely you didn't come here just to quiz me about my love life?'

'You live here all alone?'

'Not quite. Old Mr. Kleiner has his room. Actually, I'm very worried about him. I might have to call in a doctor if he doesn't snap out of this.'

Lindsey was startled. 'Who's old Mr. Kleiner?'

'This is the Kleiner Mansion. It was his, his family's. They were an old Oakland family. Nineteenth-century settlers, merchants, real estate. They lost everything in the Depression. Including the mansion and the Duesenberg.'

Lindsey looked around for someplace to sit. He opened his pocket organizer on a low table and leaned over it. He said, 'You mean to tell me there's actually a Mr. Kleiner? What can you tell me about him?' He poised his pencil above his organizer.

Jayjay Smith sat opposite him. 'Well, I

don't know very much about Mr. Kleiner. And I don't know how much it would be right to tell you. However, there's a historical pamphlet about the mansion.'

She found a brochure in a polished breakfront and handed it to him. He slipped it into his jacket pocket. 'Thanks.'

'It doesn't really tell you much, but it has a couple of nice photos in it, and a little history of the mansion. Anyway, when the Kleiners lost all their millions they couldn't keep up the taxes on the mansion. There was quite a scandal.'

Lindsey scribbled notes, mainly reminding himself to check on the Kleiner family. Tax records should still be available from the 1920s, and records of real estate transfers. And there had to be a local historical society. They might have something.

Jayjay Smith went on, 'I don't really know all the details of what happened. Just what Mr. Kleiner told me. And some of the members of the Smart Set.'

Lindsey nodded encouragingly.

'Apparently Mr. Kleiner had his lawyer draw up a paper deeding the mansion and all of its contents, as well as the garage and the Duesenberg, to the city in lieu of all taxes. The city had to forgive any other taxes that the Kleiners owed, and give Mr. Kleiner lifetime residence in the mansion, and they had to employ him for life. As chauffeur.'

'And the city went for that?' Lindsey jotted down: *Kleiner lawyer? Newspapers for '29?*

'I guess they figured it was a good offer. If this house were in private hands today the city couldn't afford to buy it. And then the owners would probably knock it down and build rotten condos here.'

'How much did the Kleiners owe the city?'

'I don't know. Must have been plenty, to give up this house. Today you couldn't touch it for any amount. The lawns, Lake Merritt in the backyard — it's priceless.'

'Looks like a good bargain for Oakland. How do they handle the use of the car?'

'The city sold the car to the club. Let somebody else worry about what to do with it. Let them worry about Mr. Kleiner, too.'

'Mr. Kleiner? I still don't — '

There was a stirring from another room. Jayjay Smith stood up. 'I'm sorry. I have to see if he's all right.'

She disappeared through a dark wood doorway. Lindsey stood up and looked about him. Porcelain figures and display china dishes with eighteenth-century ladies and gentlemen painted on them, done up in their satin clothing and powdered wigs.

He heard Jayjay Smith's voice. The tone was warm, coaxing. Almost motherly. And in the pauses, the hint of an old voice, thin and dry and weak. That had to be Mr. Kleiner.

Why in the world had Mr. Kleiner insisted on that odd arrangement, living in cramped quarters in the mansion that he'd once owned, and caring for the Duesenberg and acting as chauffeur of the car that had been his personal property?

But the Dusie was the property of the New California Smart Set. Probably, Kleiner had been unable to interfere when the city sold the car, for all that he might have disapproved. But the club was also tied into the mansion.

It was like something out of an old movie. Yes, that one with Gloria Swanson and William Holden and the young Jack Webb. And who played the chauffeur? Erich von Stroheim!

He ran back to his pocket organizer and scribbled: *Sunset Boulevard!!!*

Jayjay Smith's voice still came from the other room. Lindsey heard the sound of a telephone hitting its cradle, and Smith came partway back into the room where he was. She looked pale.

'I just called for an ambulance. I hate to send the poor man to the hospital. He doesn't want to go, but he has to.'

Lindsey stood near her and she put her hand on his cuff. He said, 'What is it?'

'Since Saturday he's been beside himself. You don't know how much he loves that car. He hasn't been eating or sleeping right, and he won't get dressed.'

'How old is he?' Lindsey asked.

'He was born in 1904, the year after the Wright brothers flew. He used to talk about that all the time. He always said he could remember the '06 earthquake, but I never believed him as he would only have been two years old. That makes him eighty-five now.'

'And he was still working as a chauffeur?'

'He still has a license. And he's always been spry. Sharp as a tack. Until Saturday. Then he just changed. He used to spend every day working on the Duesenberg, polishing it up, cleaning the engine. He has a full set of tools in the garage, all sorts of old Duesenberg manuals and spare parts. When they stole that car, it was like they killed him.'

'But — I can't see an eighty-five-year-old man working as a chauffeur.'

'Well, in fact he only drove the car once or twice a year. The night of the 1929 Ball and maybe another occasion, maybe in a parade. I worry about him myself, I'll admit. But he never so much as scratched a fender.'

From outside the Kleiner Mansion, Lindsey heard an ambulance whooper. The whooper stopped and there was a pounding on the mansion's front door.

5

Lindsey stood with Jayjay Smith, watching the ambulance disappear along Lakeside Drive. The old man hadn't wanted to go, but he didn't resist the two attendants for long. He could barely have weighed a hundred pounds, and he was on his way almost before he knew what was happening. A metaphor for human existence.

Old Mr. Kleiner was hardly an Erich von Stroheim, after all.

Lindsey looked at Jayjay Smith. Her eyes were bright with tears. How could he comfort her? He hardly knew the woman . . .

Jayjay Smith solved the problem for him. 'Goddamned sons of bitches!' She turned toward Lindsey. 'Whoever stole that Duesenberg didn't know they were killing that man, but they were. Murderers! I hope they shoot the bastards when they catch them!'

Lindsey followed her back into the mansion. She led him into a room he hadn't seen before, opened a liquor cabinet and pulled out a bottle of Johnny Walker black. 'You want some?'

Lindsey shook his head.

Smith filled a squat glass with scotch and drank off a hefty portion of it. She put her glass down and wiped her eyes with a cocktail napkin, holding the bottle by its neck all the time. 'You don't do that to an old man,' she said. 'Let him live out his damned life, let him die in peace. I hate this town and the thieves and whores and pimps and pushers! Bastards, doing that to an old man.'

Lindsey wondered if she'd be all right. He said, 'Uh, will you have dinner? Do you have food?'

She put the bottle down and raised the glass to her lips. 'I'm really all right,' she said. 'Thanks for offering, but I'll just take a sandwich and climb in bed with a book. Unless you want to . . . '

He didn't know what she was going to say, and he didn't know how he would react. 'No, I have to get home,' he said.

'Mother, you see. She . . . '

Jayjay Smith laughed and saw him to the door. He picked up his pocket organizer on the way. 'I'll need some more information. Not now, of course. But I'll need to know where the Duesenberg was kept. Is the garage here on the grounds or . . . '

'Yes, yes. Another day. I want to phone the hospital now. You get in touch when you need to.'

She almost shoved him out the front door. Rush hour was starting. Civil servants and lawyers and ordinary citizens were pouring from the county courthouse across the street. Commuters were rushing for home or to the bars on Fourteenth Street.

Lindsey walked back to Broadway, found his car in the garage where he'd parked it and paid the fee, carefully filing the receipt to accompany his expense account. He headed for the freeway and started for home.

He got home drenched with sweat. The air was chilly and moist, typical for March, and the stress of dealing with freeway traffic got worse every year.

Lindsey left the Hyundai standing in the driveway, let himself in, and heard the sound of something frightening coming from the kitchen. Mother was standing at the kitchen sink, singing. 'Ha-ha-ha-haa-ha, ha-ha-ha-haa-ha, it's the Woody Woodpecker song!'

Lindsey sighed in relief. She'd been watching cartoons on TV. They were the only things that she would watch in color. Everything else had to be black and white or she became agitated, almost hysterical. There had been color movies in her girlhood, but no color television. Movies on TV therefore had to be seen in black and white. But cartoons could be in color. Go figure.

After dinner, Mother made coffee. Lindsey asked for a cup and Mother frowned. 'You'll stunt your growth, Hobo. You want to be big and strong when Daddy gets home from Korea.'

He looked into her eyes, searching for a pathway into her mind. Were clouds gathering there again? Was she slipping back toward the days when her husband was still alive, when Lindsey himself was not yet born?

Lindsey settled for a cup of cocoa rather than upset Mother even more. They washed the dishes and put them away together. Afterwards they settled in front of the TV. Mother found a movie that she liked, a gangster film with John Garfield and Linda Darnell. It was full of car chases, and every time an old car roared across the screen Lindsey thought about the missing Duesenberg.

When the movie ended Lindsey got Mother to bed. She settled in with a Vera Caspary novel and told him good night, and it seemed that she knew who he was.

His sleep was troubled and in the morning he felt groggy even after two cups of coffee. Mrs. Hernandez was on time for once and he left Mother in her care and headed for the International Surety office in Walnut Creek.

There were half a dozen entries on the KlameNet log and he looked through them, turning the ones that didn't require his attention over to Ms. Wilbur. He filled out forms, dictated letters, made a few telephone calls. Harden wasn't pestering him about the stolen Duesenberg. At least not yet.

He looked up the number of the Kleiner Mansion in his pocket organizer and punched the call. An unfamiliar voice answered and told him that Ms. Smith was out. Lindsey asked the voice to have her return his call, please.

He was relieved to learn that there were other people working at the mansion: a housekeeper, handyman, probably some people to take visiting school children on guided tours of the splendors of the past.

He phoned his friend Eric Coffman and asked about having lunch at Max's Opera Plaza. Coffman said he was working in his law office, waiting for a jury to come in. Sure, Max's was fine.

It would be good to spend a while with Eric again. He was Lindsey's best friend — just about his only friend. He didn't get out much, and he didn't invite friends over very often. Not with Mother likely to decide it was 1953, or 1968, or some other year.

But Eric had been his friend since their

school days. If Lindsey were to swap places with anyone he knew, it would be Eric Coffman. He was a husband and a father. He understood about Lindsey's mother. He was a busy man, but somehow he always had time to listen to Lindsey, to swap stories with him, to give him a sane view of reality when Lindsey needed it most.

* * *

Lindsey looked across Max's and saw that Eric Coffman had arrived before him. The lawyer stood up and waved as Lindsey crossed the room. His perfectly cut three-piece suit and solid gold cuff links gave him a look of elegant grace despite his rotund form. Lindsey always felt shabby in Coffman's presence.

'Lindsey! Have a drink!'

'Don't mind if I do.' Lindsey slid into a leather chair.

'I'm one ahead of you.'

'So I notice. How can you drink those things, Eric?'

A waitress had arrived, and Lindsey

ordered a mineral water.

'What's the matter, Lindsey? Work? Lousy love life? You mother again?'

'No, she's doing all right. You know, she gets a little better, then she gets a little worse.' He told Coffman about last night's incident, about his mother singing the Woody Woodpecker song.

'And you thought she'd gone round the bend?'

Lindsey nodded.

'But you say she was all right after all?'

'Well, yes. And Mrs. Hernandez is there. But lately Mother's even well enough that Mrs. Hernandez can leave at four most days. Mother can stay alone for a few hours now without getting into trouble. And Joanie Schorr comes over when I need her to help out. But I can't help thinking, one of these days . . . ' He made a vague gesture.

'Just hang in there, pal. What about Marvia — you still seeing her?'

Before Lindsey could answer his mineral water arrived, and they ordered their meals.

'I have a funny claim,' Lindsey said

when the waitress had bustled away. 'Somebody stole a car in Oakland Saturday night — a 1928 Duesenberg. It's worth $425,000.'

'You do get the odd ones, don't you? What was that weird case you had a while ago, the stolen comic books?'

'Yeah. They were worth a quarter million. And they got a couple of people killed, too. A UC professor wound up in jail for murder. He's there now.' Lindsey didn't tell Coffman that the comic book killer had also been involved in the death of Lindsey's own father thirty years before.

'And now you've got an even bigger one,' Coffman said. The food had arrived and Coffman's steak knife flashed. 'Any clues? You getting any help from the cops?'

'I don't know about clues.' Lindsey speared a couple of bay shrimp. 'I don't know about clues,' he repeated. 'I talked to a man who saw the car being driven away, but he was drunk at the time and he couldn't tell me much. And I talked to an Oakland cop. I don't know if he's going to help me much at all.'

A telephone burbled from under their table and Coffman pulled a morocco attaché case onto his lap, opened it, lifted out a handset and muttered into it. He put it back in the case. 'Gotta go, pal. Jury's in. We'll settle up next time, hey? And I'll hear more about your love life.' He wolfed the rest of his steak and wiped his mouth delicately with a linen napkin before moving away from the table, looking distinctly like Raymond Burr.

Back in the office, Ms. Wilbur said, 'Ms. Smith called you from Oakland. Message on your desk.'

Lindsey grunted.

'You're a grumpy one this afternoon. What happened, get stuck with a lunch tab you can't write off?'

'None of your business.' Lindsey sat down. The message read: 'Going to visit Mr. Kleiner at Kaiser Oakland. Call me there if you want.' There was a telephone number and an extension.

Lindsey decided not to phone. He wanted to talk to Kleiner himself as well as Jayjay Smith — if Kleiner were in any shape to talk.

He parked near the hospital and stopped at the desk to ask for Mr. Kleiner's room number, and was directed to a bank of elevators.

The old man turned out to be in a ward. Jayjay Smith sat in a straight-backed chair, conversing softly with a middle-aged man. Kleiner was sleeping.

Jayjay Smith turned toward Lindsey. 'Bart! I thought you were going to phone. Why did you come here?'

'Well, I thought Mr. Kleiner . . . '

Jayjay shook her head. The middle-aged man shot Lindsey a peculiar look. The man looked vaguely familiar.

Lindsey turned his glance to Kleiner, then back. There was a definite resemblance even though the old man was a wizened figure, while the younger one was broad-shouldered and beefy.

Jayjay said, 'Bart, this is Morton Kleiner. Mr. Kleiner's grandson.'

Morton nodded to Lindsey. 'You're the insurance man, hey? You going to pay out for my grandfather? I don't think the old bird's ever going to fly again.'

'As far as I know, we don't carry a life

policy on your grandfather. Ah, aside from which, I don't think it would be in the very best taste, anyway, to discuss that while Mr. Kleiner is still alive. And might recover.' He looked at Jayjay Smith for information.

'They want to do some more tests. The doctor said it's just his age, and if he's so depressed about the car that he's lost his will to live, I don't think he'll recover.'

'Anyway, listen.' The younger Kleiner reached across the bed, pointing a finger at Lindsey. 'I want to find out what's coming to me, and I want to get it. Don't you think just because — '

Jayjay stood up abruptly. 'Stop it!' she hissed. 'Let's go somewhere else before you get us thrown out.'

They took the elevator to the lobby and found an alcove furnished with chrome and imitation leather couches.

'Now,' Morton Kleiner said, 'you're going to weasel out of the old man's insurance are you? You insurance guys are all the same. Best friend when they're trying to sell you a policy, don't know you from a dog turd when you have a claim.'

Lindsey took a deep breath. 'I tried to explain upstairs, Mr. Kleiner. I'm not here about a life policy on your grandfather. I don't even know if he has one. Do you know,' he added, turning to face Jayjay Smith, 'if he has a desk at the mansion? Any kind of files or records? Maybe a safe deposit box at a bank?'

'I think he has a box of papers.' She pressed her hands to her eyes.

'You ought to check there, Mr. Kleiner.' Lindsey took out his pocket organizer and offered Kleiner an International Surety card. 'That's my office number. If you think your grandfather has a policy with us, phone there and we can put it into the computer and find out, even if you don't turn up the policy itself. International Surety is a legitimate, ethical company. We have branches all over the world, millions of policies in effect. If your grandfather is insured with us, and if he dies, International Surety will pay. But I'm here to get information about the stolen Duesenberg. That's another matter altogether.'

'Why don't you get out and look for it,

then, if the goddamned car is so important to you? Why are you hanging around
Kaiser sniffing after my grandfather? Or
are you sniffing after something else?'

6

Lindsey got nowhere with Morton Kleiner other than taking the man's address and telephone number. This Kleiner lived in Petaluma. Lindsey hoped that he would be able to avoid further dealings with him.

But the hospital visit hadn't been a complete waste of time. Mr. Kleiner's doctor was an Indian woman who spoke English with precision. She had agreed with Jayjay Smith's ideas.

'You are dealing with a very old man who is attached emotionally to a single treasured possession that seems to be his chief link to a world that has largely ceased to exist. Without his precious automobile, he has no reason to continue living. Do you not think you can retrieve the lost vehicle for Mr. Kleiner? Or could you obtain another of a similar nature for him?'

'We'll get the car back if we can. But I don't think we could replace a Duesenberg. That isn't International Surety's job anyhow. We'd pay off the claim, then maybe the club could find another Dusie — but even for the amount the car was insured for, it wouldn't be easy. Those things are museum pieces, doctor.'

The woman pursed her lips. 'Actually, I would not normally advocate lying, but perhaps in this case . . . '

'If we told him we'd got it back . . . ?'

'It might help him a great deal. He must want to live, or he will surely die.'

As Lindsey hesitated, Jayjay Smith said, 'I guess it's my job. Really should be Morton's, but I wouldn't trust him for the time of day.'

'He's Mr. Kleiner's next of kin?'

'Only kin, as far as I know. Sometimes old Mr. Kleiner talks about his family, but I never could get the story straight. His parents were great aviation enthusiasts, he told me. They named him for a German aviation pioneer. That's what he told me, anyway. A martyr who was killed trying out an experimental glider. Otto Lilienthal Kleiner, that's Mr. Kleiner's full name.'

'Yes, sure. But what about Morton?'

'Well, that's where it gets a little fuzzy. There were an Eva and Brunhilde and a Georg Kleiner. That's like George without the final e. I could never get them all straight. Maybe Mr. Kleiner's a little confused himself, I don't know. Anyway, he got married and I think he had a sister and a son. Some of the Kleiners moved into San Francisco, and I think some records were lost in the earthquake in 1906. And then there was the terrible Oakland hill quake around about 1923. Mr. Kleiner told me about it. Hundreds of houses destroyed up near what's now Tilden Park.'

Lindsey had taken out his pocket organizer and was jotting notes. When Jayjay Smith stopped, he looked up at her to see why.

The tiny Indian doctor was still there. She said, 'I must see my other patients. But please think about what you can do for Mr. Kleiner. There is very little that *I* can do for him!'

Jayjay Smith blushed. 'I'm sorry. I guess I got carried away.'

'I understand.' Lindsey put his hand on

the back of hers. 'Look, Morton's gone back to Petaluma or wherever he went to. Mr. Kleiner doesn't seem to know whether we're here or not.'

'No, I don't want to leave yet. Let me check on him once more. Then . . . '

'Then I'd like some more information. If you don't mind.'

She went back to the ward. Lindsey found a pay phone and dialled East Bay Quality Insurance Ltd. This time Elmer Mueller was in. Lindsey identified himself and asked if Mueller knew about the Duesenberg theft and the claim on the Smart Set's policy.

'Not my problem, mac.'

'You sold the policy, Mueller. You have a responsibility!' Lindsey was pretty annoyed.

'Look, cars get swiped every day. If things like that didn't happen there'd be no insurance business and we'd both have to get an honest job. So get the man back his car or pay off the claim, right? My job is selling insurance, yours is settling claims. I do my work, you do yours. Now I'm kind of busy, if you don't mind.'

Lindsey did mind. He wanted more information on the policy, information on when it was written, who purchased it in behalf of the Art Deco Society, how long it has been in effect . . .

'Look, suppose I come to your office. You're still on Broadway, right?' Lindsey read Mueller the number. 'How about tomorrow some time?'

'Sure. We'll do lunch. On you.'

Jayjay Smith came back into view. She was carrying her long, slate-gray coat. She turned slowly, looking for Lindsey.

'Okay. Noon.' Lindsey hung up and headed back toward Jayjay Smith, waving his hand.

She looked at him, her face drawn. 'He didn't even know me, Bart. He just lies there. They have him on intravenous.'

Lindsey took her by the elbow. 'Come on. You want to go back to the mansion?'

She shook her head. 'Not yet. It's closing for the day right about now. They can handle that without me. I'll go back in a little while. You don't have to take care of me. I appreciate it, but really . . . '

'No, I tell you what.' Lindsey took her

coat and helped her on with it. It was a chilly day, heading toward early darkness and a chilling rain. 'How did you get here from the mansion?'

'I walked over to Broadway and took a bus.'

'I've got my car here. Let's stop at the Regency for a cup of coffee. You'll feel better. Then I'll drop you off.'

She managed a barely audible, 'Okay.' She pulled her coat tighter, tugged a hood over her tawny hair. She took his arm and for a fraction of a second pressed her head against his shoulder.

Lindsey felt heroic.

★   ★   ★

The cup of coffee wound up in a graceful glass with a shot of Irish whiskey in the bottom and a dab of whipped cream on the top.

'What do you think of the doctor's idea?' Jayjay Smith interrupted Lindsey's musing. 'I don't know what we can do when he comes home. But we'll lose him before that if we don't do something fast.'

Lindsey shrugged. 'If you think it will help, tell him whatever you think is right.'

She managed a smile. 'All right, I just hope he makes it. If I tell him we've got the car back and it helps him recover, then we'll have to deal with what happens later.'

'You were going to give me some more information.' Lindsey had his ballpoint poised over his pocket organizer. They were sitting in the cocktail lounge at the Hyatt Regency. 'Is the grandson taking responsibility for the old man?'

'Mr. Kleiner has insurance. City of Oakland pays for it. I signed him into the hospital. I phoned Morton because I had his name and number.'

'You'd met him before?'

'He came to the mansion a couple of times. All he wanted was money from his grandfather. Poor Mr. Kleiner didn't have any money. The city pays him some miserable salary; he's got a civil service rating of some sort. And he gets social security, and the Smart Set pitches in, so he's all right. But he doesn't have any real money.'

'Why does Morton think he has?'

'He thinks that old Mr. Kleiner has money hidden away and he knows where it is, and Morton wants it. He was really harassing the old man. I finally told him if he didn't leave his grandfather alone, I'd go to court and get a restraining order against him. So he stopped coming around.'

Lindsey signalled the waitress for another round. To Jayjay Smith he said, 'What missing money is that? I thought the Kleiners lost their fortune in the Depression.'

'Yeah, right.' The softer light made Jayjay Smith look ten years younger than she had under the hospital fluorescents. She was an attractive woman.

'It's probably just a fairy tale, Bart. They owned hotels, department stores, theaters. Oakland didn't always have the problems it has nowadays. Anyway, when the Kleiners went belly up, there was a rumor that they got together and skimmed their holdings, converted a lot of their wealth into cash. Which then disappeared.'

'So there's a fortune hidden in the mansion? Roberts ought to hear about that, he'd love it. Make a movie out of it.' Lindsey paused to reflect. 'But it doesn't have to be in cash. Maybe the Kleiners bought some valuable paintings, or stamps. People invest in all sorts of collectibles.'

'You think the Duesenberg was it then? No way. I don't know what the car cost originally, probably something like $25,000. Mr. Kleiner could tell you exactly, if — ' Jayjay Smith pulled a handkerchief from her purse and dabbed at her eyes. 'God damn it, I'm sorry. I hate crying.'

'You're allowed.'

'Anyway, the Dusie couldn't be the missing money. For one thing, it's a '28, and the Depression didn't hit until '29, and the Kleiners didn't really get into bad trouble for a couple of years. A lot of people held on for quite a while. They kept thinking that the Depression was just a passing fancy.'

'Then what's the story on the missing money?'

'Well, nobody knows for sure. I think somebody at UC did a thesis on the Kleiners before my time at the mansion. But Mr. Kleiner told me about it. This graduate student came around asking him questions. Claimed to have all sorts of papers and records, claimed that there were millions of dollars unaccounted for. Millions in 1931 dollars. What would it be today?'

* * *

Driving toward the Kleiner Mansion, Jayjay Smith said, 'Did you get all the information you need?'

'I will need some more information, but I guess it's getting too late today.' The sky was completely black, a light mist was falling, the streets were slick, and the lights of street lamps and oncoming vehicles reflected off their surfaces. Driving to Walnut Creek was going to be difficult.

As they neared the mansion, Lindsey asked, 'One thing I meant to ask you — who started those stories about the missing fortune?'

'It was a different time, Bart. There was some Klan activity out here; there were some German-American Bund types, anti-Semites. The Kleiners were Jewish. It was part of the worldwide Jewish bankers conspiracy. That kind of stuff.'

'But what about the graduate student? Why would an economics student care about some fairy tale?'

'It was a sociology major who came around. That's what interested him — the social attitudes involved, the idea that people believed that the Jews were hiding all this money. That they were responsible for the Depression; had brought it on deliberately for some reason.'

'Then there was no missing money after all.'

'No — yes. The grad student decided that there really was money missing. But he wasn't really very interested in trying to track it down. He was studying group dynamics and prejudice, that kind of thing.'

He pulled into the driveway at the mansion and put the Hyundai in park. 'You've been a lot of help,' he said.

Jayjay looked away, toward the mansion, then back at Lindsey. 'Would you like to come in for a few minutes? The mansion is an interesting place at night.

It's almost like living in the days when it was built.'

Lindsey felt a tiny shiver pass. 'I'd like to,' he said. 'But I have to get back to check on my mother.'

★ ★ ★

The next morning Lindsey had a call from Harden. He placated his boss as best he could. At least the Smart Set hadn't been raising too much of a ruckus, probably because it was a club and nobody's full-time occupation. But that wouldn't go on for long; the club members would begin to grumble soon enough.

Ms. Wilbur gave him a sympathetic glance. When he got off the phone with Harden she said, 'You getting anyplace on that car — really?'

Lindsey shook his head. 'I've had a couple of ideas, but I don't have anything solid.'

'Well, let the company pay it off, for heaven's sake!'

'Now you're starting to sound like Mueller.'

'Little Elmer?'

'You know him?'

'Of course. East Bay Quality, right? Little bantam type, likes to strut around. He wrote the policy, right? It was on the KlameNet report.'

'You know Mueller personally? I'm supposed to have a meeting with him today, try and figure out what to do.'

'Pay the claim, Bart!'

'Yeah. Maybe we should. It's just — this is a Duesenberg, Ms. Wilbur. You can't just drive it around, it's no commonplace car. Somebody would spot it in a minute. So where is it?'

'You can hide a car in a garage,' she suggested.

'And never drive it? Just walk around it every day and look at it, like in a museum?'

'No?'

'Wait a minute!' Lindsey jumped up in excitement. 'Yes! Where do you see great paintings? In an art museum! And where do you see classic cars? In a car museum! Maybe that's where it is.'

7

Lunch with Elmer Mueller couldn't have been worse. Lindsey kept thinking about the Duesenberg being at a museum. What was that Poe story, the one about hiding a purloined letter so out in the open that everybody saw it but nobody noticed it? What if the purloined Duesenberg was in a car museum where thousands of people would look at it and nobody would notice it; nobody would realize that it was the stolen Dusie?

' . . . was already in effect when I took over the agency, see, so I don't know what you really want from me. Hey?' Mueller reached across the restaurant table and rapped Lindsey on the forearm. 'Hey? Son of a bitch, you drag me down here to ask me questions and you aren't even listening to me!'

'I'm sorry. I was just thinking — '

'I'll bet you were. Listen, I'm going to have another beer. You want one? Hey, you're paying, might as well enjoy.'

'No. Uh, no thanks. One's plenty for me. I'm sorry, what were you saying about the policy?'

Mueller said, 'Like I just told you, the policy was already in effect when I took over the agency. The car used to belong to the City of Oakland. When they sold it to that dumb club they took out the policy, and it's been in force ever since. But I didn't write it. Old Stannard did, the poor bastard. Cancer. Stannard wrote the policy. I just collect my commission every time it's up for renewal. Not much, but what the hell; money for no work is always okay with me, right?'

Lindsey said, 'Right. Did you ever deal with the club members, Elmer? I mean, face to face?'

'No, mostly by mail. You know, we used to bill directly. Had a girl in the office type up renewal notices and stuff. Then the companies started taking over billing, and everything got computerized.'

Mueller drained his glass and put it on the table. 'Got to make a pit stop now. Then I got my appointment.' He looked at his watch and started to stand up.

'So you never met anybody from the club?' Lindsey asked.

'Nah.' Mueller disappeared into the restroom.

Lindsey caught the waiter's eye and ordered two coffees, one to drink, one in the hopes that Mueller would drink it.

The coffee arrived at the table before Mueller returned from the restroom. Mueller slid into his chair and lifted his cup, took one sip and put it back down. 'Jesus, I've had rotten coffee in my life but this is the all-time champ.'

Lindsey sampled his coffee. For once he agreed with Mueller.

'Hey, I just remembered something.' Mueller dumped half a jar of sugar into his coffee. 'That helps a little. Phew! When I was standing there giving back their beer I just remembered something. I did meet a couple of those club people once. The policy came up for renewal and the computer recommended they increase their coverage and that bumped up the premium and they came in to see me about it. What a pair! Dressed like the

Duke and Duchess of Windsor and acted like they thought they were, too!'

Lindsey had his pocket organizer open and his gold pen poised. 'That would be the van Arndts.'

'I don't think they called themselves that.'

'How about Ollie and Wally?'

'Yeah!' Mueller grinned. 'That was it. Like Laurel and Hardy, Martin and Lewis, whatever. Dressed up like the Duke and Duchess. Drive up in this amazing car, a '46 Ford Sportsman. I checked on it — they don't have that insured with us, they got some other policy. But the club owns this Duesenberg and they drove all the way over from Pacific Heights to argue about a twenty-buck bump in their premium.'

'And did they go along with it?'

'Yeah, I talked 'em into it. Inflation, higher costs, the usual stuff. Plus, people don't want to buy stocks and bonds anymore, they want to buy collectibles. Well, they got to insure 'em or they're in trouble. So they went along. But you know, I got a read on them two.' He checked his watch again. 'Hell, I got to make my appointment.'

'Wait a minute! What about the van Arndts?'

'Okay, you just walk me out to my car.'

Lindsey dropped a bill on the table, and regretfully opted for hearing the end of the story rather than wait for his change.

'They're phonies,' Mueller said as they stepped onto the sidewalk. 'Those sparklers that the wife was wearing. They were paste. I used to be in the business. That's how I got into insurance. Diamonds, emeralds — paste. Gold settings — rolled. Husband — same thing. Fancy cuff links — phony. That Sportsman was real enough, but those two are phonies. Check 'em out.'

★   ★   ★

Ms. Wilbur was staring into her computer screen when Lindsey walked back into the office. She swung around, rubbing her eyes. 'There you were in Oakland and you had a call from the Oakland Police Department. I left it on your desk. Your friend Gutierrez wanted to talk to you. You could have gone to see him.'

He picked up the phone and dialled Oakland Police. Maybe Gutierrez had some good news for him.

'Look, Mr. Lindsey,' Gutierrez said, 'I'm not sure this concerns you but I think it does. Can you come in here? Right now, this afternoon? We want to talk to you and get some things straight.'

'Uh — I suppose so.' Lindsey frowned. 'Is it about the Dusie?'

'Please, Mr. Lindsey. I'd much rather talk to you in person.'

'Well, all right.'

'Don't come to my office. Phone up from the lobby. I'll meet you there.'

Lindsey shrugged at Ms. Wilbur. 'Back to Oakland again. Why doesn't anything ever happen in Walnut Creek?'

* * *

It was Lindsey's second time in the Oakland Police Headquarters. He didn't have to phone up from the lobby. Gutierrez was there waiting for him. He

94

guided Lindsey through the sign-in and visitor's badge routine and hustled him to the elevator before Lindsey had time for half a sentence.

In the elevator Lindsey managed to ask if there was news about the Dusie.

Gutierrez said, 'Sort of. We're almost there.'

'There' wasn't Gutierrez's office. Instead the frosted glass in the dark door said Homicide. What the heck?

They were greeted by a man with rumpled clothes and dark, wavy hair in disarray. Gutierrez said, 'Here's Mr. Lindsey.'

'Thank you, sergeant. Thank you for coming, Mr. Lindsey.' The rumpled man smiled. 'I'm Lieutenant High.'

'Is this about the stolen car?' Lindsey asked.

High said, 'More or less. Something terrible has happened, Mr. Lindsey. I hope you can help us with this.'

He led the way to a private office outfitted with battered filing cabinets and an ancient, scratched wooden desk. He motioned Lindsey to a shabby couch. Lt. High sat behind the battered desk.

Sergeant Gutierrez stood near the door.

'Mr. Lindsey, what are your feelings about Morton Karl Kleiner, the grandson?'

'Well, I only met him yesterday. At the hospital. I went there because Ms. Smith asked me.'

'Yes, yes. You went to see the old man. You didn't even know him, but Ms. Smith asked and you went. You're a very compassionate man, Mr. Lindsey. I admire that. But you met the grandson while you were there.'

'Briefly.'

'And your impression?'

'He is not a very nice man, Lieutenant. There was his grandfather in the hospital, maybe on his deathbed, and Morton trying to beat me out of a life insurance settlement. I don't even know if old Mr. Kleiner has a life policy. I was there because of the stolen car.'

'Well, I'm glad that you told me about your conversation and your feelings about him. From what I hear, he was not a nice man at all. Not anyone you would want for a friend.'

'Say, how do you know about our conversation?'

'Well, Ms. Smith was there, wasn't she? For part of the time, anyway. And the receptionist there in the hospital lobby — she told us that you and Mr. Kleiner were quarreling rather loudly. They're picky in hospitals, almost like libraries.'

'You've had Jayjay in here?'

'Earlier.'

'So I stood up to Kleiner. He needs someone to put him in his place. He's a bully and a parasite.'

High tilted his head. 'I think putting him in his place is hardly the way to describe what happened.'

'What happened? I told the guy to get lost and I took Jayjay back to the mansion.'

'Not directly.'

Lindsey thought for a moment. 'No, we stopped at the Hyatt. We had a drink. It was a miserable day. Cold and wet. And she was depressed. So I bought her a drink. So what?'

'You went from Kaiser to the Hyatt, from there to the Kleiner Mansion, and from there home to Walnut Creek. Right?'

'Listen, are you accusing me of something? What's going on? Aren't you supposed to read me my rights or something?'

High tilted his head again and cast a mournful glance at Gutierrez. Gutierrez took a plastic card out of his pocket and started reading it. For a second Lindsey went into shock, then he found himself laughing.

'I don't see what's funny, Mr. Lindsey,' said High. 'You don't mind if I turn on this tape recorder, do you?' He continued, 'You left Ms. Smith at the Kleiner Mansion and returned directly to Walnut Creek?'

'Yes, I — '

'And you remained there until noon today, when you drove to Emeryville to keep your appointment with Mr. Mueller?'

'Yes, I — '

'Do you want a lawyer, Mr. Lindsey? We can stop right now while you get a lawyer, if you want one.'

'No, I — I don't need a lawyer. Well, maybe Eric Coffman. No, I don't. What did I do? Am I under arrest? What about Mother?'

High rubbed his earlobe between forefinger and thumb. 'What about your mother? You spent the evening with her? She can testify that you didn't leave your home again until this morning?'

'No, I mean I'm worried about Mother. We ate dinner together last night, late, after I got home from Oakland. From dropping Ms. Smith at the mansion. We watched a movie on cable. I remember it. *Two Knights from Brooklyn*. William Bendix as a cabbie, Sheldon Leonard as the Frisco Ghost.'

High nodded encouragingly. 'That could help. And you didn't go out again? How could she be sure of that, Mr. Lindsey?'

'I don't think she could give much testimony anyway. She's, ah, mentally confused.'

High looked toward Gutierrez and grunted. 'You sure you don't want your lawyer? What did you say his name was?'

'Coffman. Eric Coffman. He's really in civil practice, but he's my friend; he does whatever we need in the family. That's just Mother and me.'

High held a telephone handset toward Lindsey. 'Call him if you want to.'

Lindsey reached for the handset. 'What am I accused of?'

'Nothing.'

'What happened? Is this all about the Duesenberg?'

'No, Mr. Lindsey. That's why you're in my office, not Sergeant Gutierrez's. Morton Karl Kleiner is dead. You had an argument with him yesterday, his body was found this morning, the coroner estimates that he was killed early this morning. Say, three a.m., give or take an hour. You're not accused of anything, you understand, but you certainly would have had time to do what needed to be done.'

'But I didn't! I hardly knew the man. I met him once and I didn't like him, I'll admit that. He was greedy about his grandfather's insurance, and I told him I couldn't do anything for him. But I didn't kill him, for heaven's sake!'

'No, no, of course not.' High's shoulders sagged as if he bore the weight of the world. He sighed. 'It's just that . . . well, I have to do my job, Mr. Lindsey. Just like you have to do yours. Sergeant Gutierrez is trying to help you with the stolen car; won't you help me a little with my job?'

Lindsey spluttered.

'Just put yourself in my shoes, Mr. Lindsey. One, you quarreled with Morton Kleiner at Kaiser Hospital. Two, you went out drinking afterwards. Three, Mr. Kleiner is killed a few hours later and the only person who can testify as to your whereabouts at the time of his death is your mother. Who was presumably sound asleep in her own bed at the time, and wouldn't have heard you leave your house if you were careful. And who is also, according to your own statement, not mentally competent.'

'But I didn't kill Kleiner! I didn't know he was dead until you told me. I didn't — uh — what did he die of?'

'Can't you tell me that?' High stood up and walked to a window. He stood with his hands clasped behind his back, twirling his thumbs. His shoulders seemed to droop even more. He peered down into street. The room grew silent. 'Can't you tell me how Mr. Kleiner died?' High pleaded.

'Give me the phone.' Lindsey dug in his pocket organizer for Eric Coffman's office number.

'Eric! You have to help me! This is urgent. Yes. Oakland Police Headquarters. Yes, yes, for heaven's sake, get off the Freeway at Broadway, it's right there. Yes I know you do civil work. Homicide. Lieutenant High. Eric, please! Okay. Okay, Eric, thank you. No, no I won't. Yes, yes I did. Yes they did. No I won't. No. No. Thank you, Eric.'

'Do you want to tell us anything else, Mr. Lindsey?' asked High.

He shook his head.

'Nothing new on the Dusie?' asked Gutierrez.

Lindsey shook his head. Not another word until Eric got there. Not one more word.

8

'Am I turning into an alcoholic, Eric?'

Coffman laughed. 'After that little scene, you're entitled to a couple of belts.'

Lindsey said, 'Yeah. How about you?'

'Not me.'

Lindsey signalled the bartender. 'Another.' Then, to Coffman: 'Listen, thanks for getting me out of that.'

'They didn't have anything. They were just fishing. Hoping for a lucky hit. You know the murder rate in this town. They get a body every day or two. Sometimes two or three a day. They're years behind. High must have figured, 'Hell, I'll needle this guy and see if he yelps.''

'Sons of bitches. You know they phoned my office and left a message for me to come in? Is that how they go after murder suspects? No wonder they never catch anybody!'

'Why use an officer and a unit when you can get your man for a nickel phone call?'

Lindsey yielded a grudging grin. 'That two-bit minor-league Columbo. Could you help me out with this, Mr. Lindsey? And all the time he wants to fry me.'

'Don't take it personally, Bart. High is a decent enough guy. What if you had killed Kleiner? He put together his little case, it wasn't so bad for a quick try. Thought he'd try it out on you.'

They were sitting on red leather bar stools in the Mexican restaurant across the street from Police Headquarters. Coffman hadn't been eager to go there — or anywhere — for a drink after leaving High's office, but Lindsey had said he'd go alone if Coffman didn't go with him.

'You didn't kill this Kleiner fellow, did you? I'm only asking because I'm a civil lawyer. I won't represent you if you come to trial for murder. If I were going to do that, I'd never ask if you had done it. I'd just assume you were innocent and work to make a case for you. But since I won't represent you, I can ask.'

'No, I didn't kill the man. I told High, I told you, I hardly knew him. I met him exactly once. The guy winds up dead. I'm sorry, but I didn't kill him, period.'

'Creepy, really creepy. I'll risk one drink.' Coffman signalled to the bartender. 'I'll buy.' He laid a bill on the wood. 'Okay, I'll absolutely accept that. You didn't kill this Kleiner personage. You went from Kaiser to the Hyatt to the mansion with Jayjay Smith, then alone to Walnut Creek. Then and you stayed home the rest of the night. You didn't sneak back to Oakland and shoot Morton Karl with your little bow and arrow. How was he killed, by the way?'

'I don't know how. That was the game High was playing with me, and I never did find out.'

'Then who did kill him?'

'I have no idea, Eric.'

Coffman poured his dark beer from bottle to glass. 'What was Kleiner doing in Oakland last night anyhow? Why didn't he go home to Petaluma?' He paused. 'What time did he leave Kaiser?'

'I don't know. Jayjay and I left around around four-thirty. I didn't see Kleiner leave. Maybe he hung around the hospital, maybe he left right after Jayjay and I did. Maybe he didn't go home at all. Whoever killed him, it wouldn't make any sense to kill him up in Petaluma and then drive fifty miles back to Lake Merritt to dump the body.' Lindsey closed his eyes. 'Poor Jayjay! Of all people to find the body!'

'You haven't spoken to her today?' Lindsey shook his head. 'You got something going there, buddy?' Coffman lifted his glass and grinned at Lindsey over its rim.

'What the hell are you talking about?'

'Chill out, buddy. I guess we family men just assume that you swinging bachelor types live a wild and crazy life. Weren't you an item for a while there with a lady cop? Now that's really something.'

'Marvia's a fine person, Eric. We just, well . . . after a while we figured that we didn't have as much in common as we thought we did. We're still friends.'

'Okay, Bart. I'm sorry.' Coffman drank his beer.

'Can we talk about this case, Eric? I want to know if anything else is going to happen. Do I need to hire you or somebody else? Is there going to be more of this?'

Coffman said, 'I don't think High is going to go after you. Probably you can just forget it. If he does pester you, I'm your attorney of record. I'll get you a criminal guy if you need one.'

'Thanks. That's reassuring.'

'That lady cop was really nice, Bart. I really liked her. She was in homicide, wasn't she?'

'Not at first. But after that Patterson killing they put her in it. Yeah.'

'Maybe you could get some ideas from her.'

'I'm not a cop or a P.I., Eric. I still walk with a limp, thanks to that mess. I got shot in the foot and I don't want to get shot again anyplace else. I'm just an insurance adjuster, and all I want to do is get back a stolen car so my company won't have to shell out half a million bucks.'

'Okay. Just a thought.' Coffman looked at his watch. 'Time for me to be getting back to the 'burbs.' He hoisted his more than ample weight off the bar stool. 'Like a lift in the old family bus?'

'Thanks, I've got my car here.'

Driving back to Walnut Creek, Lindsey thought about the case. Maybe Coffman's idea hadn't been so bad. He hadn't seen Marvia Plum in a long while. He felt a little guilty about it, but where were they going? A white suburban paper-shuffler who'd spent his whole life in the state of California, pushing middle age and still living with his mother. A black female homicide officer, ex-military, used to dealing with the turmoil and weird energy of a town like Berkeley.

He hit the brakes to keep from plowing into the back of a jeep. Maybe he would call Marvia after all. He'd like to see her again. Sex had something to do with it, sure, but that was only part of it. There was something about her that seemed real, attached. When he saw her he felt the ground under his feet, tasted the air. He felt more alive when he was with Marvia.

And she was a homicide cop. She had shown brains and fortitude and persever-ance in the Patterson killing.

He had dinner with Mother and

afterwards she found a channel that showed old Liberace programs. She sat there, delighted. He closed his eyes and thought about the Duesenberg theft case, now the Morton Kleiner murder case.

He knew that the cops didn't like private citizens interfering with criminal investigations, and he couldn't prove that the stolen Duesenberg and the Kleiner killing were connected. But what had Marvia's old boss, Sergeant Yamura, always said? *I know there are coincidences in the real world but they make me very nervous. I like connections that make sense a lot better.*

Right. The Duesenberg is stolen from the Kleiner Mansion. Old Mr. Kleiner winds up in the hospital, Morton Karl Kleiner comes to visit him and winds up adding his name to the honor roll of murder victims in Oaktown USA . . . As dislikeable a man as Morton Karl Kleiner had been, that hardly warranted a death sentence.

Lindsey picked up the telephone and punched in Marvia Plum's number. He could see the Raggedy Ann quilt on her bed as he sat there listening to the phone ring, waiting for her to pick it up.

★   ★   ★

Marvia wasn't at home, but she'd put in an answering machine and just hearing her voice made Lindsey think about things he'd started to forget.

By the time she called back Mother had gone to bed and Lindsey was looking at the late news. Marvia apologized for calling so late but Lindsey was glad to hear from her. They arranged to have dinner the next night. That was the important thing. He'd ask her advice on the Kleiner killing, the Duesenberg theft. He'd look into her eyes and . . .

That was not the way to go.

He turned off the TV. The theft of the Duesenberg had made the local media, just as the theft of a quarter-million dollars in comic books had made the media in the Patterson case. The newscaster's closing comment had been about what a shame it was that nothing rare and beautiful was safe anymore, and hoping that the

Duesenberg was insured. It was insured, all right!

He climbed in bed but he had a hard time falling asleep. He kept seeing Marvia Plum's dark face on the pillow.

★　★　★

In the morning Ms. Wilbur took one look at him and said, 'They give you the third degree down there?'

He shook his head. 'Just a misunderstanding. Their homicide detective just wanted to try out a theory. It didn't work; he dropped the whole thing.'

'Sure. How come you look so lousy, Bart?'

'Didn't sleep too well.'

Before Lindsey's second cup of coffee he had a call from Gutierrez. 'What can I do for you today, Officer Gutierrez?'

'I thought it was Oscar and Bart.'

'After yesterday? Come on, Gutierrez. High was gunning for my tail, and you were handing him the ammunition. What went on there?'

'Your friend Jayjay Smith got up early

yesterday and went for her regular jog by the lake. And here's Morton Karl Kleiner out for an early splash, only the back of his head is strangely concave.'

'He didn't drown?'

'No, coroner says there's no water in his lungs. He was dead from the blow to the head. Massive, traumatic brain damage.'

'And she called you?'

'She had my card, same as you did. Phoned me. I took a quick report and sent a unit for her; met her at High's shop.'

'Hah! For her you send a car, for me you telephone.'

'Yep. Oakland Police Department provides service for Oakland residents. Why pester Walnut Creek when your fingers can do the walking?'

'Look, Oscar, you didn't call me to chat. What's up?'

'Well, I just wondered if you had anything new for me, as a matter of fact. The Duesenberg seems to have vanished from the face of the earth. We get car theft reports in here like Chernobyl got fallout after the meltdown. They come in by the hour. I don't normally pay a lot of attention to one case. But this one intrigues hell out of me.'

'Me too.'

'So I put my feelers out, Bart. You develop contacts after a while, used car dealers who like to make friends in the right places. And who don't want to move hot merchandise. A couple snitches here and there. Most stolen cars turn up on their own, they abandon them. One way or another, we get most of 'em back, unless they're shipped over the border into Mexico or unless they're cannibalized. But this Duesenberg, it's too conspicuous to move and it doesn't make sense to chop it up, so where is it? It really bothers me!'

'I'm as much in the dark as you are, Oscar. I'm still working on the club members. I still think it must have been an inside job. And somehow I think the dead Kleiner fits in somewhere.'

'Just be careful, Bart. That's what I have to warn you. You don't carry any gun, you don't own any license. You find the car if you can, but don't mess with the

Morton Karl Kleiner case, okay?'

'I'll try not to. But if it's all tied in, I can't help it, can I?'

'Don't cross High, Bart.'

'No, I wouldn't.'

★　★　★

Lindsey ordered a sandwich for lunch. Ms. Wilbur took her break so Lindsey was alone in the office when Harden phoned.

'No, Mr. Harden, I haven't found the Dusie yet. No, the Oakland Police Department hasn't found the Dusie yet. No, Mr. Harden, I'm not mixed up in another murder case. No, Mr. Harden, this isn't Terry Patterson and the comic books all over again. And No, Mr. Harden, I haven't heard from Ms. Johanssen at National; I'll let you know if I do. Yes. Right. Absolutely.'

Ms. Wilbur returned during Lindsey's conversation with Harden. He hung up the phone, shaking, grunted at Ms. Wilbur and headed out for a walk until he calmed down.

For the rest of the day he flinched every

time the phone rang, but Johanssen never called.

Even Mother realized that he wasn't right. She fussed around him, making things worse with every pat and question. He finally phoned Joanie Schorr to come over and stay with Mother. Joanie brought a cassette of *Seven Brides for Seven Brothers*. At least that would keep Mother quiet and happy. Joanie made dinner for herself and Mother, and Lindsey was able to get away and shower, put on fresh clothes, and head for Berkeley and Marvia Plum.

★　★　★

Berkeley was the same place it had been the last time Lindsey was there: a mix of staid, rock-ribbed residential neighborhoods, old money, semi-industrial slums, yuppified shops and restaurants, and of course the university. And the fast-food joints and trendy clothing stores that catered to the university community. And of course the crazies who flocked to Berkeley's welcoming arms. The political crazies and the hophead crazies and junkies and alcoholics and the plain garden-variety lunatics.

Lindsey parked the Hyundai outside where Marvia lived on Oxford Street and climbed the familiar steps. He lifted the old brass knocker and rapped it against its base.

Marvia was wearing tight jeans and a plaid button-front shirt that showed off her figure to spectacular advantage. There were strings of beads woven into her black hair, bright brass and red and green glass. Her dark face made him catch his breath, totally against his will and resolve.

She must have made the first move, because he was standing awkwardly on the porch and then he was inside the Victorian vestibule embracing her with no sense of having moved and no sense of time having passed. She turned her face up to him, smiling. It was hard to believe that she was close to his own age, and not a high school girl.

'Come on upstairs. Can we relax a little before we leave?'

She led him by the hand. A couple of

her housemates were sitting in the common living room. Someone had put a CD on the player, a smooth saxophone gliding over a bass and percussion.

Upstairs he looked around Marvia's familiar room, the Golden Age comic books with their portraits of black athletes and superheroes displayed in their mylar protectors, the posters of Billie Holiday with an orchid in her hair.

Marvia drew him down into her easy chair and sat opposite him in her Raggedy Ann bedspread. Her room was not overly spacious or furnished. 'How have you been, Bart? It's been a long time.'

'I'm sorry. You know how it is. International Surety demands a lot. And then there's Mother.'

'How is she?'

'I'm sorry about how she could never, ah . . . '

'I understand that, Bart. It's a lot harder to take from some people than from others.'

9

It was Marvia's town so they took her '67 Mustang. She picked a place in El Cerrito that she said had a friendly bar and generous portions of plain food. Lindsey was relieved; he'd half-expected her to name one of Berkeley's exotic restaurants.

The place Marvia picked was called the Silver Dollar. The bar was dark and three-quarters full. A juke box glowed the same colors as the decorations in Marvia's hair.

Marvia nodded to the bartenders. There were two of them. A Bloody Mary appeared in front of her; the bartender lifted an eyebrow at Lindsey and he ordered an Irish coffee. Lindsey could feel the eyes on the back of his head. El Cerrito was an old-fashioned town; interracial couples could still draw stares, if not worse.

When their bartender turned away to pick up the pot of coffee, Lindsey saw that he was wearing a leather belt with his name burned into it. His name was Robert. The bartender leaned on his elbows. 'How you doing, Sarge?'

Marvia said, 'Good. Busy. Tired.'

He turned to Lindsey. 'I'm Robert. Who are you?'

Lindsey gave his name.

Robert extended his hand. 'That your regular drink?'

'I'm not sure. Seems to be getting to be.'

'I'll remember it. Excuse me.' Robert went to fill an order at the service bar.

Lindsey turned toward Marvia. 'You're a sergeant now?'

'You didn't know? O'Hara finally retired, Dorothy Yamura got promoted to lieutenant, and I made sergeant.'

'Congratulations.'

'I don't know. I really enjoyed my work before. Something new every day, meet lots of interesting people.'

'Including the dead ones?'

'Sure. Now . . . now I'm turning into a bureaucrat. Sit at my desk and do paperwork all the time.'

'Yeah. Welcome to the club.'

'But you have to keep moving up. I guess.' She lifted her glass and sipped. 'That's what they always taught us, anyhow. I'm not so sure.'

Over dinner Lindsey said, 'I've got an odd case, Marvia. You remember that other one, the comic books. Now somebody's stolen a 1928 Duesenberg. You know International Surety. They don't want to pay off.'

'So you're playing detective again.'

'I guess that's what it amounts to. Anyhow, I thought maybe we could just — I don't know — maybe talk it out a little. You helped me so much last time. So . . . ' He shrugged.

'Not a Berkeley case, is it?'

'Oakland.'

'Who're you working with?'

'Oscar Gutierrez, mainly. And a Lieutenant High.'

'High? In auto theft? I thought he was in homicide.'

'Well, he is.'

Marvia put down her silverware and looked him in the eye. 'Now we're getting somewhere. I thought this was a date. It's a private consultation, isn't it?'

Lindsey felt himself blushing.

'Are you trying to solve another murder, Bart? That last one was a fluke. Believe me, it's tough enough for professionals. Amateur detectives solve murders in paperback novels but they don't do it in real life. Once in a blue moon!'

He picked up a piece of French bread to keep his hands busy.

Marvia reached across the table and took his hand in hers. 'You're not just playing detective, are you? You're in trouble. Why else would High be involved?'

He told her everything that had happened.

When he finished, she said, 'I don't think you have to worry. Your friend Eric Coffman sounds pretty solid to me. If he walked you out of there with nothing more on paper, if he says you're clear, he's probably right.'

'It's still pretty scary. Do you think the murder is connected with the Duesenberg? I keep remembering Sergeant Yamura.'

'I think so, too. Did High tell you if Morton Kleiner was robbed? Anything taken, any other sign of assault or activity? Marks? Ritual activities?'

'No, I didn't think of asking him all those things, but he would have told me, wouldn't he?'

She grinned at that. 'Well, he might have. But he told you the cause of death, and I'd think he'd have held that back too if he was going to hold back. What about Kleiner's home?'

'He lived in Petaluma.'

'I'm sure High's been in touch with the people in Sonoma County. Probably has a report on his desk right now. Huh.' She poked her fork at a green bean. 'So you're not really out to solve this murder.'

'Not really. But if I'm going to find the car and save International Surety its money, I think I have to consider it at least.'

'Yes. Look, tell me about this New California Smart Set.'

He described the party at the mansion and the members of the club he'd met: Ollie and Wally van Arndt, Joe Roberts, Martha Bernstein. He mentioned Elmer

Mueller's theory about Ollie and Wally.

'You keep running into these UC connections, don't you? That sweet Professor ben Zinowicz and the stolen comic books.'

'Don't remind me! My foot still hurts.'

'You think Martha Bernstein has something to do with ben Zinowicz?'

'I doubt it. The University of California is big.'

'Even so, they might have known each other. They might have served on interdepartmental committees, or been faculty club buddies, whatever. It's a long shot, but it wouldn't hurt to check it out.' Marvia pursed her lips. 'Bernstein might be able to give you some help, though.'

'And Mueller's idea?'

'That the van Arndts might have stolen the car?'

'No, I saw them at the mansion. They couldn't have.'

'But they might have arranged something. Hired a couple of professionals to take it and deliver it. Sort of an inside-outside job.'

Lindsey looked at his watch. It was twenty after ten.

They ordered coffee, passed up dessert.

Marvia said, 'You want me to talk to Lieutenant High, don't you?'

Lindsey shrugged.

'I don't think I can do that. It's his case. You see, if he came to me — well, it's his case. He has the right to ask for help. If there were any Berkeley connection, he'd probably call Dorothy Yamura and I might wind up involved. But I don't see how I can push into an Oakland case.'

Lindsey tightened his lips. He wasn't surprised to hear that, but he'd been hoping.

The night had turned cold. In the parking lot they stood beside the Mustang for a moment and embraced. Lindsey could see his own breath and Marvia's in the air.

They climbed into the car and headed back toward Berkeley.

Waiting at a traffic light, Marvia said, 'I could ask Tyrone about that car.'

'Your brother?'

'He knows everything about cars. Especially old cars.'

'Ought to get him together with Gutierrez.'

'Well — it's up to you.' The light turned green. Marvia started the Mustang forward.

'You think he could help me?'

'There has to be something about that car. You told me yourself that nobody would just drive around in a stolen Duesenberg. So, where is it? And why did they steal it? Like stealing the Mona Lisa. You can't show it off, you can't let anybody know you have it, and you can't sell it — at least, not easily.'

A late train whirred overhead as the Mustang passed under its elevated tracks. Passengers were silhouetted for a few seconds: couples headed home from dinners out, workers headed home from late shifts.

Lindsey said, 'A serious art collector won't stop at buying stolen goods. If he can't show his prize off publicly he'll show it to a few choice friends sworn to secrecy. Or he'll just keep it to himself, keep it in a secret place and just look at it. Maybe touch it.'

Marvia laughed. 'You make it sound like sex. Something secret that they do in

125

the dark of the night, a hidden pleasure.'

'I guess so. Anyway, you want to give me Tyrone's number?'

'I'd better have him call you, okay?'

The radio faded as they drove through the Solano tunnel. A few minutes later Marvia pulled into a parking place less than a block from her house. They sat in the car a while longer, talking. Lindsey realized that Marvia had said little about her work despite her recent promotion, and less about herself.

He got up his nerve to say, 'I've missed you, Marvia.'

She took his hand. 'You should have called me.'

'I know it. I just — I'm sorry.'

She said, 'I have to get up early tomorrow. I enjoyed it, Bart. Thanks.' She turned her face up toward him.

He put his hands on her cheeks and kissed her.

At length Marvia pulled away. 'What if a cruising cop stops and shines a light on us?' She laughed. 'I really have to go.'

He walked her to her door and held her again, like a boy half his age reluctant to let his first flame out of his company.

Marvia said, 'Not tonight. Please don't be angry.'

He released her and waited while she fitted her key to the lock. 'I'll have Tyrone phone you,' she said.

*   *   *

In the morning Lindsey phoned Jayjay Smith. She'd been in touch with Dr. Mukerji; Mr. Kleiner's condition was unchanged.

'What about telling him we got the Dusie back?' Lindsey asked.

'He's not responding well to stimuli, Bart. I don't think he's aware enough to reach him.'

'Jayjay, about Morton Karl Kleiner . . . I saw Lieutenant High yesterday.'

'He told you I found, ah, the body.'

'Do you think Morton's death is connected with the Duesenberg? You have any idea who did it?'

She didn't answer.

'High acted as if he thought I was the one,' Lindsey offered. 'He didn't push me too hard, but he did enough. I had to get my lawyer in there. Then High backed off.'

'He really thought you killed Morton Kleiner?'

'My lawyer, Eric Coffman, thought High was just fishing. I looked like a likely fish, so he tried to haul me, but it didn't work.'

'You had an alibi? After you dropped me off, I mean? Do you know what time he was killed? I went out for a run by the lake around six o'clock. And there he was. He must have been floating around in the lake and he somehow drifted back to shore. I think it was just coincidence that he wound up at the mansion. Unless he was trying to swim to the mansion. But he was fully dressed. I don't know what to make of it.'

She's rambling, Lindsey thought. *Just running on because she's upset.* 'I think Lieutenant High said Kleiner was killed around three in the morning. Have you talked to him again?'

'No.'

'He said they did an autopsy and the

coroner said he didn't drown, he was killed by having his skull caved in. He was dead when he was dumped in the lake.'

Jayjay Smith whispered, 'Oh, my God!'

'So High tried to pin it on me.'

'But you're okay now.'

'Yes. I'll stay in touch.'

Even before he hung up another light was flashing on his telephone. He punched the button and heard an unfamiliar male voice. 'Mr. Hobart Lindsey? My name is Tyrone Plum. I'm Marvia's brother.'

'Uh, how do you do, Mr. Plum.' Tyrone Plum! The legendary car authority, the man Marvia said had bought an old hulk of a classic Mustang and restored it to creampuff condition for his sister!

'Marvia says you need some expertise. What kind of car you having trouble with?'

Lindsey told him.

Tyrone Plum whistled. 'A 1928 SJ,' he repeated. It was the same tone Lindsey had heard comic book collectors use when they spoke of a *Captain Marvel* Special Edition or a New York World's Fair Comic.

'I'm in the insurance business, Mr.

Plum, and a policy-holder has reported an SJ stolen.'

'What can I do for you?'

'Maybe you can tell me why somebody would take a car like that?'

Lindsey recited the by-now familiar reasons why it didn't make sense to steal a car like the Duesenberg. He ended with, ' . . . unless he's just a fanatic to wants to have it and keep it hidden. But I'm hoping that there's another reason. Something about this particular car. It's not just a beautiful, powerful collectible. What makes this car so special?'

'You mean this model of car? Or this particular car?'

'Either one. I don't know. Maybe we can get together. Maybe you can figure it out, or help me figure it out.'

There was a long pause. Then, 'What's in it for me?'

Lindsey smiled. 'We can pay a consulting fee. International Surety is always fair about business dealings.'

'Sure it is. Well, do you want to come to my office and we'll talk about it?'

'All right. Where would that be?'

Plum gave him an address near the Santa Fe tracks in Berkeley, just off the foot of University Avenue. 'But look,' Plum continued, 'don't come by today. I'm going to be up to my elbows in a Ford Skyliner. In fact, maybe after hours would be better. You don't want to spoil your nice suit with a lot of nasty grease.'

'Well, all right. But when — '

'I'll call you back tomorrow. Listen, how much of a consulting fee you think you can afford?'

Lindsey had taken heat from Harden about hiring high-priced consultants with company funds. He decided to hold back. 'How much do you charge?'

'Well, for mechanical work, a hundred twenty-five an hour.'

Lindsey ran a finger around the inside of his collar. 'I'll have to clear it with Regional, but all right. Shall I phone you back, or — '

'I'll call you tomorrow.'

Lindsey was staring at his telephone when it burbled at him still again. He was ready for almost anything by now.

It was a female voice, sounding slightly

slurred. Lindsey peered at his Seiko. It was barely ten o'clock. 'Hobart,' the woman's voice said, 'this is Wally. You remember me, don't you? Ollie and I want to invite you on a little picnic.'

Lindsey held the telephone away from his face and stared at it again. From the earpiece a tiny, sloshy-sounding voice was saying, 'Hobart? Wouldn't you like a nice day in the country?'

10

Lindsey had responded to Wally van Arndt's invitation by asking if the occasion was to be purely social in nature. At that point Wally turned coy, Ollie took over the conversation, and Lindsey repeated his question.

'Not quite, old man,' Ollie said. 'I am the president of the club, you know, and we're pretty concerned about our stolen automobile.'

The van Arndts' invitation had been followed by a call from Lieutenant High of the Oakland Police Department. 'Mr. Lindsey, I've just had some interesting information from Petaluma.'

'Morton Kleiner lived in Petaluma.'

'That's correct, yes. Police up there checked Mr. Kleiner's house after we'd informed them of his death. They agreed that it's our case, not theirs, but they checked out his house for us, and they found some things that might give us a lead.'

Lindsey said, 'What was that?'

'Well, I want to see it for myself. They've sealed the house but I talked to the chief up there, all I have to do is go by his office and pick up the key.'

'Yes. And — ?'

'I thought you might like to come along, Mr. Lindsey.'

'You mean, lure the suspect back to the scene of the crime and wait for him to give himself away?'

'You've been watching too many old movies, Mr. Lindsey. You're not a major suspect.'

'Then why do you want me?'

'Well, you were one of the last people to see him alive.'

'Jayjay Smith and me, right.'

'Are you suggesting that she killed him?'

'You're the cop. I'm just an insurance adjuster, as everybody likes to remind me.'

'Please, I know you're interested in the Kleiner family because of your own job, and maybe you can help me a little with mine. If you don't want to go . . . '

Lindsey glanced at Ms. Wilbur, who was observing him with amusement.

'Matter of fact,' he said, 'I just had a call from the Van Arndts, Mr. and Mrs. He's the president. They signed the insurance policy for the Duesenberg, so I suppose they're technically my clients. They invited me on a picnic.'

High laughed. 'I envy you all the luxury of going on a picnic on a working day.'

'It's just given me an idea. All of us are working on this case from our own angles. So I thought we could all — if the van Arndts don't mind, which I don't think they will — ride up to Petaluma together and see whatever it is at Kleiner's house.' He caught his breath. 'He lived alone, I take it?'

'Yep.' High paused, then: 'I think this is passing strange, but all right. Where were you planning to assemble?'

'Their apartment. In the city.'

'All right. Suppose you meet me here in Oakland, and I'll give you a ride over to their place.'

* * *

The day sparkled, a cool onshore breeze bringing clear air in from the Faralones. The bay itself was dotted with freighters and the white sails of small pleasure craft. The Marin headlands loomed craggily ahead. Ella Raines's rich, energetic voice gave way to the marshmallow baritone of Buddy Clark.

'You ever hear DAT tape, Lindsey?' Oliver van Arndt had his arm draped across the back of the Ford's seat. 'Sounds as good as compact disk. Had to get the machine from Japan. They won't sell 'em here — afraid of too many bootleg transfers.'

Lindsey admitted that the music sounded remarkably good for transfers of forty-three-year-old recordings. It was strange that van Arndt seemed equally comfortable with the past and the future, but ill at ease with the present. Something that Martha Bernstein, Ph.D. would love.

They stopped in downtown Petaluma and Lieutenant High disappeared into the police headquarters building to make his bureaucratic obligations and pick up the key to Kleiner's house. While they waited,

Wallis van Arndt walked to the back of the Sportsman. She returned carrying a thermos bottle and a pair of plastic stem glasses.

'A little martini?' She smiled.

Lindsey looked at his watch. 'Uh, I'm afraid it's a little early in the day for me.'

'None for me, my dear,' Ollie put in. 'I'm driving.'

Wally made a mock pout. 'You know it isn't good to drink alone.'

She poured herself a drink, put the thermos away and added an olive from the picnic basket to her glass.

The door of the Depression-era police building swung open and High strode down the steps. He took one look at Wally van Arndt, leaning against the Ford's front fender, and said, 'We'll have to wait while you finish that. Can't drive with an alcoholic beverage in the car.'

'I'm driving,' Ollie pointed out. 'I'm not drinking.'

High shook his head. 'Doesn't matter.'

Wally downed the last of her drink and deposited her empty glass in a public trash container. 'All gone,' she trilled.

'Now we can go.'

Morton Kleiner's house was isolated, up a dirt road northwest of the city of Petaluma. And the 'house' itself was clearly a onetime church. The steeple still rose into the clear air. There was no belfry — when the building was a working church, it must have belonged to a tiny and dirt-poor congregation.

Most of Kleiner's neighbors were apparently chicken farmers, but the only productive land near the abandoned church was behind the building. There had once been a burying-ground there. Fragments of wooden markers lay on the ground; clearly these people had been too poor to afford tombstones. And the graveyard had apparently been turned into a garden patch. Lindsey noticed some holes where plants seemed to have been torn out by the roots.

Lt. High squatted and fingered the loose soil. He studied it, then lifted it to his nose.

'Really, Lieutenant.' Ollie van Arndt stood over High, his studiedly casual elegance contrasting with High's shabby civvies. 'What can you learn by smelling a handful of dirt?'

High pushed himself to his feet, grunting softly. He brushed his hands together, dislodging the fragments of soil. 'Not much question what Kleiner was growing. Nobody's going to come by and steal your tomato plants in the dead of night. Or maybe, since Kleiner is dead himself, they might have come in broad daylight.'

Van Arndt grumbled: 'Did we really drive up here to investigate the case of the stolen vegetables?'

High smiled faintly. 'He was growing marijuana here. This patch was behind the house here in the old graveyard, hidden from the road. Unless the state drug people spotted it from a helicopter, Kleiner was pretty safe. It doesn't take a big patch to be worth a lot of money.'

Lindsey said, 'You think he was killed in a drug war?'

High smiled ruefully. 'I don't know. It's possible. But wait till you see what's inside. At least according to the local authorities.'

'Too much coincidence makes me uncomfortable in a case like this,' Lindsey said.

High raised an eyebrow. 'That your own opinion, Mr. Lindsey?'

'Uh — actually, I got it from a police officer I know in Berkeley. Dorothy Yamura.'

'I know her well. Good police officer, good detective. But let's take a look inside.'

High led the way to the front of the old church. Except for the steeple it was a one-story building that he been erected decades before by some hopeful congregation — Baptists, Methodists. It didn't have the look of the Russian Orthodox churches that had appeared in this region before the gold rush brought Americans west. Sold off, perhaps foreclosed, then converted into a house and used by a series of progressively less hopeful families, its paint peeling, the wood cracking here, rotting there, the onetime church was working its way gradually back into the earth.

High broke the paper seal on the front

door, inserted his key and pushed the door open. He ushered the van Arndts in, then Lindsey, then followed them.

Lindsey looked about him. There were electric lights in the room, but they were not turned on. Enough sunlight filtered into the room to give it a sense of ghostly presence. Countless tiny dust motes wove an intricate pattern in beams of sunlight.

He heard Wally and Ollie gasp simultaneously as their eyes adjusted to the gloom. The pulpit and baptistry had been converted into a kind of museum, and a crude table had been draped with what looked like an old bedspread to create a makeshift altar.

The rear of the baptistry had been converted into a portrait gallery. Two cheap paintings made a diptych in the center. They were of men in World War II uniforms. The one on the left wore rather Spartan brown, with a leather belt over one shoulder and a Swastika armband on his sleeve. The other, a less familiar face, wore the midnight-blue jacket, white shirt and black tie of a naval officer. Hobart Lindsey did not know the details of Nazi navy regalia, but the amount of trim on the man's uniform and the gold stripes around his lower arms indicated that he was a very big shot.

Smaller portraits flanking the paintings of Adolf Hitler and the naval officer showed middle-aged men with stern visages dressed in the gray or black uniforms of different Nazi services.

Behind Lindsey, Lieutenant High's voice said, 'After the local police found this shrine they sent an officer down to look up the admiral in the town library. His name was Karl Dönitz, Chief of the German U-boat fleet from 1935 onward. Became Grand Admiral of the whole Nazi navy in 1943. When Hitler died in '45, Dönitz became Reichsführer and promptly surrendered to the allied powers. He served a few years in prison as a war criminal, then lived quietly until a few years ago. Was almost ninety when he died.'

Lindsey looked around for someplace to sit. The pews had long since been removed but Kleiner had furnished the place with a bed and a scattering of chairs. Lindsey lowered himself into one.

He said, 'I don't get it.'

'Always been a certain amount of right-wing activity around here,' High told him. 'You must have heard of things like the Aryan Nation and the NAAWP. And there's a certain kind of sick individual who just worships the old Nazis. Skinheads. I guess Morton Karl Kleiner was one of those sick ones. So who killed him? Rival drug farmers? Or somebody else in the Nazi underground? Remember George Lincoln Rockwell? These people kill each other, too.'

Wally van Arndt asked, 'Did you say that admiral's name was Karl Dönitz? Mr. Kleiner's name was Karl, too. Do you think there was a connection there, Lieutenant?'

High shook his head. 'I don't think so. President Kennedy's daddy and Stalin and Jesus's earthly father were all named Joseph and I don't think they had much of a connection.'

He walked to the makeshift altar. The cloth was covered with thick dust, but spots showed where some object had prevented the dust from accumulating and had been removed. 'The Petaluma police left those pictures up there because they're somebody's property now. Most likely old Mr. Kleiner. Your friend Ms. Smith, Mr. Lindsey, she probably ought to apply to the court for a conservatorship. I don't think there are any other heirs. Don't think there's anybody left from the family.'

He looked from Lindsey to the van Arndts. 'There were other things here, quite a display. German bayonets, various guns, one of those old coal-scoop helmets, all sorts of Nazi regalia. All down at headquarters. If I seemed to take a long time picking up the key to this place, I was looking over the weapons.' He shook his head.

Ollie van Arndt frowned at High. 'I don't see what this all has to do with us, the Smart Set or with the stolen automobile.'

High shrugged. 'Maybe it's just my way of getting out of a stuffy office and off to the country for a picnic.'

Mr. van Arndt grunted. 'What do you think, Lindsey? Are you part of this fellow's scheme, or are you as puzzled and annoyed as Wallis and I?'

Lindsey walked to the front of the room and stood gazing up into the old baptistry, studying the portraits. They all looked vaguely familiar. Probably Mother had watched them a hundred times on *Old Newsreel Theater* or some other nostalgia show, or on one or another of the history programs she loved to watch. Only she thought they were current events, not history at all.

'Why do you think he has Dönitz up there with Hitler?' High was standing behind Lindsey, slightly to one side.

Lindsey shrugged. 'Maybe Kleiner was named for Dönitz. You know, Wally's notion.'

'Hmph. Or maybe because he was the last so-called 'legitimate' führer. But if Kleiner had some kind of apostolic succession in mind, he might put Dönitz right up there with Adolf.'

Lindsey looked at High. 'If that's what he had in mind, it doesn't make much sense. Hitler was their big leader — they worshipped him. You said that Dönitz was

145

just the head of the navy.'

High rubbed his chin. 'You may be right. Still — I just don't know.'

Wally said, 'I'm getting the creeps, Ollie. Can't you make that man let us out of here?'

Mr. van Arndt said, 'He's not making us stay, my dear. We're not under arrest. We're just here on a picnic. Shall we repair to the car?'

The van Arndts had reached the door, and as it swung open, Lindsey heard Ollie mutter something to his wife. Something like, 'After all, my dear, he's from Oakland. One mustn't expect too much.'

High grinned at Lindsey. 'There was one other thing. A video cassette.'

Lindsey looked around the room, then back at High.

'I see you got the point, Mr. Lindsey. There's no VCR here. There isn't even a television. So why would he have had the cassette, do you think?'

'Because it was something he wanted to save. Something that he could take to a friend's house and watch whenever he wanted to see it.'

'Very good! Now, the Petaluma police have the cassette. They screened it. It was a feature film, story film, whatever they call them. Made in Germany during the war. There's a fellow on the force who was raised in Germany and knows the language. He translated the title for me. Here, let me see what he said it was.'

He fumbled for his notebook. It didn't look that different from Lindsey's pocket organizer. High flipped the notebook open. 'It's called *U-Boats Westward*. Remember, Karl Dönitz was head of the Nazi submarine fleet, the U-boats, before he became head of the whole navy.'

Lindsey waited for High to continue.

'It's a war story from the Nazi viewpoint. Nasty treacherous British fleet against the noble heroic Germans. Toward the end of the movie the surviving Nazi submariners get a medal from the big admiral himself. He actually played a part in the movie — played himself; made a little patriotic speech and handed out the medals.' He tilted his head toward the portrait gallery and gestured with his thumb. 'Admiral Dönitz. What do you make of that?'

* * *

They were halfway across the Golden Gate Bridge, headed home from the odd picnic, before it hit Lindsey. He was staring out the Ford's window, watching fog swirl in through the Gate, distractedly thinking that it was going to be a cold night.

He turned to Edward High and said, 'The Kleiners were Jewish.'

11

After Lt. High dropped him off at Oakland Police Headquarters, Lindsey had driven to the Kleiner Mansion and asked Jayjay if he could talk with her after closing. She'd agreed, but first Lindsey asked if he could use the phone. He needed to check up on Mother. And he had another call to make.

When Mother answered the phone she'd been distraught. She'd been watching a historical show on TV and she was terrified at the outbreak of war.

'What war, Mother?' Lindsey tried to slow her down.

'In Poland! They're invading Poland! Those horrible Nazis, I saw them. They're using horses to draw the artillery, and those terrible Stuka airplanes, diving down and dropping bombs on people. Everybody is trying to run away, people are running away from Warsaw!'

'Mother, Mother, calm down! Is Joanie there with you?'

'And the Russians are coming from the other side! It's terrible!' Mother was beside herself. 'They're just as bad, they're just as bad. That Stalin is just as bad as Hitler. He shot all those people just a little while ago, I saw it on the news. Trials right there in Moscow, and they took them right outside and shot them — '

'Mother, is Joanie with you? Can I speak to her?'

'Of course.' Mother's tone underwent a sudden change. 'I don't really know if I should let her see this — it's so terrible. Should children be allowed to see this? But I suppose they need to know. It's all part of their education, isn't it?' He could hear her, off the phone, talking to the teenager. 'Here, you talk to little Hobo. He's all upset about something. Maybe you can figure it out.'

Joanie took the phone.

Lindsey said, 'Joanie, what's going on?'

'Oh, it's all right.' In the background Lindsey could hear the sound of TV jingles. 'I've got the TV on that movie channel now, Mr. Lindsey. I'm sorry; she got involved in this documentary on the beginning of World War II. I was watching, too. I'm doing a paper for my history class.'

'And she thought it was the evening news?'

'I'm afraid so. I should have switched it over when I saw she was getting confused. But there's something else coming on now. Let me look it up.' He could tell that she had put down the telephone. There was a shuffling sound; she had to be looking something up in the cable TV monthly.

'It's *One Hundred Men and a Girl*. 1937. Deanna Durbin, musical comedy.'

That sounded good. That would calm Mother down and keep her calm. Lindsey said, 'Joanie, can you stay for a while? I'm not sure what time I'll get home tonight.'

Joanie said, 'Sure, Mr. Lindsey. I brought my laptop. I can work on my paper here. I'll get Mrs. Lindsey to bed if you want me to. Are you stuck somewhere? I could stay over and sleep on the couch.'

Lindsey wasn't sure that would be

necessary. But he asked her to take care of Mother. And if he wasn't home by eleven . . .

He looked up at Jayjay Smith. She was ostentatiously busy dusting the antique furnishings of the room. Lindsey said, 'One more call, all right?'

'I'm sorry. Should I leave the room? If it's personal . . . '

Before he could reply she disappeared.

He dialled Berkeley Police Headquarters and asked for Sergeant Marvia Plum. When she answered he told her about his earlier conversation with her brother Tyrone. 'Can we get together? Maybe that's a good idea, to ask Tyrone about the Duesenberg. But he seems a little reluctant to meet me.'

Marvia said she'd call Tyrone and set something up. Was Lindsey at home?

'No, I, ah — I'm at the Kleiner Mansion in Oakland. I'm still working on the missing car. I came over here to talk to the, ah, curator of the mansion. The car was stolen from here, you know, and — '

'Bart, you don't have to explain

anything. I'll phone Tyrone and set something up. You want me to call you there at the mansion or at your office in the morning?'

'The morning will be fine. I'll be at International Surety in Walnut Creek. I — '

'Bart, are you all right? I know where you work. Look, I have to go now. Bye.'

He hung up and went to look for Jayjay Smith. He found her standing before the mansion's huge fireplace. An ornate clock fitted with scrollwork hands and decorated with naked cherubs ticked sedately.

'That's a beautiful clock,' Lindsey commented.

'It's well over a hundred years old. The Kleiners knew something about furnishings of quality. It's lovely ormolu work, isn't it?'

Lindsey said, 'Ormolu work?'

'The metal. Ormolu. It's gold, thinly laid down over bronze. Gives it a very distinctive color and texture.'

Lindsey said, 'I'm impressed!'

'I have a funny kind of memory. Took a course in metallurgy in college — learned all the atomic weights, melting points, and so on. It's never been one damn bit useful, but I still remember it all.'

'Nobody ever tries to take the things from the mansion? Like that clock?'

'We keep a pretty close watch on rooms open to the public. Only the staff and myself have the use of the rest of the mansion.' She turned toward Lindsey. She'd opened a bottle of winery and stood with a glass in her hand, smiling at Bart. 'Would you like some?'

She was wearing a champagne-colored shirt and a pair of tan slacks that showed off her figure. The top couple of buttons of the shirt were open.

Lindsey accepted a glass of the wine and tasted it.

Jayjay said, 'I saw Mr. Kleiner today.' She had added a couple of huge floor pillows to the old polished wood and upholstery. She lowered herself to one of the cushions and put the bottle carefully aside. 'He was a little better,' she continued. 'He's still on IV. Dr. Mukerji says he has maybe a fifty-fifty chance. But he was conscious a little bit, and he drank some warm soup.' She made a rolling motion with her head. 'This is really uncomfortable, having to crane my neck to see you.'

He felt flustered. 'Uh, I'll, uh, sit.' He took a couple of steps and lowered himself gingerly to the cushion adjacent to Jayjay Smith's.

'Please don't put your shoes on the cushion.' She reached for his shoes, tugged at one of the laces. He pulled away, looked at her, then reached down and slipped off both shoes. He placed them neatly beside the cushion, their toes carefully aligned.

'You don't need that coat and tie, either. Are you hungry? Did you eat dinner yet?'

'The picnic was pretty big. And we didn't eat it until after Kleiner's house.' Lindsey slipped his arms out of the jacket and undid his tie. 'Could the old man talk?'

'A little. He didn't tell me anything useful, though. He's eighty-five years old and very weak.'

'Maybe I could see his room. Or the

garage. You said it was part of the mansion? Maybe if I see the place where he worked on the Duesenberg there'd be something to tell us something.' He sipped his wine. 'I'm not making much sense either, am I?'

'What happened today?' she asked.

He told her about the picnic and about what the authorities had found in Morton Kleiner's Petaluma home.

'That son of a bitch.' She looked at Lindsey. The angle between them made the firelight reflect in her eyes. They were light brown, barely darker than her hair. Her eyes, her hair, the fire and the furnishings of the room were all colors in a warm tapestry.

Lindsey sipped some more wine. 'Not a nice person at all. But who would have thought he was a Nazi? You told me the Kleiners were Jewish, Jayjay. How could Morton be a Nazi?'

She shrugged her shoulders. He could see her breasts rise and fall against the cloth of her shirt. 'Maybe he decided he was more German than Jewish. Maybe he converted to another religion. I don't think the real Nazis would have cared about that. Hitler and his gang. They had weird theories about race; it didn't matter if you were a religious Jew or became a Christian. They didn't care.'

Lindsey shook his head. 'I can't figure out people like that.'

He watched Jayjay Smith as she carefully put her glass down. She walked away and switched on some music, then turned back toward him. 'Is this all right?'

He nodded. She came back and sat beside him, watching the fire. The music she had switched on was a medley of show tunes.

'You know what?' Lindsey said. 'I think that graduate thesis might have something in it.'

'It might.' Jayjay Smith was leaning against him. He could see her face close in the firelight.

'You don't remember the student's name or the title of the thesis?'

'Not a bit.' She turned and put her hands on his cheeks, then drew his mouth to hers. He could taste the wine in her mouth, and maybe something spicy. He managed to put his glass down without spilling it on the cushions. He could feel Jayjay Smith's fingers in his hair and running down his neck.

* * *

He woke up early, staring briefly at the ceiling. Jayjay Smith lay beside him, her head on his shoulder and her leg across him. He flinched as she pinched his chest with her fingernails and pulled herself closer to him.

There was a clock beside the bed, its glowing digital readout showing 3:56 a.m. He relaxed and felt Jayjay Smith do the same. He had one arm around her and he closed his hand on her, feeling the warmth and solidity of her flesh. The room was chilly but there was a thick comforter on the bed, somehow thrown aside during the night. He was able to reach it with his free hand and draw it over their bodies.

Jayjay Smith made a sound in her sleep. She pulled herself against him, ground her body once against his, then lapsed back into quietness.

Should he feel guilty? He wasn't married, didn't have a committed relationship to anybody . . .

Why was he kidding himself? He wasn't thinking of 'anybody.' He was thinking of Marvia Plum.

He hadn't made any pledge to her, nor she to him. If he didn't see other women when he wasn't with her, it was because . . . well, because that was his particular lifestyle. It wasn't a moral thing. For all he knew she saw other men when she wasn't with him.

By the red light of the digital readout — 4:11 a.m. now — he looked at Jayjay Smith. He let his eyes close. When he opened them he was alone in the bed. He turned to the clock and saw that it was eight o'clock. He could hear sounds coming from another room. He slid his feet over the edge of the old bed and stood up.

Jayjay Smith's voice said, 'Hey, you're up. Good morning!'

Lindsey said, 'I'll be late for work.'

'Sorry about that. How about some

scrambled eggs and toast?'

'Harden might call. And Mother! Joanie has to get to school.' He fumbled for his clothing.

Jayjay Smith appeared in the doorway, looking fresh and smiling. She wore a different shirt and tight jeans. 'Bet you'll feel better after a shower. And you can borrow my razor.'

He felt fierce pressure from his bladder. He ran to the bathroom naked. A little later he towelled off, emerged and dressed in yesterday's clothing. He made his way to the kitchen.

'Breakfast's ready,' Jayjay Smith said. 'Here, sit down. Take a look at the paper.'

He scanned the *Oakland Tribune*'s front page. It was full of politics and crime but there was nothing about the murder of Morton Karl Kleiner. Yesterday's news. There were a couple of drug-war shootings reported in Oakland and a drug-connected bombing in Colombia.

Jayjay Smith poured two cups of coffee and sat down opposite Lindsey. She smiled at him and touched him on the back of one hand. 'You know something,' she said,

'I'd say you were a little bit ugly.'

'Thank you very much.'

'Don't knock it. How come you're so sexy?' She put scrambled egg on a corner of toast and ate it, watching him all the time. 'What the hell, Jack Palance is old and ugly and he's absolutely gorgeous. You've got something to shoot for.'

He looked at his watch. It was almost nine o'clock. 'I have to call my office.' He'd had a flash of inspiration. He punched in the Walnut Creek number and Ms. Wilbur answered.

'Well, good morning. And what can I do for you today, Mr. Lindsey?'

'I, ah, I'm in Oakland, working on this Duesenberg claim. I'll be back in the office this afternoon. If, ah, Sergeant Plum of the Berkeley Police Department calls, just take a message, okay? I'll see you this afternoon.' Click.

'You have to go?'

'My mother isn't very well. I want to see her before I go to my office.' He wolfed down the rest of his eggs and pushed himself away from the table.

Jayjay Smith stood up and Lindsey put

his arms around her. He held her lightly, feeling her shoulder blades in the palms of his hands. He kissed her on the cheek. 'I — thanks.'

She said, 'Come again.'

When he got back to Walnut Creek he found Mother happily watching a *Dennis the Menace* rerun. Joanie had stayed the night, breakfasted with Mother, and gone on her way.

12

At the office Lindsey confronted his incoming telephone calls. There were none from Harden at Regional or Johanssen at National, thank heaven. But there were some calls that Lindsey had to make. In fact, it looked as if he was going to spend most of the day on the phone.

Among the incoming calls was one from Oscar Gutierrez at Oakland Police Headquarters. That one Lindsey returned.

'I had a little talk with Lieutenant High,' Gutierrez said. 'You went on a picnic together? You had a couple of those Art Deco people along, right, Bart?'

'It was their idea. Ollie and Wally van Arndt.'

'Uh-huh. Your insurance company's policy is in Mr. van Arndt's name, isn't that right?'

'The policy is in the name of the club. It's not uncommon. The payment goes to the corporate entity, not to the officer who signs the application. What's your point, Oscar?'

'Nothing really.' Lindsey believed that like he believed Nixon wasn't a crook. 'It's just that I thought you might have found something out about the Duesenberg.'

'I don't think so. Presumably High told you about Morton Karl Kleiner's home?'

'His church, you mean? He said it was pretty strange.'

'That's putting it mildly.'

'Do you see a connection?'

'You call me up and you want me to do your job for you? Don't they pay you guys? Who made me a detective, anyway?'

'Now, now,' Gutierrez soothed. 'We call on citizens for help all the time. Besides, you help me out, we get your car back for you and you don't have to pay any insurance claim.'

Lindsey sighed. 'I don't think Morton Kleiner had anything to do with the car. I think maybe he got mixed up with a bunch of Nazis and they bumped him off. Look, Oscar, what else can you tell me? Are you making any progress at all?'

'We're still working on it.'

Right. Sure they were. 'Thanks a lot, Oscar.' He hung up, annoyed.

He called Martha Rachel Bernstein before he took his morning coffee break. She was in her office and he asked her about the graduate student who'd done the thesis on Otto Lilienthal Kleiner.

A pause, then: 'Oh, sure, I remember that. It wasn't a thesis about Otto Kleiner. It was called something like 'Anti-Semitism in Times of Economic Stress'. It wasn't really about Kleiner; it was a case study of a phenomenon. He just happened to be the case.'

'Right. Can I get a look at that? Would there be a copy in the library there at the university?'

Bernstein said, 'I'm sure there would. They have all graduate theses on microfilm and hard copy both. Be easier for me to get than you. Let me have a little time and I'll call up a copy. You can look at it here or you can take it home with you.'

'How long?'

'Certainly by tomorrow first thing. You

can come in and look at it here if you want to. Give me a call first, please.'

He said he would. Good! Another piece was falling into place.

He punched in Marvia Plum's number at Berkeley police. A civilian clerk took the call and said that Sergeant Plum was out of the office. Could she take a message?

'This is Hobart Lindsey. When she calls in — '

The clerk cut him off. 'Sergeant Plum left a message for you, Mr. Lindsey. She says that she and Mr. Tyrone Plum will meet you at Mr. Plum's place of business at seven o'clock.'

'Okay, thanks.' He'd have to face Marvia now. He'd hoped to get it over with on the telephone, but he'd have to face her tonight.

But — her brother would be there. Maybe they'd be so busy, he wouldn't have to talk about last night. That was something to hope for.

★　★　★

He had lunch with Eric Coffman again. Coffman got to the restaurant first and was sitting with a martini in one hand, a copy of the *Contra Costa Times* in the other, his briefcase telephone balanced against his ear and a pencil in his hand.

He saw Lindsey arrive and waved him to silence. He mouthed a few words into the telephone, then put it back into his briefcase. 'Good to see you, buddy. Have a seat. I'm one ahead of you in the libation department, can I order you something?'

'No, uh — I've got too much to do this afternoon.'

Coffman waved his hand and a waitress approached. Coffman already had a menu. He handed it to Lindsey. Lindsey glanced at it abstractedly, then ordered a sandwich almost at random.

Coffman frowned through his beard. 'Your mom okay?'

'She was all excited about a commercial she'd seen on TV. Something about a 50s rock-and-roll revival. She asked if I wanted to go to the show.'

'I think I saw the same commercial. And they have a big ad in today's *Times*.

You going to go?'

'No. I mean, I don't know. She said maybe Dad would be home soon and they'd take me. It's upsetting.'

'I understand. But — there's nothing can be done for her?'

The waitress brought their meals.

Lindsey shrugged. 'I took her to the doctor. He sent us to a psychiatrist. He put her through a battery of tests. He gave me a lot of babble. But what it came to was, Dad's death upset her so badly that she just refuses to accept it. So she keeps pretending that he's still alive. So she keeps wandering into the past, into the time when he was alive.'

'Sure. But you've known that for years. What does he want to do about it?'

'Well, he offered two suggestions. Bring her in for an hour of psychotherapy four or five days a week. I can't afford his rates. And I don't think she wants it. I won't do that to her. She's pretty happy as she is, reading old magazines and watching TV.'

'You said the shrink had two suggestions.'

'Oh. The other was to, ah, institutional-ize her, put her away. You hear these horror stories about abusing patients. No way I'll do that.'

'Yeah.' Coffman's plate was empty. He folded his newspaper and handed it across the table.

Lindsey took the paper and looked at the page Coffman indicated. 'That the ad you mean?' He was happy enough to change the subject. He read partway into the ad. ' "The good old days of rock and roll are back! A giant night of fun with all your favorite stars!" '

Coffman grinned.

'Maybe I'll pick up a couple of tickets,' Lindsey said. 'I wonder if Joanie Schorr would like to go with Mother? Or maybe I ought to go. Might be fun.'

'Better check on it then. I think those things sell out fast.'

Lindsey studied the ad. 'Something here for Dr. Bernstein's temporal dis-placement cases.'

'What's that?'

'Just thinking about one of my professor friends. Doing a paper on people who can't cope with the present and have to live in the past. Or the future. I don't suppose any of the Art Deco people are involved in this. Too modern for them by twenty years. Joe Roberts, though — he might want to see the show. Maybe I'll ask him about it.' He held the paper back toward Eric Coffman.

'Keep it,' Coffman said. He signalled the waitress. As she headed toward their table he said, 'Got to go, Bart. Got the other guy on the ropes this time. We were in court all morning. I think he's ready to throw in the towel. I think we can settle up before we go back in there.'

He took the check from the waitress and disappeared toward the cashier's station. Lindsey left a tip on the table.

* * *

Joe Roberts phoned Lindsey before he could phone Roberts. 'Hey, I just got back in town. Had to take a meeting with the network in LA. Wondered if there's anything new here.'

'About the car?'

170

'Right. Oh, and — you getting along all right with Jayjay?'

Lindsey felt his cheeks getting warm. 'Ah, she's very helpful. She's been keeping in touch with old Mr. Kleiner. Nothing new about the Duesenberg.'

'Yep. Say, I didn't mean to abandon you at the mansion like that. I just, ah . . . '

'No, it's okay. I didn't mind.'

'You going to spend any more time at the mansion?'

'Why? Is this about the Duesenberg?'

'Well, I just thought if you were headed over there, I might kind of tag along.'

The last thing Lindsey wanted to do was return to the mansion with Joe Roberts in tow. You don't spend the night with a woman and then just show up on her doorstep with another man who's been chasing after that same woman, and whose previous approaches have been unwelcome. Still, he didn't want to offend a potentially valuable ally.

He said, 'Maybe I ought to phone Jayjay and see if it's all right with her.' He felt himself beginning to burn.

171

Roberts said, 'Maybe we could go over there tonight. I mean, I'm on my own here. I don't have to punch in and out or anything. But if you're stuck in your office . . . And the mansion doesn't close to the public for another couple of hours.'

'Sorry, I can't go over there tonight. I've got a meeting.'

'Oh?'

Nosy character, Lindsey thought. 'But maybe tomorrow. If it's okay with her, you want me to set it up for tomorrow? Or as soon as I can.'

Roberts said that was all right. He sounded a little disappointed.

Lindsey had to deal with his own feelings. His night with Jayjay had been different from any he had experienced in his life.

Not that he'd had experience with many women. Marvia Plum had been the first woman he'd ever had an intimate relationship with, the one who had shown Lindsey what a woman was like. He felt comfortable with her. There was no challenge, no demand, just a mutual sharing and giving of affection and of pleasure.

172

Jayjay Smith had been exciting. Her lovemaking was daring and accomplished — and he felt that he had pleased her. Certainly she'd invited him to return.

But she was not like Marvia Plum.

Joe Roberts said, 'Okay. You want to see about it and call me back? I'm at my office.'

Roberts's voice had broken Lindsey's reverie. 'Yes. Oh — Joe. I saw this commercial on TV and the ad in the paper. This 50s-60s rock-and-roll revival at the Coliseum Arena.'

'Oh, yes. Doo-wop, shoo-bop. You betcha.'

'Is it going to be tough to get tickets to that?'

'You interested in that show?'

'Actually, it's for Mother. I'll come with her, of course. She couldn't go to it alone.'

'Nah, you shouldn't have any trouble getting tickets. Going to be a good show, but it'll take a while for those tickets to go. This is old timers' night. Look, just hold off. I can probably get you a couple of comps through the network.'

'You planning to attend?'

'I might. But you go ahead and phone Jayjay Smith, and I'll phone the promoter's office. I'll see what I can do for you.' Roberts clicked off.

Lindsey looked at Ms. Wilbur. She smiled at him. He wondered about Roberts. What was going on between Roberts and Jayjay Smith? From the things she said about Roberts, she didn't like him and had not welcomed his past advances. But Roberts had been eager to get back into the mansion.

And Roberts had been the one who brought Lindsey to the mansion previously, set him up with Jayjay and taken a disappearing powder. Was that a maneuver? Did Roberts have something else in mind? Did Jayjay?

He phoned the mansion and asked Jayjay if he could come over again. She said he could. He said he wanted to look at the garage and look over Otto Kleiner's work area and the stock of tools and spare parts that he worked with. Jayjay said there would be no problem. When did he want to come?

He wasn't sure. He'd phone and let her know. He started to ask if he could bring Joe Roberts along, then decided not to say something that might stir up a hornet's nest. He'd talk it over with Roberts before he called Jayjay to set the time.

Lindsey had an early dinner with Mother and left her sitting calmly in front of the TV. He kissed her on the cheek and told her to phone Joanie Schorr if she felt worried or upset. She squeezed his hand, then turned back to the TV screen.

Lindsey got into the Hyundai and headed for Tyrone Plum's garage in Berkeley. He hummed to himself as he drove. He checked his watch, got out of the Hyundai, and rapped on the sheet-metal door. The sign on the top of the building read Classic Auto Restorations Unlimited.

Tyrone Plum opened the door and let him in.

13

Tyrone had sent Lindsey to his personal travel agency, an outfit on College Avenue. Lindsey didn't like doing business in Berkeley but he didn't want to alienate Tyrone. And Tyrone had insisted on researching the Duesenberg. Lacking access to the stolen car, Tyrone insisted, the next best place to go was the automobile museum in Reno. Tyrone knew they had a Dusie there, and a technical library and a staff of mechanics who could answer the toughest questions.

The travel agent assured him that the Metroliner was a safe, modern aircraft. Sky West Airlines favored it for short hauls and short-runway operations. It was perfect for flights between Oakland and Reno.

If they left Oakland International at 9:40 a.m. they could be in Reno before eleven and check into Harrah's Hotel and Casino by mid-afternoon. They could spend the rest of the day at the automobile museum, Tyrone huddling with the technical staff, and have an evening on the town. Return the next day.

The only problem was Marvia's schedule. Lindsey could get away; Ms. Wilbur ran the office with perfect competence when he was absent. And Tyrone said that Classic Auto Restorations Unlimited operated by appointment only; he had more business than he could handle, anyhow. But cops worked by duty roster, and Marvia was more than lucky to have a Monday-through-Friday schedule. She could leave on Saturday, return on Sunday, report for duty Monday.

When Lindsey told Ms. Wilbur his plans, she frowned. 'I don't know, Bart. Have you cleared that with Mr. Harden?'

'Do I have to?'

'What happens if the voucher hits Regional and Harden bounces it? You ready to reimburse International Surety?'

Lindsey took a few deep breaths, then nodded. 'I guess you're right. We have any of those expense authorization forms around? I'll fill one out and send it up to

Regional. Let Harden play little tin god while I go after the money.' Of course, by the time Harden saw the request, Lindsey would have gone to Reno and come back. Let the big-time leader say no then!

★　★　★

Meeting Tyrone Plum at Oakland International, Lindsey barely recognized the man. Fortunately, Tyrone was with Marvia, and Lindsey would know her anywhere. She wore a quilted vest over a heavy shirt to travel; the March morning was chilly and damp.

Tyrone looked like a perfect yuppie, not the grease-covered mechanic Lindsey had last seen emerging from beneath a 1939 Hudson convertible brougham. Lindsey had arrived at Tyrone's restoration garage and been captivated by the car.

But now they were flying east to Reno. Lindsey got to share a seat with Marvia. Tyrone sat across the aisle.

Even though the propellers were powered by turbines and ran almost as quietly as jets, Lindsey imagined them as old-fashioned piston engines. He watched the wings for dancing chorines and found himself humming a tune from *Flying Down to Rio*, but the dancing girls failed to appear.

Marvia broke his reverie with a poke in the ribs. 'People are staring at us.'

Lindsey reddened and fumbled in the seat pocket for something to read. Somebody had left the previous day's Reno paper in the pocket, and the cleaners had missed it. He turned the pages and found an ad for the same big rock-and-roll revival show that was coming to Oakland. Apparently it was coming to Reno, too.

They took a cab into town and checked in at their hotel. They took two rooms. Both the desk clerk and the bellman had assumed that Tyrone and Marvia were a couple that Lindsey would be staying in a single. Maybe he would — but when they reached their floor Tyrone told the bellman that he wanted the single. Lindsey looked at Marvia. She said nothing.

Inside their room, the bellman put their suitcases on stands, pulled the drapes, showed them how to work the temperature controls, and waited. As he tipped him, Lindsey asked where the automobile museum was. The bellman said the museum was in temporary quarters in Sparks.

Downstairs, they grabbed a sandwich without leaving the hotel. Lindsey picked up a pocketful of quarters from the cashier and lost them in a slot machine. Then they rode to the museum in a free shuttle. Harden would approve.

The cars were housed in a huge, incredibly ugly industrial building, an abandoned factory or warehouse surrounded by a dirt parking lot. Lindsey was appalled. When he paid his admission he asked the cashier for a receipt. And he asked how a world-famous collection wound up in a place like this. The cashier said that they were building a permanent home for the collection in downtown Reno; these were temporary quarters.

But if the exterior of the museum was unimpressive, its contents were overwhelming. Lindsey stopped in front of a magnificent black Chrysler — Al Jolson's personal 1931 model. Marvia took his hand. They wandered from aisle to aisle, peering at an American-built Rolls Royce, a scarce air-cooled Chevrolet, a Stutz Bearcat.

Tyrone appeared at his shoulder. 'Look, you want me to find out what's so special about that '28 Duesenberg. I'm going to look at the Dusie, then head for the research department. You want to come along?'

The Duesenberg was magnificent. Lindsey could imagine John Barrymore or Margaret Dumont cruising majestically through the roaring 20s in just such a car, dispensing wealth to the eager masses. Some plutocrat from Joe Roberts's *Jazz Babies* series might own such a car. It was spectacular, overwhelming — but he could see nothing about it that told him who stole the Dusie from the Smart Set.

Lindsey looked at Tyrone. 'What do you see?'

'I see a great car. I'd love to get my hands on it — see what makes it tick. Take it out for a ride.'

'Sure. But nothing to tell us why

someone stole the one from the Kleiner Mansion?'

'That was a '28 Phaeton. Not quite the same model. But close to it. Can't be picky.'

Lindsey and Marvia accompanied Tyrone into the reference department. Tyrone immediately made friends with a technician who was more than willing to talk cars. Soon the technician and Tyrone Plum were deep into talk of manifolds and connecting rods.

Lindsey whispered to Marvia, 'Do you know what they're talking about?'

She shrugged. 'I only know Tyrone built that Mustang for me out of a junker.'

They left Tyrone talking with the reference technician and looked at fabulous cars for another hour. When they got back to the reference library, Tyrone and his new friend were deeper than ever into manuals and charts. Tyrone looked up and said, 'Carter here is going to stay after they close. I'm going to get under that Dusie's hood. You two can hang around if you want to, else I'll see you back at the hotel.'

Lindsey said, 'I think I really ought to

stay here. I mean, I'm on company business.'

Carter looked up from a manual. 'I read about that stolen Dusie. Too bad. You got any clues? You a dick?'

'No clues. I'm an insurance adjuster.'

'Guess you'll have to pay, then.'

'We may. I was hoping Mr. Plum could learn something by studying one of your Duesenbergs that might point us the right way.'

Marvia said, 'This is fun but I'm getting pretty tired. You see any reason for hanging out here, Bart?'

He didn't, really. They left Tyrone and went back downtown.

The day had been cool and damp in Oakland. In Reno it was hot and dry. The sun was setting over the desert to the east. The city didn't have very much pollution but it wouldn't be possible to see much of the night sky because of the casino lights.

They walked the neighborhood. It was like being in the middle of Mardi Gras. Mobs of people surged along the sidewalks, across the streets, pouring in and out of casinos. Every establishment seemed to have at least a row of one-armed bandits.

Lindsey and Marvia Plum wound up back in their hotel. They passed on the unlimited cheap food of the buffet and opted for a slower and more expensive meal in a pleasanter setting. The hotel boasted several restaurants; they settled on one with a nautical theme.

They lingered over brandy, then wandered through the casino again. Neither was eager for the day to end. But Lindsey caught Marvia stifling a yawn. 'You want to go . . . ?' He left the sentence there.

She held his hand and nodded.

In their room she drew the thin curtain but left the lightproof drapes open. Lindsey spent a while in the bathroom, came back wearing pajamas. Marvia Plum disappeared. Lindsey turned on the room radio, found some quiet music, climbed into bed. When Marvia came back he was in bed, the covers pulled up.

Marvia wore a — what did they call those things — a teddy. It looked something like the corsets that actresses wore in '90s musicals. It was far more arousing than nudity would have been.

She stood between him and the window. The lights of Reno, softened by the translucent window covering, silhouetted her. Lindsey sat up in bed. He felt himself trembling. His heart was thumping. He started to speak but Marvia held her finger up to her lips.

He said, 'But — Marvia.' He wanted to tell her a million things. He wanted desperately to tell her about being with Jayjay Smith.

* * *

When he woke up the room was light with morning, the radio was still on, and the telephone was burbling.

Tyrone Plum's voice said, 'You lover birds going to sleep in or you feel like some breakfast today? International Surety is buying, right, Hobart?'

Lindsey laughed. He saw Marvia lying beside him, smiling. To Tyrone he said, 'We'll meet you downstairs in a little while. I guess we can get a disk of oatmeal

185

somewhere in this town.' Then he slid down in the bed again, and put his arms around Marvia.

Later, over a sizable breakfast, he asked Tyrone Plum what his hours at the automobile museum had produced.

Tyrone shrugged. 'Not much. Carter says the '33 Weymann fish-tail had pretty much the same mechanical parts as your '28 Derham Phaeton. I crawled all over and under that thing. I studied the specs and then I spent some time under the hood and underneath the car again. Your company's getting its money's worth.' Tyrone sliced a slab of ham.

'But you didn't learn anything.'

'I learned plenty, Hobart. Plenty! Maybe I should pay you. I learned that anybody who wants one of the greatest cars ever built would have plenty of reason to steal that '28 Phaeton. But I don't know who it was.'

Lindsey groaned.

Marvia said, 'Do you think the trip was a waste, Bart?'

He looked at her. 'No.'

She smiled.

To Tyrone he said, 'Well, tell me some more.'

Tyrone said, 'Well, the cars cost around $8500 new. That was for what Duesenberg sold you. With the coachwork, that just about doubled the price. They were built in Indianapolis, the engines were built by Lycoming. Cars had a three-speed manual transmission, really easy to operate. That was one reason why people loved them so much — you could get a high-performance car and drive it yourself.'

Lindsey had his golden International Surety pencil in his hand and was trying to take notes, but he hardly knew what to write down.

Tyrone said, 'You could get to 110 miles per hour in second gear, up around 130 in high. They weighed around 4500 pounds; the engine and transmission alone weighed about 600 pounds. They were all straight eights, and with the supercharger they got up to 320 horsepower.'

Lindsey had his hand to his chin, the other still holding the pencil. 'Who owned the things?'

'Movie stars loved 'em. Clark Gable, Gary Cooper, Jean Harlow. And millionaires. Anybody with a ton of money who just wanted a great car. The Dusie was right up there with the Rolls Royce. People who own them still love them.'

All Lindsey could say to that was, 'Somebody loved this one too much.'

14

They got back into Oakland a little after five, and stopped at a Mexican restaurant for dinner. Marvia invited Tyrone and Lindsey to her apartment afterwards, but Tyrone begged off.

At Marvia's place on Oxford Street, Lindsey said, 'I was going to ask you — the other night, after we had dinner out, then you said it was a bad idea for me to come up. I guess it was.'

'But then in Reno I went to bed with you. You seemed to like it.'

'I loved it. I — I think I love you, Marvia.'

'I love you too, Bart. What are we going to do about it?'

'People in love still get married.' It took all his courage to say that, and it came out in little more than a whisper.

'I know. But — maybe that was what I was thinking when I said it would be a bad idea. If you came up here that night, we would have wound up in bed. And

189

then we would have wound up right where we are now, anyhow.'

'Marvia — I've been with — uh — with other women.'

She grinned. 'I just hope you're careful.'

'You don't mind?'

'People should keep their promises. You didn't promise me anything, you didn't have to keep any promise.'

'Then — '

'But marriage?'

'I know that Mother would be a problem. And where to live. Would you want to commute from Walnut Creek? Would you still be a cop?'

'That isn't all of it either.'

Lindsey took a deep breath. 'I know you must have been with other men. What you said about promises — that goes both ways, Marvia. You never promised me anything. But now . . . '

'You still don't know anywhere near everything.'

'Tell me, then!' He stood up. For a moment her face appeared to be superimposed on the Billie Holiday poster behind her, so that Billie's orchid seemed pinned in Marvia's hair.

'Not now, Bart. Please.' She leaned against him. He could feel a hot place on his shirt, and looked down and saw that it was wet from Marvia's tears.

'Well then, when?'

'I don't know. Maybe never. I'm mixed up.' She dropped to her knees on the carpet and he put his arms around her shoulders.

'It's because I'm white, isn't it?'

She shook her head. He could feel it against him.

'Then what?'

'Please go home now.'

He stood up and went to the door. She didn't see him downstairs. He just walked to his Hyundai and got in it and headed for Walnut Creek.

What could Marvia's secret be? How terrible could it be? Lindsey felt like a character in a soap opera, and it didn't feel good.

When he got home, Joanie Schorr was sitting with her laptop computer on the kitchen table, working on her high school paper. She looked up and smiled at

Lindsey, then returned to her computer.

Mother was watching an old Jack Benny show on TV. Lindsey bent over and kissed her on the cheek. He stood behind her with his hands on her shoulders. A familiar voice caught his attention and he looked back at the TV set. Jack Benny was doing a gangster skit with — Humphrey Bogart? Lindsey watched incredulously. Yes, it was Humphrey Bogart, all right. Looking old and sick. It must have been near the end of his career, near the end of his life, but he was still working.

Joanie hit some switches and folded down the screen of her computer. The whole thing was smaller than an attaché case. She said, 'I guess I'll be going now.'

Lindsey said, 'Has she been all right?' He indicated Mother with a move of his head.

Joanie said, 'I guess so. I was pretty involved in my homework. I'll be starting college in the fall, Mr. Lindsey. I don't know if I'll be able to come over after that. I'm sorry.'

Lindsey nodded. He didn't appear to

be listening to her words.

'I think maybe she's getting a little more mixed up than she used to be.' Joanie was at the doorway, her computer in one hand, a notebook in the other.

Lindsey said, 'Are you keeping track of your hours, Joanie?'

She said yes. She let herself out, slamming the door as she left.

★　★　★

At the office next morning Lindsey phoned UC and reached Professor Bernstein. He asked if she had located that graduate thesis about the Kleiners. She had. She would be in her office this afternoon if he wanted to look at it there, or take it home with him. He said he'd be in.

The fax machine burbled and whirred and Ms. Wilbur held up a sheet of paper and laughed. She marched over to his desk and dropped the fax before him. It was a memo from Harden at Regional turning down his request for authorization for a trip to Reno and for hiring Tyrone Plum.

Ms. Wilbur said, 'What are you going to do?'

'I don't know. I guess I can pay for it out of my pocket.'

'We could fudge the office supplies budget.'

'No. I'll pay it.' Lindsey looked at her. 'I'm going to get that car back.'

'But if you do get the car, how's that going to get you reimbursed? What's this costing you, Hobart? Must be a couple of thousand dollars at least. Can you afford that?'

'Of course I can't. But once I get that car, save International Surety a half-million bucks, Johanssen will want to know all about it. Harden will want to look like a hero. He'll know that she'll find out about this Reno caper and he'll make sure that I get my money before that. You just wait and see, Ms. Wilbur.'

'I will.'

After a sandwich lunch he headed into Berkeley to see Dr. Bernstein. She welcomed him to her office and plumped back into her chair. She picked up a yellow pencil and tapped it against the cover of an inch-thick book. 'Here it is.'

Lindsey pulled the book toward him. It was merely a typewritten manuscript in an elaborate binding. The title was 'Ethnic Scapegoating in an Economically Stressed Period: A Case Study, Oakland, California, 1929–1935'. The author was one Irving Israel Iskowitz.

Professor Bernstein grinned. 'How could anybody forget old Three Eyes? Brilliant kid. We were junior faculty members together before he went off to Vietnam.'

Lindsey looked up from the book. 'I didn't think they drafted students.'

She shook her head. 'He wasn't a student by then, and he wasn't drafted anyhow. He volunteered. Everybody was against the war. He said no, the South Vietnamese were trying to build a democracy and we were there to help them and he enlisted.'

Lindsey nodded and made a sound.

'Poor guy. Three Eyes because of his name, but he wore these thick glasses too. Nobody could figure out how he got past the physical. Made Woody Allen look like

Arnold Schwarzenegger.'

'And after the war?' Lindsey asked.

'There was no 'after the war'.' Bernstein frowned. 'Not for Three Eyes. The day after he arrived in 'Nam he somehow wandered away from his unit. By the next morning they had him listed as AWOL and by the next night they found him in an alley. Somebody stuck a knife between his ribs. Didn't take his wallet, didn't take his ID or his money or anything else. Just a little message to Uncle Sam to go home. That was how much the brave democratic South Vietnamese people wanted our help.'

Lindsey said, 'That's a sad story. But it doesn't prove the Vietnamese didn't want us.'

Bernstein waved her hands. 'Let's not get into that, okay? You came to look at the paper, look at the paper.'

Lindsey leaned over the bound book, turned to the table of contents. It was a bunch of gobbledegook and academic jargon. But then he turned to the index and struck paydirt. There it was — Kleiner, Otto Lilienthal. A series of page references. And

Kleiner, Morton Karl. One reference. And most intriguingly, Kleiner, Brunhilde Lottchen and Kleiner, Georg Maria and Kleiner, Eva Strauss.

Here was a chance to learn more about the Kleiners — who was who; and if he was lucky, who would be likely to do what, and why.

He looked at Dr. Bernstein. 'You said I could take this home if I needed to?'

She nodded.

'I think I will, then. Do I have to sign out for it or anything?'

'No. Faculty privilege. Just slip it in your little case there. Take care of it, though. They'd slap my wrist if it didn't come back intact.'

'I'll be careful.' He started for the door. 'I'll, ah — '

'Listen,' Bernstein said, 'you getting anywhere on that stolen car?'

'I don't know.' He turned around, his hand still on the doorknob. Was Martha Bernstein was going to give him a lead? 'Morton Kleiner was murdered,' he told her. 'Did you know that?'

'He the fella they found in Lake

Merritt? Sure. Saw it on the Channel 2 news. Did he steal the car?'

'I don't think so, but I think he was connected. His grandfather Otto Kleiner was the chauffeur. He was also one of the Kleiners who used to own the Kleiner Mansion.'

'Very interesting. They find out who did it? Same guy who took the Dusie?'

Lindsey shrugged. 'Nobody knows. Lt. High — he's the homicide cop in charge of the case — isn't sure if there's any connection at all. But he's looking for one. We went up to Morton Kleiner's home, High and the van Arndts and I, to look around. It looks as if Morton Kleiner was some kind of Nazi. It's like a jigsaw puzzle, but nobody can figure out how the parts fit together.'

Martha Bernstein said, 'You ever read mystery stories?'

'Once in a while. I don't read many novels. I'm pretty busy with my work. When I relax I mainly watch TV.'

'Then you probably never heard of Ross Macdonald.'

'Ronald McDonald.'

'Ross Macdonald. Christ, Lindsey. You've probably seen some movies based on his books, anyhow. Look, the point is, he wrote these gloomy books about lost, sad people. There had to be a murder somewhere in the plot, they were mysteries, but they were really about things coming out of the past to screw up people's lives.'

Lindsey said, 'What are you telling me?'

'I don't know, Lindsey. Maybe you'll find something in Three Eyes's thesis there. Do me a favour — keep me posted. This is getting interesting.'

As he reached for the doorknob again she stopped him. 'You said Morton Karl Kleiner was some kind of Nazi — you want to tell me about that? Come back, have a seat. Tell me about that.'

Lindsey described Kleiner's home in the former church, the Nazi paraphernalia that he'd seen there, the weapons cache that Lt. High said the Petaluma police had seized.

Martha Bernstein smiled crookedly. 'What do you know,' she muttered. 'What do you goddamned know about that.'

'What do you make of it, Dr. Bernstein?'

She smiled again. 'I don't really know. But it's fascinating, I'll tell you that much.'

Lindsey sensed she was dying to tell him what she thought; she just wanted to be coaxed. 'Won't you try? Surely you have some idea.'

'Okay. What is a Jew?' She didn't wait for Lindsey to answer. 'He's an eternal outsider. Wherever he goes. So here's Morton Karl, living up in Sonoma County. There's a lot of right-wing crap going on up there anyhow. He comes across these Hitler nuts, maybe in a bar.'

Lindsey had flipped his pocket organizer open and was jotting furiously.

'Kleiner has to make a quick decision,' Bernstein went on. 'He can just keep his head down, slope out of there and leave those bums to their own devices. If he confronts them he risks getting pounded into hamburger meat. Or,' he added with a bitter smile, 'he can suck up to 'em. They don't know he's Jewish. His name is more German than Jewish. He introduces himself to the scum, makes some remarks about undesirable liberal types — and suddenly he's one of the gang.'

She held her hands up as if she'd just made a brilliant point in a classroom. 'Inside of five minutes he's gone from being an outsider to being an insider. Something everyone yearns for. He's no longer one of the despised group, he's one of the group that does the despising. You think he wouldn't turn his back on his heritage, wouldn't turn against his own people? I could show you case studies of light-skinned blacks who turn into black-haters. So Morton Karl Kleiner, scion of the Oakland Kleiners, becomes a Nazi in Petaluma. Makes me ashamed to be one of the chosen people, Lindsey. It surely does that.'

★   ★   ★

Lindsey held the book Bernstein had loaned him on his lap that night, sitting on the living room sofa with his notebook opened on the coffee table. Across the room, Mother watched *Daddy Long Legs*

201

on cable. She clucked and fretted because Fred wasn't dancing with Ginger, he was dancing with this young girl Leslie Caron, half his age. But she seemed to enjoy the picture anyway, in all its black and white glory, the TV set's controls set to keep Technicolor reality from intruding on Mother's nest in the past.

Irving Israel Iskowitz indicated that he had interviewed Otto Kleiner at length. The anti-Semitic incidents were the main focus of Iskowitz's work. He quoted Kleiner's recollections of them, thirty years after the fact. He reproduced clippings from the *Oakland Tribune* and the *Berkeley Gazette* and other papers and Anti-Defamation League newsletters. It was like reading something from the early years of Hitler's Germany, but it was Oakland.

But it didn't tell him who killed Morton Kleiner or who stole the 1928 Duesenberg Phaeton.

But apparently Iskowitz's interviews had ranged more widely than the cross burnings and stink-bombs of the 1930s. He delved into Kleiner history and into the Kleiner fortune that was crumbling away in those Depression years.

The fortune did include theaters — at least six in Oakland, two playhouses and three motion picture houses and one self-styled opera house. There was a department store, originally a 'dry-goods emporium'. It had gone through a series of takeovers until the Kleiner name was totally obliterated. There was even some light industry — a couple of small fabricating plants and a foundry. All of them gone.

And the Kleiner family. Lindsey turned to the index and found the entries for Morton, Brunhilde, Georg and Eva. He jotted down the page references and searched them out. He looked up and saw that *Daddy Long Legs* had ended and Mother was watching *Old Newsreel Theater*. What was going to come up there?

'Almost bed time, Mother.'

The newsreel switched to a feature on college football in the leather-helmet era and Mother lost interest. Lindsey was able to get her to bed.

He came back to the living room and looked up the Kleiner family again in Iskowitz's thesis. There were some surprises here.

First, who was Eva Strauss Kleiner? She was barely mentioned because she had died in 1926, three years before the Great Depression began. But Iskowitz had traced out family members, even put in a Kleiner family tree that Lindsey copied into his notebook.

Otto — old Mr. Kleiner — had married Eva in 1925, when he was twenty-one and she was nineteen. They had had a son, Georg Maria Kleiner, the following year. And Eva had died the same year.

Question: what became of the son? From Iskowitz's interviews with Otto in 1966, it would appear that Georg was still alive, at least up to then. Who had raised him, Otto alone? According to Otto Kleiner and Irving Iskowitz, Georg had married one Edith Hopkins in 1944. Edith was older than Georg, born 1920. Georg would have been 18, his bride 24. Surprising that Georg wasn't off fighting World War II in 1944, but there must have been a reason for his staying out of the service — or maybe he was assigned to some job in the United States, pounding a typewriter or driving some bigwig's sedan. No indication of what had become of Edith, either.

Question: Where were Georg and Edith? They must have departed from the Oakland Kleiner scene. Jayjay had made no mention of them, and if they were in the area they would surely have visited Otto Lilienthal Kleiner at the mansion once in a while. And old Otto would have mentioned them to Jayjay — passed along tidbits of news, or even complaints of their neglecting him.

Jayjay had never mentioned Georg and Edith. That made it a pretty safe bet that they were either dead or had moved away and lost touch with Otto.

Next item: Georg and Edith had a son, Morton Karl Kleiner, born 1946. All right, Lindsey knew what had become of Morton Karl!

But he made a note to have another chat with Lieutenant High. High might want to check out Georg and Edith. Not that they were likely to have bopped their son on the head hard enough to kill him, then dumped his body into Lake Merritt. But at the very least they were entitled to notification. If Morton Karl Kleiner had never married, and there was no indication that he had, they would probably have a claim on his estate. Such as it was.

Ah, Brunhilde Lottchen Kleiner. Otto's sister! Born 1909, that would make her five years younger than Otto. And what had become of her? Iskowitz gave her a good deal of space.

Lindsey rubbed his eyes. They were growing weary. He looked at his watch. It was after midnight. He went into the kitchen and made himself a cup of coffee, then carried it back to the living room and set it next to his notebook.

Otto's little sister. Apparently he'd doted on her. There were anecdotes in Iskowitz's book, childhood stories from the days of the First World War. Otto defending Brunhilde — and himself — from bullies who accused them of being German spies. Kaiser Bill! Family dinners and lectures about using the right terms for food dishes. The senior Kleiners — Otto and Brunhilde's parents — buying Liberty bonds and converting the Kleiner Foundry to war production, building engines for Jennies.

Ahah, here was an answer! According to the thesis, Brunhilde had taken the place of the deceased Eva Strauss Kleiner, and raised her brother's child Georg following Eva's death in 1926. But then, in 1931 — she would have been twenty-two, a legal adult — Brunhilde disappeared from the story. What became of Brunhilde? Was this another problem for Lt. High? No, wait a minute — the index showed another entry for Brunhilde.

Lindsey turned the pages.

1931. The American economy had crashed in '29; by '31 the nation was deep into the Great Depression and sinking deeper every month. Hoover was president and trying desperately to convince the people that the Depression was just a dip; was going to end any day now. The Democrats were maneuvering for the following year's election and Franklin

Roosevelt of New York was playing his cards close to his chest. In Europe the scars of the First World War remained raw and bleeding.

And Brunhilde Lottchen Kleiner returned to Germany.

Why would an American-born Jew want to go back to Nazi Germany? But it wasn't Nazi Germany then. These were the last days of — Lindsey racked his brain, trying to remember history lessons that had meant nothing to him at the time — the Weimar Republic.

The Kleiner family's enterprises had been in decline in America since the beginning of the Depression in 1929. Was Brunhilde going back to look up relatives and ask them for help? Did she think the future was brighter in Germany than in America? But the Depression was world-wide, as bad or worse in Europe than in the United States.

And this was just about the time that the Kleiner fortune — the rumored 'missing millions' — had disappeared. Maybe there was something to the legend. Maybe Brunhilde had got hold of the money, taken it in gold — gold was still legal tender in those days, although not for much longer — and fled to Europe with it.

What did Iskowitz say?

What did Otto Kleiner say?

Lindsey's eyes were burning. He didn't want any more coffee, but he didn't want to give up and go to bed, either. There was no way he'd be able to sleep now. He put on a warm jacket and stepped outside, onto the little flagstone path that led from his front door to the sidewalk.

There was no traffic at this hour, and the surrounding houses were dark. A couple of street lamps cast puddles of illumination. The air was so heavy with moisture that after walking a few yards Lindsey found his face wet, even though it wasn't raining yet. Well, good. That felt better anyway. He took a couple of deep lungfuls of the damp air and went back to work, refreshed.

Otto Kleiner had told Iskowitz that he'd had a few letters from Brunhilde. She had met a man she thought he was wonderful. He was older, and from an aristocratic German family.

Otto wrote back, warning Brunhilde about coming events. Ever the older brother, the guardian.

Brunhilde said nothing about politics in her letters. They were about the beauties of Germany and the happiness she was enjoying with her new friend. She said nothing in the letters about marriage, and Otto suspected that Brunhilde's lover was a married man.

Otto Kleiner tried again to warn her of her peril if she stayed in Germany, but she refused to leave. Eventually she stopped answering Otto's letters, then the letters started coming back unopened.

Of course, once the United States entered World War II, there was no point in even trying to write to Brunhilde, and when Otto made inquiries at the end of the war, he could learn nothing. He'd even gone to the local office of his congressman. That, at least, brought him a letter, dated August 8, 1946. The US forces in Germany had investigated the whereabouts of Brunhilde Lottchen Kleiner, working from the last known address Otto had furnished. That address was in the Russian zone of occupation and the Soviet authorities had provided no information in response to the American request.

The congressman added that Brunhilde had likely been killed, either by the Nazis, or in an Allied bombing raid, or by Soviet forces in the closing months of the war.

That was the end of Brunhilde.

Lindsey closed the book and leaned back. He closed his eyes to rest them. So much about the Kleiners, but he'd learned nothing about the stolen Duesenberg. He had a feeling that it had to have something to do with the Kleiner fortune, the legendary missing millions. Unless Brunhilde had managed somehow to get the money to Europe with her. Otherwise, where was it? Hidden in the glove compartment of the Duesenberg?

'Hobo?'

Lindsey jumped. 'Mother!'

She stood in her dressing gown, smiling. 'Hobo, it's after your bedtime. I know you want to wait up for Daddy, but you need your sleep. He'll come in and kiss you good night. Come, little Hobo, let's get you into your jammies and then bed.'

He ran his fingers through his hair. 'You're right, Mother, it's late.' He looked at his watch. It was almost four o'clock. He'd been reading Iskowitz's dissertation and making notes for almost six hours.

He got Mother to go back to bed, put the Iskowitz dissertation and his notebook in his attaché case, and went to bed.

He had trouble sleeping. He imagined Brunhilde as a child during World War I, Eva as a bride in 1926, a mother, and then dead within the year. What had killed her? Either Iskowitz didn't say or Lindsey had overlooked it, but flu was a common cause of death in the '20s. Flu, or childbirth, or killed in the crash of a flivver.

And Georg Maria Kleiner, the middle Kleiner, Otto's son and Morton's father — were he and his wife Edith living somewhere in California now, unaware of their son's death? Did they know that he had been a Nazi, lived in an abandoned church in Petaluma, furnished his home as a shrine to the Führer and his dead henchmen?

Have to call Lt. High was Lindsey's last thought as, to his own astonishment, he felt himself slipping down the slope of sleep.

15

The Pacific storm arrived in full force before Lindsey had his breakfast. Mother sat opposite him, watching the rain fall.

'That rain's a relief,' she said.

'Make driving terrible,' Lindsey said. 'Be a lousy commute.'

Mother smiled. 'You only have to drive downtown. If you weren't so lazy, you could walk to work. Besides, if the drought keeps up we'll have a lot worse problem than a few traffic jams. Be thankful for a little rain!' She carried the coffee pot back to the table. 'Want another cup, Hobart?'

He nodded and she poured for him. Last night she had been thinking he was a child, thinking his father was coming home. This morning she knew that he was a grown man and knew where he worked and knew about the California drought. Amazing.

He finished his meal and looked

worriedly at his watch.

Mother said, 'You go ahead, Hobart. International Surety needs you. I'll let Mrs. Hernandez in when she gets here.'

From his office he phoned Lt. High. He told him about the Iskowitz dissertation and asked if High knew about Morton Kleiner's parents.

'Georg and Edith? Yes, in fact I do know about them. It's helpful of you to call, though. Did you know them?'

Lindsey said he'd only come across references to them in Iskowitz's dissertation.

'How did you get a copy of that?'

Lindsey told him.

'From Rachel Bernstein? Who's that?' High's voice sharpened.

'Uh — Dr. Bernstein's a prof at UC in Berkely.'

'How did she get involved, Lindsey?'

'She's a member of the Art Deco club. I met her through — '

'Yes. All right. And you found out about Morton's parents that way.'

'Isn't that okay? Is that how you found out, Lieutenant?'

'No. I wouldn't normally let you in on police methods, Mr. Lindsey.' At least he was back to Mister. 'But if you'll keep this under your hat, we just check records. Driver's licenses, auto registrations, voter rolls. We got Georg and Edith off Morton's birth record. Highland Hospital, January 23, 1946.'

Lindsey said, 'Oh.'

High said, 'Why are you interested in Georg and Edith, Mr. Lindsey?'

'Well, since nobody seems to know who killed Morton, or who took the Duesenberg from the mansion . . . '

'Are you investigating crimes, now? You shouldn't really be doing that.'

'I appreciate that. I'm just trying to get back the car. Sergeant Gutierrez hasn't had any luck so far, and my company has a lot of money at stake.'

'Of course. As long as you're not getting into the police business.'

'I'm not.' Lindsey frowned. 'But what about Georg and Edith?'

'We check death records, too. Edith Hopkins Kleiner died in 1980. Georg Maria Kleiner died in 1986. There don't seem to be any brothers or sisters.'

Lindsey said, 'Oh. Thanks, Lieutenant.'

'Keep me posted if you get any more good ideas, Mr. Lindsey. Georg and Edith were a good idea. Goodbye.' He hung up.

Lindsey tried unsuccessfully to get involved with routine work. Something kept itching at the back of his brain. There was somebody he hadn't thought about who just didn't fit in. Who?

In his mind he traced his involvement with the case back to the Saturday night that the Duesenberg had been stolen. He could see the Kleiner Mansion, the faces of the Oakland police officers, of Joseph Roberts, Jayjay Smith, the van Arndts, the old man in the Ike jacket . . .

The old man in the Ike jacket! He picked up the phone and called Oscar Gutierrez. 'Oscar, this is Hobart Lindsey. Listen, you got a copy of the Smart Set membership roster, didn't you? You know everybody who was at the mansion the night the Dusie was stolen. Did you notice an old guy in a World War II uniform? You did? Did you get his name?'

Gutierrez said, 'Hold on a second.' At

length: 'Here it is. Hammersmith, Andrew Joshua. What about him?'

'Didn't it strike you as odd that the rest of the club was pretty much lily white, and all in tuxedoes and evening gowns, and here's this one black man in an old uniform?'

'Well, just a little, yes.'

'Did you follow it up?'

'Nothing there, Bart.'

'You sure? Maybe I ought to talk to that guy — you have his address handy?'

Gutierrez hesitated briefly. Then he said, 'Club membership roster just shows him as care of Oliver van Arndt.'

'And you talked to Hammersmith?'

'Nothing there.'

Lindsey ended the call and phoned the van Arndts' apartment. He identified himself and asked to speak to Ollie.

But Ollie was out — 'Keeping tabs on his investments, the old silly,' as Wally explained.

Lindsey told her he was trying to get in touch with Hammersmith.

'Oh, you mustn't bother dear Andy.'

Lindsey said, 'Does he live with you

218

and Ollie? The club list gives your address.'

Wally laughed. 'Hardly, Mr. Linden. He's a very sweet man, but really . . . '

'I need to talk with him. It's important.'

'I'm sorry, I'd love to talk with you more, Mr. Lyman, but I have an appointment with my hairdresser. Perhaps some other time.' She hung up.

Frustrated, Lindsey phoned Gutierrez again and asked about Hammersmith.

Gutierrez laughed. 'Right. He isn't in our computer, DMV doesn't have him. That uniform was a good clue, though. The VA refused to give out his home address on right-of-privacy grounds.'

'But you told me you found him.'

'Right. Turns out that he got mugged a couple of times. Usually SFPD doesn't even bother with those cases — some junkie rolls an unfortunate type for small change or food stamps or a bottle of T-bird. But this one they recorded. Hammersmith has a plastic leg, did you know that?'

'No.'

'Service injury. Second or third time he

got mugged, they took his prosthetic leg. Can you imagine that? Knocked him down, stole his money and his TV, held a knife on him and took off his leg and left.'

'You've got his address?'

'Hammersmith lives in a crummy hotel in the Tenderloin.' He gave Lindsey the address on Taylor Street. 'These were burglars. Never caught them, of course. But the cops took Hammersmith to San Francisco General. He'd been hit pretty hard. General put him to bed for a while, didn't do anything for him, he came around by himself and they sent him down to the VA hospital at Laguna Honda. They got him another leg and sent him home.'

Lindsey said, 'Jesus. You have a phone number for him?'

'He doesn't have one. The hotel has a phone but he doesn't like to talk. I had to go see him.'

Lindsey took the hotel's number anyway.

* * *

After lunch with Eric Coffman, Lindsey tried to concentrate on more International Surety routine, cases, but all he could think about was the Kleiner mansion, the stolen Duesenberg, and the dead Morton Kleiner.

Early that afternoon, Lindsey got a call from Joseph Roberts. 'How was everything in the great glitter capital, Joe?'

'Lousy,' Roberts grumbled.

'What happened?'

'My show,' Roberts moaned.

'Something happen to *Jazz Babies*?'

'Goddamn network brass. Nobody wants to make stories anymore. That bunch of bean-counters looked at the demographics again, decided that the '20s wouldn't pull enough bell cords. Whole new concept.'

'Are you still on the project?'

'By my fingernails, Bart. I think I might have to get a new license plate. That makes a real impression, you know.'

'Sure. What's the new one?'

'They want to move the show to the '60s. Gonna call it *Luv Beads*. All about flower children, hippies, psychedelics. I figure we can get a great sound track. Sixties nostalgia, that's the coming thing, you know.'

'So they're forcing this on you, Joe?'

'Well, it was their idea, but actually I kind of like it. Might be something really big. Girls in long hair and granny dresses, guys in beads, get some great drug episodes in there. But nonviolent, see. None of this *Miami Vice* stuff.'

Lindsey said, 'Right.'

'I didn't really like that *Jazz Babies* idea anyhow. Just something for the old farts in their rocking chairs. Not enough people left in that pop group anyhow, half of 'em in retirement homes, they don't spend any money. We need the younger earners and spenders — people who are building homes, having kids, buying cars, using credit cards, travelling. Right?'

Lindsey said faintly, 'Right.'

'But you know who really spends? It's the thirty through fifty-five group, they go for the big ticket items. That's what the advertisers want. Networks have to deliver audience, Bart — you see that, don't you?'

Lindsey said, 'Yes.' He looked beseechingly at Ms. Wilbur. He caught her eye and she winked at him and turned back to her work.

Roberts said, 'Everybody remembers the '60s. The kids who were demonstrating on the college campuses, now they're in their forties; they're right there in the pop group we want.

'Have to get the rights people into action, start clearing music for us. Yeah, not to be too obvious, you know, everybody knows about the Beatles and Janis Joplin. For the soundtrack we'll go for the other second-rate bands. They'll sound familiar but they won't distract the audience, see. They'll keep their attention on the product where it belongs. Besides, we can get the rights cheaper.'

Lindsey said, 'That sounds terrific, Joe. Is that what you called to tell me?'

Roberts said, 'Oh. Got carried away, didn't I? Look, I always like to do a favor for a friend. This show at the Coliseum — I know you wanted to go, and I got a promo kit from the producers. An old chum of mine is emceeing. Oldies deejay,

223

got a following of his own. Maybe you've heard of him. Buddy Barton. Appeals to overaged hippies and Elvisoids. Got the kit right here on my desk right now.'

Lindsey said, 'Uh-huh.'

'You know, trade courtesy. Buddy told 'em to put me on the list. Came through the network. They send these to the papers, the radio and TV people. So here's a box on my doorstep this morning, from the promoter, thanks to old Buddy. Pair of complimentary tix, all the usual press kit stuff, and a T-shirt with a tour logo and a baseball hat with a picture of Leslie Gore on the front.'

'Leslie Gore?'

'Big singing star. Specialized in teenage angst. Used to wear big hair, big chest, party dresses. Real fave with the fourteen-year-old girls. Tell you what, you want, you can have the whole shmear.'

'Aren't you going to the show?'

'Thought I told you that. Hot doings at the network. I have to head back down to helltown end of the week. I can't afford to go to music shows, don't have the time. But you can have my package. You want to come over and pick it up tonight?'

Lindsey's mind was racing as he tried to keep up with Roberts. 'Can't you, uh, can't you send it to me?'

'Not enough time. Show's this weekend anyhow. Two big nights, Friday and Saturday. Comps are for Friday night. Choice seats. Take your girlfriend, or that mom of yours you're always talking about; she should love this. Fats Domino, the Chordettes, Little Richard, Leslie Gore. Great show. Your mom'll love it. All you have to do is come by and pick 'em up tonight.'

'Well — '

'Oh, look. One other thing, Bart. You want to head over to the Kleiner Mansion again, you can leave your car at my place; there are a couple of visitors' spots. We can head over to the mansion in the Porsche.'

'Oh — okay. I guess we can do that.'

'You'll phone over there then, okay? Set it up with Jayjay so she'll know you're coming. Don't mention me though, all right? I want to surprise her.' He finally stopped talking and hung up.

Ms. Wilbur said, 'What was that all about?'

'Oh, just one of the Art Deco club people.'

Ms. Wilbur raised her eyebrows. 'You mean you're actually getting somewhere with that case? This fellow has something for you?'

Lindsey shrugged. He phoned the Kleiner Mansion and got Jayjay Smith on the phone. She seemed pleased that he was coming over. He said, 'Anything new on old Mr. Kleiner?'

'He's still in the hospital. I told him a little white lie, Bart. I told him that the police had recovered the Duesenberg.'

'Did it work?'

'I think so. I guess the IV did him some good. I stopped at a hobby store and got him a little scale model Duesenberg. I put it in his hands and he opened his eyes and looked at it and smiled.'

'Good. What did Dr. Mukerji say?'

'She says it made a real difference. She thinks he may be able to come home in another week or so.

'Only, what happens when he sees the

car isn't here? I can stall him a while, and tell him that the police have to dust it for fingerprints or whatever they do.'

'Well, maybe we will get it back.'

'Do you have any leads?'

'We'll talk about it tonight, okay? I'll come over in the evening, after dinner.'

He phoned home next. Mrs. Hernandez said that Mother was doing fine. He phoned Joanie Schorr's house. She was working on her paper. She agreed to go over to Lindsey's house for dinner and to stay until he got home, or until Mother's bed time.

★　★　★

Arriving at Joe Roberts's waterfront condo, Lindsey found a parking place and knocked on the door. Roberts had already made a shaker of martinis and offered one to Lindsey. Lindsey declined.

Roberts said, 'Jayjay expecting us?'

'She's just expecting me. Maybe you should call her first and ask if you can come along.'

'No way.' Roberts sipped off his

227

martini. 'Jayjay's a little peeved with me, you see? If I ask first, she might say not to come. But if you show up with me in tow, she'll let me in.'

'But she doesn't want to see you. You know that.'

'I'll level with you, Bart. I got the hots for her. I just want to give it one more try. If she doesn't want me hanging around, I'll bow out.' He sat on the cloth-covered couch, his arms spread across its back. He gave Lindsey a quizzical look. 'You're not after her, are you, Bart?'

Lindsey didn't answer. He felt himself growing flushed.

'By God, you're banging her, aren't you?'

Lindsey said, 'I don't think I ought to answer that. As an adult, what she does is up to her, isn't it?'

Roberts shook his head, smiling bitterly. He drained his glass.

Lindsey said, 'I guess I'll head over there now. It's getting a little late. I have to get home to Walnut Creek in a while.'

Roberts pushed himself up from the couch. He headed for the closet and took out his jacket and put it on.

'I don't think you should drive,' Lindsey said. 'You've been drinking. If you won't stay here, then we'll take my car. That's final.'

Roberts swayed slightly, then shrugged. 'All right. My God, we're good little law-abiding citizens, aren't we?' On the way to the door he passed a table with a square white box on it. He'd missed it on the way in. He stopped next to the table. 'Here.' He picked up the box and handed it to Lindsey. 'Still friends, hey? Here's the present.' He closed one eye and tapped his forehead with his forefinger. 'Say, just had a wonderful idea. Why don't you take Jayjay to that show with you? You're so hot for each other, why don't you go together. As my guests. Choice seats. Compliments of Joseph Roberts, screenwriter and lover.'

Lindsey took the box. He put it in the trunk of the Hyundai. He was thoroughly annoyed. He made sure that Roberts was buckled in, then went to the driver's side.

He parked in the driveway at the Kleiner Mansion. He stood before the great door, Roberts at his side, and rang the bell.

Jayjay opened the door, a smile on her face. She started to move toward Lindsey, then saw Joe Roberts and froze. 'What's he doing here?'

Before Lindsey could answer, Roberts said, 'Bartie was just over at my house for a dink. I mean a drink.'

Jayjay frowned. 'I didn't invite you over here.'

'Kleiner Mansion's public property, isn't it?'

'Public hours are posted, Mr. Roberts.' Jayjay drew her breath, then said, 'Well, come on in, both of you. Bart, I thought you were coming alone. If I'd known this — ' She shuddered and made an inarticulate sound. 'If I'd known this person was with you, I wouldn't have invited you over.'

Lindsey started to apologize, but Jayjay said, 'You don't have to stand out here in the rain.' She stood aside and let them in, closing the door behind them. She was wearing a cherry-colored shirt, open to show her generous cleavage, and tight pale gray jeans.

She led them through the public rooms of the house, ghostly and museum-like now, and into the living quarters. Roberts sprawled on a sofa. Lindsey sat uneasily on the edge of a chair. Jayjay stood.

'I didn't know you two boys were such good chums.'

She had built a fire once more, and Lindsey couldn't keep from watching her, thinking of her body beneath the thin clothing. She'd set out a couple of trays of finger food. Lindsey had no appetite, but Joe Roberts was munching on a piece of celery.

'We're not exactly chums,' Lindsey said. 'Joe was helping me get some insights in the car theft. I thought we could all sort of talk it over.'

Roberts said, 'Yeah. We could all sort of talk it over.'

Jayjay's face was white. 'I don't think there's anything to say.'

'Well, I — what about Mr. Kleiner?' Lindsey felt that his question was feeble, but he didn't know what to say.

'He used to keep the car right here, din' he?' Roberts slurred.

Jayjay made a minimal gesture with one thumb. 'In the garage. It's cold and wet out there. There's nothing there but some tools. But you want to look, go ahead.'

Roberts turned toward Lindsey. 'Le's go, Bartie. Le's see what ol' man Kleiner has hidden away in his secret workshop.'

Lindsey looked at Jayjay. Her facial expression said, *Go ahead, you fools. I don't care.*

Lindsey stood up. Roberts followed suit, lurched and caught himself on Lindsey's arm.

Jayjay put on a heavy quilted jacket and pulled its hood over her hair. She led them outside and walked through rain to the garage. It stood behind the mansion, between the main building and the edge of Lake Merritt, where the body of Morton Karl Kleiner had been found. She opened the garage with a heavy key and flicked on a light switch.

Lindsey gaped. It was like a trip into the past. The room — garage — looked like a picture of a service station from one of the oldest magazines he'd brought home for Mother.

The garage looked like something out of a 1930s *Fortune*. The nation might have been suffering the worst financial collapse in its history, but there were plenty of wealthy individuals who did just fine in those days. There were ads in those magazines for ocean liners and luxury automobiles and expensive radios and fur salons and elegant hotels.

The Kleiner establishment featured a hydraulic lift, machine tools, wrenches and hammers and filters, all of them laid out or hung on wall racks in perfect order. A block and tackle hung empty. The place was immaculate, and cavernous.

There were shelves of spare parts. Under a heavy tarpaulin something large lurked. Lindsey walked over and tried to lift the tarp, but it was tied down.

Roberts leaned over Lindsey, said, 'Wha's that?'

'I don't know.'

'Well, le's have a look.'

The tarp cord was held in place by an old padlock. Lindsey asked Jayjay if she had a key for it. She did.

With Roberts at one end and Lindsey at the other, they lifted the canvas. Even Jayjay's curiosity had been roused. She stood watching. She said, 'What is it?'

'Don't you know? Did you ever look under the tarp?' said Lindsey.

'Mr. Kleiner was very protective about these things, very possessive. He didn't like me coming out here, and the few times I did — when he was here — he never lifted that tarp. And I would never sneak out here like some kind of spy. I had too much respect for Mr. Kleiner to ever do that, Bart. I'm sorry to learn that you'd think I would.'

Lindsey didn't want to get in a fight with Jayjay. He said, 'Maybe we can figure it out ourselves.' The thing was thickly coated in black grease. If only Tyrone Plum were here. After his visit to the technical department at the auto museum and his examination of the Duesenberg on display there, he'd know for sure. But Lindsey thought he could identify it. 'It's an engine and transmission. Isn't that something! He's had a whole extra engine and transmission here all these years, coated in this thick gunk. What is it?' He sniffed. 'Creosote, I think.'

'Sure,' Jayjay said. 'That's what the block and tackle were for. Mr. Kleiner showed it to me. If the engine ever wore out, he could pull it with the block and tackle and put in a whole new one. Or the transmission; he'd use the lift. I don't think one man could do it alone, even a young man, and certainly not poor Otto. But he could have got a helper. He never needed to. I guess they really built those old-timers to last.'

They put the tarp back in place and locked it again.

'Too cold out here,' Roberts muttered. 'Le's go back in the house. Maybe Jayjay'd be a good hostess and be nice to us, maybe make us breakfas' in the morning.'

'Not a chance. You boys learn anything useful?'

Lindsey said, 'I'm afraid not, but you can never tell.'

Roberts said, 'It's really cold out. You sure you wanna send us away, Jayjay?'

'Absolutely positively and without the

shadow of a doubt. Is that sure enough for you? Good night.' They were standing outside. She started toward the mansion. She halted and turned. 'If you ever want to come over again, Bart, don't bring any uninvited guests with you.'

In the Hyundai, Roberts said, 'Cold-hearted bitch. But I think she still likes me a little bit.'

Lindsey said, 'I'll drop you at your place. I'm going home.'

16

Take Mother to the Coliseum? Maybe it would be too much for her, and bring on an episode of confusion or worse. There was still time; the opening-night tickets were for a week from Friday. He decided to say nothing to her and bide his time. He left the cardboard box in the trunk of the Hyundai.

He put in routine days at International Surety, routine evenings with Mother watching movies on cable or on tape.

He met Eric Coffman for one of their regular lunches together. Coffman asked Lindsey about the Duesenberg, and Lindsey gave him a mildly expurgated version of his research expedition to Reno with Marvia Plum and her brother Tyrone.

The lawyer raised an eyebrow. 'Little weekend escape with Offissa Plum, Bart?'

Lindsey flushed. 'She's a sergeant now.'

Coffman grinned like a shark. 'I don't care if your little tootsie is an admiral now. Isn't a weekend in the Silver State a little bit of a stretch? And you actually swindled International Surety into paying for that?'

'It was research, Eric. I'm still trying to figure out why somebody stole that car. Gutierrez is getting nowhere. He doesn't even take my calls now, half the time.'

Coffman said, 'At least you got a nice trip to Reno on the swindle sheet, anyhow.'

Lindsey shook his head mournfully. 'Regional turned me down.'

'But at least you got laid, right, my friend?'

Lindsey concentrated on his lunch. They ate in silence for a while. Then Coffman said, 'Listen, Bart — are you going anywhere with Marvia?'

'I don't know, Eric. I think she's terrific.'

'You in love with her?'

'I told her I was. All the years I didn't have a girlfriend I envied the guys who did. Now I don't know whether I have one or two or none. I just don't know what to do.'

'Get it on or make your break,'

Coffman advised. 'Don't leave the lady hanging, that's not fair.'

'You think so?'

'Take it from an old married hand, Bart.'

* * *

After lunch Lindsey dialled Marvia's number. She was at her desk. Sergeants got to spend a lot more time in the office and a lot less time in the field than ordinary cops did. Lindsey told her about the revival show tickets that Joe Roberts had given him. He asked if she'd like to go with him.

Marvia turned him down.

'Are you busy that night?'

'No, Bart. As a matter of fact, I really don't have very much of a social life.'

'Why not?' As soon as he'd said it, he realized that he'd committed a gaffe. No promises, no obligations — that was the basis of their friendship. 'I'm sorry. I had no right to ask you that.'

'No, that's okay. I don't think I've been fair with you, Bart . . . Look, are you busy

Saturday night? You want to come to Berkeley? I guess I really owe you an explanation.'

He accepted. What kind of explanation she had in mind, he could only guess. She wasn't going to dump him, she couldn't be. But if she wasn't going to dump him, then what was the mysterious explanation?

★ ★ ★

Saturday afternoon Joanie Schorr came over to stay with Mother. While Lindsey fussed over what clothes to wear to see Marvia, Joanie phoned out for Chinese food. The food arrived before Lindsey was ready to leave, and when he headed for the door Joanie and Mother were deeply involved in their meal.

He kissed Mother on the cheek. She looked up from her plate and smiled at him. 'Joanie, will you look at my little Hobo! All dressed up and going out with girls already!'

A chill went through Lindsey. Every time he thought Mother was coming out of her decade-long fugue, she managed to dash his hopes with a few innocently intended words.

★ ★ ★

The roads were wet. Another storm front had arrived. It made the traffic tough, but it was good for the reservoirs.

Lindsey parked outside Marvia's apartment on Oxford Street and rang the doorbell. She was downstairs waiting for him, dressed in a pale yellow shirt and a denim skirt. He couldn't remember ever seeing her in a skirt before.

She said, 'Come on up for a little while. It's early.'

She'd left music playing in her room. It was nothing he'd ever heard before. He walked around the room uncomfortably. Finally he settled on her rocking chair. 'What's going on, Marvia?'

'I promised I'd explain, didn't I? You're a nice man, Bart. I really do love you.'

'Some way to show it.'

'Don't be angry with me. It's something you don't know about, and you can't know about it. It isn't your fault.'

'It isn't because I'm white? Or Mother?'

She shook her head. 'It only has to do with me.'

She was sitting on the edge of her bed, on the Raggedy Ann bedspread. She took his hand and said, 'I told you about my parents once, remember?'

'I do. They sounded wonderful. I envied you.'

'We're invited for dinner at their house. I told them you might not want to come, but I'd ask you.'

Lindsey pressed his hands against his eyes. 'Do they know I'm white?'

'They know you're my friend, they know about our adventure with the comic books and the professor. And they know you're white. I got mad at my mother when she asked.'

He said, 'I'll go. You thought I wouldn't want to eat dinner with a black family?'

'What would you have said, the first time we met?'

'I didn't like you then. You kind of — annoyed me.'

'Oh, Bart.' She put her hand on his cheek. It felt marvelous and he didn't want her to take it away.

She said, 'Come on, then. You won't have to suffer through black-eyed peas and chitterlings. Dad's making poached salmon.' She started for the doorway, but she stopped with Lindsey close behind her. She turned and put her hands on her shoulders. She leaned her head against his sweater and spoke so softly he could barely hear her words. 'There's something else, Bart.'

He put his hands on her back and pressed her to him. He could feel her trembling. He said, 'What is it?'

'I have a son,' she said softly.

He dropped his hands to his sides, and as he did so, he felt her dig her fingers into the heavy wool of his sweater. He felt ashamed of himself, and took her hands with his. He took a deep breath and said, 'You'll tell me when you're ready to tell me.'

She held his hand tightly with one of hers while she locked the door behind them with the other.

Lindsey felt an amazing sense of liberation. On the way down the stairs he said, 'Your father cooks?'

Marvia said, 'His company put him on early retirement. Industry moving out of Emeryville to make room for condos and boutiques. Mom still has her job, so Dad cooks. He says he always cooked better than she did anyhow.'

They left Lindsey's Hyundai on Oxford Street and took Marvia's Mustang to her parents' house on Bonar. As Marvia pulled to the curb an ancient Checker cab, converted to a private car, rattled to a halt across the street from them. The Checker was half rusted out. One crumpled fender had a texture like oatmeal. The car was three or four colors, apparently the original colors of doors or fenders cannibalized from dead Checkers.

Tyrone Plum climbed out of the Checker. He pointed a security system armer at the Checker, then slipped it in his pocket. He bounded across the street, swung Marvia in the air, planted her with a kiss, and shook hands with Lindsey.

'You drive that?' Lindsey asked.

'Gets me where I want to go. Heard you were dinner company. Ready for some down-home soul food?'

Marvia said, 'I told him we're having Dad's salmon, Tyrone!'

The house was an elderly frame bungalow. It couldn't have cost more than a few thousand dollars when it was built. Houses like this were going for fortunes today.

Marvia's father let them in. They followed him into the living room. It was comfortably furnished. Everything had the look of age to it. Not antiques, just old furniture, old carpets, an old house.

Marcus Plum was heavy-set. His hair was cropped short and had turned gray. He was in his shirtsleeves. He kissed his son and daughter, then shook Lindsey's hand. 'So you're Marvia's friend, Mr. Lindsey.'

Lindsey said, 'Ah, Bart, please.'

'Fine. Call me Marcus. My wife — '
She came through a doorway. 'Gloria. This is Mr. Lindsey. Bart.'

Mrs. Plum followed the same pattern. When he shook her hand, Lindsey noticed that she had long red fingernails. All except one that was gold. She said, 'Sit down. We'll get something to snack on.'

She disappeared again through a swinging door. She came back, preceded by a small boy carrying a tray of snacks. He broke into a grin, scurried across the room and put the tray onto a table. He ran to Marvia. She threw her arms around him.

She said, 'Jamie!'

He said, 'Mom!' Marvia was already seated on a sofa. Jamie climbed onto it beside her. He wore a striped shirt and jeans. She held her arm around him, rubbing his head. She looked at Lindsey. 'Bart, this is my son.'

Lindsey looked from Marvia to Jamie. The boy must be ten. He didn't have Marvia's chunkiness; his arms and legs were thin, and there was a wiry strength to him. But one look at his face left no doubt that he was hers.

Marvia whispered in Jamie's ear. The boy held his hand toward Lindsey. 'How do you do, sir.'

Lindsey hesitated for a second, then shook the boy's hand solemnly. 'How do you do, Jamie. A pleasure to meet you.'

Out of the corner of his eye, Lindsey caught Tyrone Plum measuring him. He looked directly at Marvia. She was smiling.

Mrs. Plum served them tea. Marcus Plum excused himself to tend to his poached salmon. The others talked about their work. Gloria Plum listened to Lindsey's description of his job. After a while she said, 'I'm in the insurance business myself. The government. Getting people to pay back social security when they get too much money. The government makes mistakes. Then we take the money back.'

'Right. Well, we try not to pay the money in the first place,' Lindsey said. 'But we have to get things back, too. Stolen goods — if we get it, we save paying off the claim.'

Marcus Plum's voice boomed from the kitchen. 'Delicate operation. I need a hand in here.'

The evening went well. When Jamie's

bedtime came he departed with minimal protest. The adults sat around the table talking about politics and sports. Marcus Plum was a basketball fan, and insisted that the Warriors were only a couple of years from being serious contenders in the NBA.

When they were getting ready to leave, Marvia went to Jamie's room to spend a few more minutes with him. Marcus and Gloria saw them all to the door. Gloria was friendly and correct. Marcus was warm. Lindsey wondered what it would have been like to have a father.

Tyrone climbed in his Checker and was off in a cloud of smoke.

Lindsey sat with Marvia in her Mustang. She said, 'You handled it beautifully, Bart. Thank you.'

'He's a nice boy. Very well-behaved.'

'It's better for him, being with them. He has a wonderful role model.'

'I liked your dad.'

Marvia laid her head on Lindsey's shoulder. He could feel her tension, feel it lessen.

'Who's Jamie's father, Marvia?'

She sat upright behind the wheel. 'James Wilkerson.'

'Is he your husband?'

'I was in the army, you know. In the MPs. Before I got my degree and became a civilian cop. I was a corporal. I'd been in the army a couple of years. James was a second lieutenant.'

'Okay. So, here you are, you're Corporal Marvia Plum, military police. And this green lieutenant gets assigned to your unit.'

'Right. We were in Germany. Wiesbaden. I thought he was just too pretty for words. I was young myself, Bart. I didn't know anything either. Oh boy, talk about the blind leading the blind. I thought it would be funny to get this guy in the sack. It was a kind of contest. A bunch of us tried. I won.'

'And he married you? Is that it?'

'Well, he did eventually.' She looked away. 'He was an officer. I was enlisted personnel. That was a bigger social difference than black and white. It just isn't done. I got pregnant. James's captain found out about it, he almost had him court-martialled.'

'Wouldn't he marry you?'

'That has nothing to do with it. Or everything. An officer can't marry an enlisted soldier. It's against the code. It's against regulations. They can't even dance together.'

'So what did they do?'

'Well, for a while they wanted to kick me out of the army for getting pregnant. But they couldn't make that stick without getting James in trouble. And he had his heart set on a career in the service. So we finally worked it out, his captain and my captain, and the JAG — that's an army lawyer. I wouldn't take any kind of discharge other than honorable, and if they tried to stick me with any other kind, James would get into it. So they let me resign from the army. He married me the next day. An officer can marry a civilian, you see — that's okay. And after Jamie was born — James Wilkerson, Jr. — we got divorced. But his dad sends money every month. He's a captain now. Almost due for major.'

'Did he ever remarry?'

'No.'

'Sounds to me as if he might want you back.'

She shrugged her shoulders. 'I don't know.'

'Do you ever see him?'

'No. I don't know that I want to.'

She started the Mustang. Its headlights cut twin swaths through the mist. She headed back toward north Berkeley and Oxford Street.

'Where does that leave us?' Lindsey asked.

'I don't know. Are you still interested in seeing me?'

He hesitated. 'Yes.'

'Thank you, Bart.' She pulled in behind his Hyundai on Oxford Street. 'Let me call you then, all right?'

He said that would be all right.

17

Saturday would be the day — the night — of the show at the Coliseum. But first Lindsey wanted to look for Andrew Joshua Hammersmith. He drove into San Francisco and put the Hyundai in a muni lot. Then he walked to Hammersmith's hotel, a rotting pile of bricks that might once have housed respectable citizens. Now it had been converted to warehouse welfare cases and newly arrived Asian refugees.

A hand-lettered cardboard sign hung in the doorway, advising one and all that no one was admitted except residents. Lindsey tried the door and found it locked. He rapped on the glass. He could see a few old men and women sitting around the lobby on faded furniture. A black and white TV set was mounted on a bracket eight or nine feet above the floor. The people in the lobby were enchanted.

Lindsey tapped again, using a coin. A

clerk leaned on the hotel counter, engrossed in watching the television.

Lindsey crossed the street, entered a restaurant and saloon directly opposite, and phoned the hotel. Eventually a sleepy female voice answered. Lindsey said he had to see Mr. Hammersmith urgently.

The voice said no visitors were allowed. Lindsey said it was worth twenty dollars. The person on the other phone dropped the receiver into its cradle.

Lindsey crossed the street once more and rapped on the front door with a coin. The sleepy-looking woman clerk dragged herself to the door. She stood there, leaning against the glass for support.

Lindsey took a twenty out of his wallet and held it up for her to see. He felt like a private eye. The door opened and he stepped inside the hotel. The twenty disappeared before he could say a word. When the clerk locked the door behind Lindsey, he said, 'What room is he in?'

'That'll cost you another twenty.'

He paid, got the number, and walked past the enchanted TV viewers and up a flight of ill-smelling stairs. He found

Hammersmith's room and knocked on the door. It cost him another twenty to meet Hammersmith, who was out of his uniform now, wearing a pair of ragged jeans and a faded plaid shirt.

Lindsey said, 'I have to talk to you. Just for a few minutes.'

Hammersmith said, 'I got nothing. Don't know nothing. Go away.'

Lindsey said, 'Then give me back my twenty.'

Hammersmith smiled. 'No way.'

'Look, I just need to know a few things about the car that was stolen at the Kleiner Mansion in Oakland.'

Hammersmith said, 'I'm too busy. Got to get my lunch.'

'You can talk to me.'

'Lunchtime. If you buy me lunch, we can talk some.'

More expense. Well, International Surety should go for it. 'Where?'

'Right across the street's okay with me.'

Lindsey sighed. 'All right.'

They got a booth at the restaurant across the street. Lindsey had a late breakfast and Hammersmith ordered a

T-bone, extra rare. Hammersmith refused to talk about anything except the Giants' prospects until the food came. Then he dug in with gusto. Finally he sat back in his seat and said, 'I could take another of those.'

'You're kidding.'

'No, sir. You want to hear me talk, ply me with steaks.'

Lindsey gave in.

Hammersmith said, 'Now, what you want to hear?'

'I'm investigating the theft of the Duesenberg; I'm an insurance adjuster. Are you a member of the New California Smart Set?'

'Charter member. Ollie van Arndt put my name down. Pays my dues. Always gets me to come to the parties. I don't mind. Lots of good food and drinks. I don't drink much, but I don't mind a little champagne now and again.'

Lindsey shook his head. 'I don't understand. How do you know Oliver van Arndt?'

'I save his daddy. Saved him in England. June 6, 1944. You know what that day was? That was D-Day. Ike took the whole armada across the channel.'

'You were part of it?'

'Oh, no. I wasn't no dogface. I was Army air force. I was ground crew. We put up everything we had, close air support for the invasion. Those planes was coming back all shot to shit, corpses in 'em, crashing on the tarmac. It was terrible.' Hammersmith attacked his meal. 'Terrible.' His eyes had a distant look. 'This P-51 comes in, holes in the wings, half the tail shot away, engine smoking. Comes in on half a landing gear, ground loops. I'm riding the rescue wagon.'

Lindsey waited while Hammersmith ate some more with relish.

'We get about twenty yards from this 51, flames start coming out of the engine, crew chief yells, 'No way,' and the wagon starts to pull away from the 51. You see what I'm telling you, Mr. — what's your name? Mr. Lindsey. You see what I'm telling you?'

Lindsey nodded.

'That engine was on fire. Meant the fuel tank was gonna blow. But I saw that pilot struggling to get out of the cockpit. I jumped off the wagon, got him out of that cockpit, drug him away. Then the 51 blew.'

Lindsey said, 'Is that how you lost your leg?'

Hammersmith grinned. 'I didn't get a scratch. But I saved that pilot. He said he'd take care of me forever. That was Ollie's daddy. Dead a long time now, but Ollie takes care of me, too. I get a little check every month. And he makes me go to those club meetings. I don't mind. Lots of good food. And champagne. I don't mind.'

Lindsey said, 'But your leg . . . '

'Well, afterward I stayed in. I figured, I made tech sergeant here; I got nothing outside. Never went to school. Never learned no trade. So I'll just stay in. They kept me. They sent me over to the Pacific; we was gettin' ready to land in Japan, but the war ended first. So they sent me back to Germany. I was in the occupation. They put me in the ground force. I got to see a lot of things.'

A waiter cleared their plates. Hammersmith ordered a slice of apple pie and a cup of coffee.

'Well, I saw those prison camps, those death camps. That was terrible. And some of them DPs — displaced persons, they called 'em. Homeless people, who wound up in the wrong country, or they tried to get away from the Rooshians, or they was POWs and didn't want to go back, or they was Jews. That was really sad, some of the things I saw.'

He wiped his face with his napkin. 'I saw some nice things, too. I saw Hitler's place at Berchtesgaden. Birdy's Garden, we called it. But it was Berchtesgaden. That's a kraut word. Well, I was ready to stay in the service for life. Then would you believe, I'm riding in a six-by-six truck and the driver's a little drunk and he rams a building with it and we get all broken up. Three men killed. I lost my leg. So they give me a new leg and a pension and they send me home. So I look up Captain van Arndt, only by then he was Mr. van Arndt, and here I am.'

Lindsey just looked at him. At length he said, 'What do you know about the car theft?'

'I saw it happen.'

'I thought Joseph Roberts was the only one who saw it happen.'

'I saw it happen. I tried to tell the police. They wasn't interested.'

'But Sergeant Gutierrez — '

'I told him I didn't see nothing. Police don't care what some old black man see. Not with all those fancy folks there. Old black man, half crazy, wearing an old uniform. They don't care.'

Lindsey said, 'What did you see?'

Hammersmith said, 'Two black Oakland boys stole that car. They bad people. They come walking up, look around, jump in and they stole it. I didn't see nothing. I don't know nothing, I don't have nothing. You have time for another piece of pie?'

★ ★ ★

Actually, the show was more fun than Lindsey had expected. Mother had been wildly excited at the idea of going to it, although the more she talked about the upcoming event, the more confused she became.

Did she think that her husband was still alive; that she was a war bride? How, in the fog-filled channels of her mind, did she account for her adult son?

Lindsey pulled off the freeway and into the parking lot at the Coliseum. The show had drawn an early crowd. The parking lot was nearly full, but he managed to find a spot between a giant Chevrolet station wagon and a vintage Volkswagen van. That spelled out the audience, he thought: middle-aged family types trying to recapture the past, and graying hippies who've never let go of it.

He'd kept the Hyundai's radio tuned to an oldies station, and the disk jockey had spent as much time plugging the revival show as selling cosmetics and gasoline. Between pitches he played old records, and Mother sang along.

Outside the car, Mother looked at the Coliseum Arena building and stopped in her tracks. She clutched Lindsey's arm. 'This is the wrong place, Hobo! This isn't where they're holding the dance.'

He put his arm around her shoulders and guided her toward the arena. 'So many people wanted to come, they had to move it here,' he said. With his free hand he pointed. 'See the people? They're all going to see the show.'

He was wearing the Leslie Gore baseball cap that came in the guest package. He felt pretty silly in it, but Mother got such a kick out of it, he kept it on. And when he looked around, he didn't feel conspicuous. At least half the people headed into the arena had got themselves up in period outfits. Men with greased-back duck's-ass haircuts. Women with bouffant hair, pedal pushers, sweater sets.

He kept Mother close to him while they found their seats. He bought Mother a souvenir program book full of photos of the stars and facsimile ads from thirty years ago.

The auditorium was huge and the lighting was dim. Joe Roberts's status with his friend Buddy Baron mustn't have been too high. Their seats were halfway up the side tier and half the length of the auditorium from the stage. The flat center of the floor, used for Warriors basketball games, was covered over with temporary seats.

M.C. Buddy Baron told some jokes that must have come from old Bob Hope kinescopes, read a few headlines from ancient newspapers, and introduced the acts. Fats Domino led off with a medley of 'Blueberry Hill' and 'My Blue Heaven', and played for half an hour. The Chordettes followed, featuring 'Mr. Sandman', and Little Richard went wild on the stage singing 'Tutti Frutti' and 'Good Golly Miss Molly'.

The program book contained a warning against taking flash pictures or recording the show. But hundreds of people, it seemed, were taking pictures. Most of the cameras Lindsey saw had big lenses and no flashes, but there still seemed a steady sequence of bright pinpoints flaring and disappearing all over the auditorium.

He took a walk with Mother during the intermission and waited for her outside the ladies' room. While he waited he watched the crowd surging to refreshment and souvenir stands. He felt a massive hand on his shoulder. He spun around. The hand belonged to a muscular giant outfitted as a '50s motorcycle tough. Martha Rachel Bernstein stood beside him, dressed as his chick.

The giant said, 'I'm Ed Mason. You must be Hobart Lindsey. Martha spotted you from across the crowd.' He stuck out a huge hand.

'Pleasure,' Lindsey managed. 'You make a great Hell's Angel. More convincing than Marlon Brando.'

Mason laughed. 'Yeah. This is a little different from my usual beat. Last time I was in this joint, the Warriors topped the Lakers. Can you imagine that?'

'I'm sorry. I don't follow basketball.'

'Smart fella.'

Martha Bernstein said, 'How are you doing with Three Eyes's dissertation?'

'It's good. Lots of useful information in it. Okay if I keep it a while?'

She said, 'Sure. Good luck.'

They drifted away. Seconds later, Mother came out of the ladies' room. Lindsey guided her back to their seats, relieved that he hadn't had to introduce her to Bernstein and Mason.

The second part of the show opened with special guests, and then came the star of the show, Leslie Gore. Buddy Barton was beside himself introducing her. She sang half a dozen songs, all of them about crying. Then she got to her all-time triumph, 'It's My Party and I'll Cry If I Want To'.

The auditorium was very dark. Flashbulbs kept popping. Mother dropped her souvenir program and started to fidget and whimper. Lindsey leaned across her and bent to retrieve the program. As he tipped his head he saw a particularly bright flashbulb go off and felt something slam into his shoulder like an Ed Mason hit.

The music was loud and Lindsey was slammed back against Mother and somebody behind him made a sound somewhere between a gasp and grunt and people started screaming.

People were shouting and jumping out of their seats. Those around them started complaining, then yelling. Ushers started converging on them and Lindsey tried to sit up with Mother's souvenir program in his hand but something hot and wet was pouring all over him. Maybe the person behind him had dumped a styrofoam cup of coffee on him.

Lindsey started to snarl at the person who'd dumped the coffee but either his voice wasn't working or there was so much noise he couldn't hear himself. Mother was grabbing him, pawing him, pulling him to herself. Something heavy fell on him, something warm and fleshy — the person who'd dumped his coffee, or her coffee. The person felt soft, like a woman. Lindsey dropped the souvenir program and groped upward with his right hand; his left hand didn't seem to be there. He felt the person. Yes, it was definitely a woman. He grabbed and felt her breast in his hand. He felt ashamed and let go. The weight was gone.

The lights were on. Security guards and ushers were pointing flashlights around, and the house lights were coming on, bank after bank. Lindsey couldn't hear the music anymore. Maybe it had stopped. He could only hear screaming and shouting, and through it the voice of Mother calling, 'Daddy, Daddy, come quick, somebody's hurt our little Hobo, somebody's shot our little Hobo!'

He was picked up by strong hands and half-dragged, half-carried across rows of rapidly emptying seats. He was laid on his back on a cold concrete floor. Somebody shined a flashlight on his face, then on his shoulder. He followed the light. The shoulder was covered with red. The light swung back to his face.

A voice said, 'Can you hear me? You doing all right?'

Behind the flashlight he could see a black face with frizzled hair and a moustache, and a security guard's uniform. 'Hey, man, talk to me.'

Lindsey said, 'Mother — she needs help . . . '

The guard said, 'Help me, we need a stretcher.'

Another voice said, 'She's all right. She's okay. Lay still.'

Lindsey said, 'What happened?'

The voice said, 'Somebody shot you. Just lay back.'

They must have got him up the stairs to the ramp. He felt himself lifted. He felt something under him. He felt it moving. It had to be a gurney. There were people around him, faces and clothing, white and black, coming and going, and the gurney kept rolling.

Somebody'd shot him.

He went through a doorway, down a dingy corridor. He was in the parking lot, and could see the gray-black clouds illuminated by the glare of lights. It was raining. He could feel the cold rain falling on his face.

He could hear the wheels of the gurney grinding over bits of gravel. He could hear voices shouting and other voices with the peculiar sound of radio speakers and doors slamming. He was lifted and more doors slammed, and he thought he must be in a dead van if he'd been shot and killed and they were taking him off to the morgue.

Something stung his arm and he turned to see what it was and saw somebody in a white costume with a needle in his arm, draining his blood out.

That must be what they did to corpses, to prepare them for embalming.

'I'm dead,' he muttered.

The person in white said, 'No, you're alive. You've been shot. This is an IV.'

He heard crashing sounds, distant, and a siren warbling. The mortician kept saying, 'Hang on, you're going to make it.'

He lost track of the lights and darkness, the swerves and jolts. He felt somebody holding his hand and he opened his eyes to too much brightness. He squeezed them shut again, then opened them more slowly.

He felt a monstrous throbbing in his left shoulder and he looked that way and saw a mound of bandages, and beyond the bandages a man peering at him. The man was familiar. Lindsey squinted at him, trying to remember who he was. Finally he figured it out. It was Lt. High.

Lindsey said, 'You're not a real doctor, you're a cop. You think I'm a killer.' Angry with High, he turned his head the other way. Somebody was holding on to his right hand. He could see his hand held by two hands, black hands. He blinked and looked up to see whose hands they were. They were Marvia Plum's hands.

Marvia said, 'Bart, you're okay.'

Lindsey said, 'No, I'm not. Somebody shot me. I'm dead. They drained my blood out. They're going to embalm me.'

Another voice said, 'He's still in shock. Don't worry. He'll be okay.'

Marvia's face got very big, coming very close to Lindsey's. All he could see was her face surrounded by her black hair, filling the world. He said, 'You're all black. You're all black.' He could see she was crying. Her tears fell onto his face and they made his face start crying too.

He passed out again. There were more strange sensations, movements and unpleasant spells and things being stuck in him, and then he passed out but good. And the next time he woke up he knew he was alive. He must have made some kind of sound, or maybe somebody was monitoring him, because a nurse came running in and looked at him. Lindsey said, 'Somebody shot me. How badly?'

'Not very. The bullet entered your left

shoulder, broke a bone and ricocheted out. They cleaned out the splinters already. You'll do fine.'

'Who shot me? Is Mother all right?'

'I don't know.'

He tried to sit up but she moved forward and laid a hand on his right shoulder. Her touch was light but it was enough to weigh him down. He managed to raise his head enough to see that he was connected to an IV and a couple of sensors. He said, 'Can I talk to somebody? I need to know . . . I need to know . . . '

His head fell back onto his pillow and he closed his eyes until somebody shook him by his good shoulder. Another person in white. This one was male. He looked young enough to be Joanie Schorr's brother.

'How are you, Mr. Lindsey? I'm your doctor.' He gave a name that sounded like a brand of gourmet pasta. 'What can I do for you?'

This time when Lindsey tried to sit up it was the doctor's hand on his shoulder that held him down. 'You're really going to be okay, Mr. Lindsey. You'll be out of here in a day or two, and back to work in a week. You were very lucky.'

'*Lucky?*'

'Well, I don't think anybody shot you from directly overhead. The police said that the shot came from across the arena. Do you remember it?'

Lindsey concentrated. Mother had dropped her souvenir program. He'd leaned over to pick it up for her. He told the doctor.

'Your lucky break. If you'd been sitting up, you wouldn't be here now. Whoever shot you must have aimed at your head. I don't see how he could do that across a huge, dark auditorium.'

'My Leslie Gore hat. I was wearing a baseball cap with a picture of Leslie Gore on it. A white hat.'

The young doctor whistled. 'That hat was a target. Without it, you'd never have got shot. And if you hadn't bent over to pick up that program, I can tell you, you wouldn't be here now, you'd be at the city morgue ... By the way, who's Leslie Gore?'

271

Lindsey said, 'You wouldn't know. Your mother might.'

The doctor chuckled, then sobered. 'Lady sitting behind you wasn't so lucky. When that bullet ricocheted it went up at an angle and got her in the throat. Severed arteries, crushed larynx, lodged in her top vertebra.'

'Then she's — '

'Than a doornail. That's how it goes. If you'd been sitting up, you'd be in dead right now, and she'd probably be at home with a story to tell her grandchildren. But you bent over, she's at the morgue, and you'll have the story to tell.'

'What about my mother? Is she all right? Was she hurt? She's a little . . . confused, sometimes.'

'I wouldn't know, Mr. Lindsey. But we're supposed to call OPD when you can talk. Can you talk now?'

'I guess so.'

An hour later High was back.

Lindsey found the control that made his bed sit up. He saw that he was wearing an angel gown. He was still hooked to the IV but there was a tray beside his bed and he was able to reach for a glass of water and sip at it.

High was wearing civvies. He smiled nervously. Lindsey spotted a hardbacked chair and gestured toward it.

High slid into the chair. 'How are you feeling? They taking care of you?'

Lindsey said, 'I don't even know what hospital I'm in.'

'Kaiser Oakland. They were going to take you to Highland but the emergency room was too full. Motorcycle accidents and crack wars. You're lucky. I understand the food at Highland is even worse than it is here.'

'I don't think I'm hungry.'

'Yeah. You don't look too great.'

Lindsey said, 'What happened? Some young guy came in here a while ago and said he was a doctor. Said somebody'd shot at me from across the arena. Do you know who? Or why? Did you catch him?'

As High fumbled for a pocket notebook before answering, Lindsey added, 'Are you sure he was aiming at me? There were something like 14,000 people out there; are you sure he wanted me? The little doctor said that a woman sitting behind me was killed, is that right?'

High had his notebook open now and referred to it. 'Angelina Tozzi, age 42, of San Leandro. At the show with her husband. Three children, one grandchild. Husband is taking it pretty hard.'

'You're sure he was after me, not her?'

High nodded. 'Akim Ibrahimi, a.k.a. Alvin Joseph Jackson of 94th Avenue, Oakland. I'll quote you exactly what he said — short, and not very sweet . . . '

Lindsey frowned as he listened to a lurid stream of low-life street obscenity, Shorn of its invective, it read:

'*** burned me, *** burn artist ***, show the ***, miles, hundreds of miles, blow *** head away *** burn me show *** burn me blow that white hat right off his *** head'.

High concluded: 'You were wearing a white hat, weren't you? Several witnesses sitting around you said as much.'

Lindsey pushed himself upright with his uninjured arm. 'Whoa! Wait a minute. Alvin J. Jackson?'

'Black male, 23 years old, unmarried.'

'Did he say why? I never heard of any Alvin J. Jackson. Or Akim whatever that other name was. You must have asked him. What did he say? Where is he now?'

High flipped his notebook shut and open again a couple of times, looking unhappy. 'He's with the coroner. Preliminary report says he was full of cocaine and alcohol with traces of marijuana, methamphetamines, and a few other funny substances. He had a very unusual weapon with him. A Dragunov. Soviet-made sniper weapon. Apparently he smuggled it into the arena disassembled, slipped it out from under his coat and put it together in the presence of 14,000 witnesses. It was very dark in there.'

'I know.'

'Took one shot at you, wounding you and killing Mrs. Tozzi. Threw the weapon away — it landed seven or eight rows from where he was sitting. He was able to run out of the auditorium and get to his car and reach the freeway.'

'Nobody stopped him?'

'Nobody knew what had happened. Nobody heard the shot except the people directly around him. Too much noise. And the arena was dark except for the stage. That's why he was able to sight on your baseball cap. There was so much confusion, so much panic, he just ran out.'

Lindsey tried to put his head in hands. His right hand flew up and smacked him in the face. 'Oh, Jesus, I'm a mess.' He wiped his forehead with his good hand. 'He's dead?'

'He is. But his driver isn't.' High referred to his notebook once again. 'Willie M. Jackson, a.k.a. Ali Watani. No known address. Alvin's brother. He's alive. He insists that he doesn't know anything about anything. His brother had a ticket for the show and told Willie he might want to leave early. Asked Willie to wait for him in the car with the engine running, and be ready to beat the crowd to the freeway.'

'You actually believe that, Lieutenant?'

Before High could answer, the telephone sounded. High picked it up. In a diffident voice he said, 'This is Mr. Lindsey's room.' Pause. 'Yes, Mr. Lindsey is here.' He smiled at Lindsey, held the phone toward his good hand.

It was Joe Roberts. He'd just got around to looking at this morning's *Oakland Tribune*. There was a story in it about the shooting. He was beside himself with remorse. It was his tickets that Lindsey had used, his Leslie Gore hat that Lindsey had been wearing. He was so relieved that Lindsey was only wounded; that he was going to recover. And yes, it was tragic about that woman from San Leandro; he couldn't feel worse. And could Lindsey ever forgive him for giving him those tickets? But anyway, had Lindsey had a chance to enjoy the rest of the show?

Lindsey managed to mutter something polite and hung up. He sighed.

'A friend?' High said.

'A lightweight. So Jackson is dead?'

'He got onto 980 headed west. Willie was driving. We got the CHP onto them. Went off the freeway at the Cypress structure in west Oakland. They were doing almost ninety. Caromed off a Toyota van and a Volvo station wagon and went over the guard rail. Willie was driving a '78 Chevrolet Camaro, black with red and gold flame decorations. Straight down to the surface, thirty feet, landed in a front yard, fortunately unoccupied at the time. When CHP got there, they were still alive. Alvin died in the ambulance. I read you his statement, didn't I?'

'Yes. What about Willie?'

'You'll get a kick out of this. He was a couple of doors from here at first. But they transferred him to Highland. He's handcuffed to his bed. Probably recover, the docs tell me. But he says he was just Alvin's driver; he's sticking to his story, and for all we know it may even be true.'

Lindsey said, 'Jesus.'

'Had an interesting arsenal in the Camaro,' High resumed, 'as well as a few bindles of heroin, a box full of crack vials and paraphernalia, and about half a kilo of marijuana. Oh, and an empty whiskey bottle. Willie's in a lot of trouble, but I don't think we can pin the shooting on him. He may have been involved or maybe not, but he's going to try and pin it on Alvin. And he'll probably succeed. Of course we'll check the weapon for fingerprints, but I expect they'll be Alvin's.'

'You know these guys?'

'Everybody at headquarters knows them. Apparently the brothers were pretty new at the dope game. We didn't have any priors on them for that. But your friend Gutierrez knows them well. Alvin in particular. He had a long record for auto theft, a few assaults and extortions . . . ' High consulted his notebook again. ' . . . a couple of atrocious assaults and two murders to his credit. Ali Watani, or Willie, hasn't racked up the record his brother has, but I suppose in time he will. Little brothers are like that. I found the murders in my files, but I'm afraid I didn't remember Akim.'

Lindsey was incredulous. 'This guy was walking the streets?'

'He was on probation for the most recent murder. Can you think of any reason Mr. Ibrahimi, a.k.a. Jackson, was angry with you? Let's assume that Willie really was just a driver. Why would Alvin call you a burn artist if he didn't even know you? Do you think the brothers were the parties who stole that Duesenberg from the Kleiner Mansion, and Alvin wanted you to stop pursuing them?'

Lindsey stared up at the bottle of clear liquid that was dripping through the IV tube into his arm. 'I wasn't getting anywhere at all on that case. If Alvin stole the car, maybe you can find it by checking him out. Where did you say he lived?'

'Ninety-fourth Avenue. We're checking out there. No luck so far, but we're still trying. My people and the auto theft folks.'

Lindsey closed his eyes. He ought to tell High that Jackson was shooting at Joe Roberts, not at Hobart Lindsey. How the hell did Jackson know that Roberts was going to be at the show and wearing a white hat? That was a puzzle, but if Jackson was in the cocaine business and Buddy Barton was as sleazy a character as Lindsey suspected, then Jackson and Barton might have been acquainted. And Barton might have shown Jackson a revival show promo kit, maybe even given him one — and mentioned that Joe Roberts would have got one, and would probably be at the show.

And if Jackson had stolen the car at Roberts's instructions, and Roberts then cheated Jackson on a promised fee, that would make Roberts a burn artist. A man of Jackson's temperament and background, hopped up on half a dozen drugs, could very well have decided to kill Roberts. And shot Lindsey because he was sitting in Roberts's seat wearing the white Leslie Gore hat. And killed Angelina Tozzi because Lindsey's mother had dropped her souvenir program.

Where was Mother? What had she thought when the shooting took place? Had she got home? There was no way she could have got the car keys from Lindsey's pocket and driven to Walnut Creek in the Hyundai. She hadn't driven for years. Who was taking care of her?

Lindsey realized that his eyes were closed. Why was he so drowsy? His eyes slid shut.

The little doctor bustled around

Lindsey, touching and humming and checking. Lindsey felt like a character in a Whitley Strieber book in the custody of aliens. He managed to open his eyes.

It was a little dark brown doctor in hospital whites. Electric light glinted off her glasses. Her hair was jet black, glossy, braided like a child's.

'I know you.'

'Parvati Mukerji. Yes. I was Mr. Otto Kleiner's doctor.'

Lindsey said, 'How's the old fellow doing?'

'I'm very sorry.'

'But Jayjay Smith told me he was getting better.'

'Yes. He *did* rally. But he was so frail, Mr. Lindsey. Sometimes at that age . . . ' She put her hand on his wrist, checking his pulse. 'Well, you have had quite an experience yourself, Mr. Lindsey. How are you feeling now?'

'Still a little woozy. Uh — ' He reached for the water glass. It had been refilled. 'What day is it?'

'Tuesday. You came in Friday night. Or early Saturday morning. The accounting office will be most interested in the exact date you were admitted.'

'I'll bet they will.'

'Anyway, you have been here almost three days. I've spoken with your doctor. You'll be going home in another day or two. Right now you should start eating the delicious food that our kitchen sends up.'

'Yeah. I'll try.'

Dr. Mukerji smiled at him again and walked out. He had another thought, and called after her, 'My mother — was she . . . ' But Dr. Mukerji was out into the hall by then, the heavy door to Lindsey's room easing itself shut.

18

The phone again. This place was busier than Lindsey's office. In fact it was Ms. Wilbur. 'Hobart, are you all right?'

'Well, I don't think I'm going to die. The doc was in and said I was lucky. They've got me eating real food now, but I'm still on an IV. Must be some painkiller in that, too. Every so often I just sort of fade out. Is that what you mean by all right?'

'Well, you're as sweet-natured as ever, so I guess you are.'

'Listen, maybe you can do something for me. I've been trying to find out what happened to Mother. She was with me when that guy shot me. I can't find out where she is. I tried calling my house and there's no answer.'

'She's in Kaiser Hospital, too. They decided she was in emotional shock, so she's there under observation.'

'She's in the same hospital I am, and

nobody told me?'

'I guess so. She's covered on your policy as a dependent adult. I checked that on the computer; I hope you don't mind.'

'No, of course not.'

'But I don't think they'll want to keep her long.'

One more thing to worry about.

'There's something else,' Ms. Wilbur said. 'This is unofficial, okay? I didn't tell you this.'

Lindsey said that was okay. Ms. Wilbur was hooked into the central nervous system of International Surety. If anybody was up to anything, she knew about it. She'd saved Lindsey's career more than once.

'Harden is coming to see you. From Regional.'

'Oh, boy. Do you know why?'

'Harden is coming out here to look over the operation. He's going to put you on medical leave.'

'What happens to my job?'

'He offered it to me. I told him, no way. I just like being office manager. I'm not a claims adjuster and I don't want to be one.'

'So then what?'

'He hired some independent agent, offered him a nice steady salary. The guy said he didn't like running an independent insurance agency, as it meant too much night work and too many weekends. He wanted a regular job. He was more interested in some other investments he has, anyhow — wants to get out of the agency business and work for International Surety and watch his investments in his spare time.'

'I have a feeling that I know who this is,' he said. 'I hope I'm wrong. Is it Elmer Mueller?'

'Hobart, you're amazing! I'm just running the office for the rest of the week, and Elmer starts Monday morning. You're not pleased?'

'Damn right.'

'Other than that, Mr. Lindsey, how did you like the show?' Ms. Wilbur asked.

'Very funny. When is Harden due in?'

'He's flying into Oakland tonight. I don't know whether he'll come out here first or go to see you, so it could be any time from tomorrow morning on.'

He hung up and rang for a nurse. When he got one, he asked about Mother and the nurse she'd check and let him know.

Somehow he napped, and when he woke up he had visitors again. It was disorienting lying in bed, never getting dressed, never getting out, living by artificial light. He was losing track of the day, even losing track of whether it was day or night. He thought of poor Otto Kleiner. It might have been better to leave him at home to die in familiar surroundings.

Visitors! Marvia Plum and her father, Marcus.

Marvia reached for Lindsey, put her hands on him, pressed her face against his. Marcus advanced behind his daughter, reached around her like a giant with a princess, and shook Lindsey's good hand. He said, 'I heard what happened to you, young man. Came to see how you're doing.'

Lindsey held Marvia against him a little

longer. When she straightened up he held on to her hand. 'Thank you. You're very — '

'My wife is at work. She couldn't get away. She sends her regards, Hobart. Are you getting proper care here?'

Lindsey nodded. 'Only problem, my doctor looks like a boy scout.'

Marcus chuckled. 'Sign of age. Next thing, you'll be looking at pretty girls and thinking that they're children instead of — '

'Dad!' Marvia dug her father with an elbow.

Marcus laughed again. 'And they start treating you like that. My own daughter, see?'

Marvia said, 'Do you need anything?'

Lindsey said he didn't, but he was worried about Mother. He explained about her being in Kaiser for observation.

Marcus Plum said, 'I'll go look in on her.'

'I appreciate that, sir, but — '

'That's another thing,' Marcus Plum said. 'When grown people start calling you sir.' He waved and left the room.

Marvia said, 'He means well. And I'm crazy about him. But sometimes I just can't handle him. And neither can my mom.'

'Maybe I could phone the desk from here,' Lindsey said, 'and get put through to Mother's room.'

Marvia said, 'Try it.'

He did. She picked up the phone herself. She didn't sound so bad. She didn't seem to understand why she was in the hospital, but she also didn't seem too upset about it. 'But how are you?' she asked. 'Don't be afraid to tell me, little Hobo. I should say, Big Hobo! I'm proud of you. I'm very proud. He's here right now, and he's proud of you, too.'

'Mother, now just tell me. Why are you proud of me, and who is there with you?'

'Why, you broke your shoulder, my poor Hobo. But you're a hero, breaking your shoulder in that high school football game. And you scored the touchdown. I'm so proud of you! Sometimes I think the boys fake the injuries just to get girls. You'll be all right. And now you'll get a girl friend, mark my words.'

'Mother, just tell me, who is there with you?'

'Why, it's your coach. That nice Mr. Plum.' She lowered her voice confidentially. 'You know, even though he's black, he looks very clean and he speaks just as nicely as a white person.' She raised her voice back to normal. 'And he says you're a real star and a hero. Isn't that wonderful?'

Lindsey finished the call and hung up. Marvia had heard his half of the conversation. He filled in Mother's half. Marvia said with a smile, 'That's my dad.'

Lindsey told her he expected to go on medical leave from his job. He took her hand again. 'Do you think you could get a few days off and help me? I want to go to LA. Mother should be able to leave when I do, and Mrs. Hernandez will stay with her. But I can't drive. Could you get away from Berkeley?'

She frowned. 'I don't know. Is this another trip like Reno?'

'Joe Roberts phoned earlier. I meant to tell High about him, but I just passed out. I think I'm being doped.'

'Don't get paranoid. Of course you're not being doped. Do you think hospitals do things like that?'

'I guess it's just a painkiller. But my mind gets a little fuzzy sometimes, and I fall asleep.'

'Well — what is it, then?'

'Do you know who shot me, and why?'

'Oh, yes. It's been in the papers and on TV. Some violent, crazed dope dealer. Alvin Jackson. A well-known character in certain circles, such as East Bay police forces.'

'Did you know he was a car booster as well as a drug dealer and strong-arm man?'

'Meaning? Do you think he has your Duesenberg stashed in his backyard? In East Oakland, or wherever he lived?'

'Marvia, I only had those tickets because Joe Roberts gave them to me. That's why I had that Leslie Gore hat, too. Ibrahimi, or Jackson, managed to make a garbled statement before he died. He was complaining about being burned, cheated on an illegal deal. It wasn't a crazy, random crime. He was aiming at that white hat. Somehow Jackson knew that Roberts had tickets for the show and would be there, in those seats, wearing a white baseball cap. He didn't know that Roberts would get so busy with his Hollywood project that he'd give away the tickets — and the white hat, for good measure.'

'So Jackson had worked for Roberts. Roberts cheated him, and Jackson tried to murder him for revenge. Only you got wounded by mistake. And that poor Mrs. Tozzi from San Leandro was killed.'

'That's what I think. Yes.'

'Tell High.'

'Maybe I should. I was about to when High came to see me, but I fell asleep.'

'Tell him now.'

'I want to check something out first. In LA.'

She looked exasperated. 'What, Bart?'

'Why hasn't that car turned up, when it's so conspicuous? If the thief tried to drive it, he'd be spotted. If he tried to sell it, word would get out. It's true, he might have hidden it nearby after he stole it from the Kleiner Mansion, but I have another idea. If Jackson stole the car for Roberts, I think it may be hidden at

Roberts's home in LA.'

'You've lost me.'

'Roberts told me he has a bungalow in LA. Or near LA. He was showing me his office in the Clorox Building and I asked him about living here and keeping up with his work down there. When he's working in Hollywood he uses the cottage, and when he's working up here he lives in his Condo in Oakland. Will you come with me, Marvia?'

'You're treading on very dangerous ground, Bart. And you want me to come along? I'm a sworn police officer.'

'Can you get a few days off, and come along with me? Strictly unofficial. No badge, no gun. Just as my friend. If you — oh, hell, I'm going to lay a guilt trip on you to get you to do what I want.'

She managed half a laugh. 'I've heard worse.'

Lindsey said, 'I just need someone to drive a car for me. To help me get around. This can't wait 'til I recover from this shoulder. I have to go as soon as they let me.'

She bit her lip. 'I have some days

coming. But I don't know. How are you going to find the car down there? Do you even have Roberts's address?'

'Can't that come out of the DMV? Wouldn't it be on his driver's record?'

'If his legal residence is Oakland, that's all the DMV will have. Either for his license or for his car registration.'

'He told me that he came from the LA area; that he didn't like it there and he moved up here because the life is better but he has to go back frequently for business.'

'Sure. But what are you going to do, just pick up the phone book and look for Joseph Roberts? In Los Angeles County?'

'I'll find him. I know some of his screen credits. I'll try the networks, the studios, the production companies. Somebody will have a home address for him.'

'Let me sleep on it, okay? I want to help you, I really do. But I don't know if I can do this, or if it'll work.'

Marvia moved toward him and took his hand with one of hers, laying the other against his face. Behind her, the door swung open and Marcus Plum came in.

'Whoops! Pardon me!'

Marvia straightened. 'Come on in, Dad.'

Marcus said, 'I had quite a chat with your mother, Mr. Lindsey. Hobart.'

Lindsey said, 'She's a little confused.'

'She's all right. Take care of her. And don't fret. You know, when I was a boy I was 'colored'. Then along came 'Negro' as the preferred term of dignity. Then that became a bad word and we were supposed to be called blacks. Many of my relatives are not black at all, they're dark brown or light brown or — never mind that. Next there will be another word, I suppose. I could tell that your mother has no malice in her, and for that I can overlook a good deal. At my age, I've learned to look beyond the word and beyond the moment, Hobart.'

Marvia whispered, 'I'll think it over. I promise. I'll talk to you tomorrow.'

★   ★   ★

Lindsey had never met Harden, but he recognized him from photos in company newsletters. And if he'd had any doubt about the square-faced, square-bodied man in the old-fashioned light tan double-breasted suit, he would have known him from his voice.

'The hell happened to you?' was Harden's sympathetic greeting.

Lindsey wasn't feeling too great already this morning. Apparently his shoulder was coming along beautifully. The little doctor had told him he'd be going home tomorrow, in all likelihood. He was off the IV, eating a normal diet, and getting only tablets for painkillers, no more magic formulas added to his glucose infusions. But his shoulder ached like blazes when he moved.

He was walking down the hall, returning from a visit to Mother. She'd been in a semi-private room, hit it off with the woman in the next bed, and had had a grand time gabbing with her and the nurses and doctors. Marcus Plum had made a big hit, too, although Mother's roommate had given Lindsey an odd look when he was introduced as a high school student.

Even so, he could take Mother home when he checked out himself, get her settled, arrange for Mrs. Hernandez and Joanie Schorr to share the task of caring for her. And then, if Marvia agreed to fly south with him . . .

Ms. Wilbur had warned him not to let Harden know what was going on at International Surety. Okay, play dumb. That would not be hard to do. Harden was just coming out of Lindsey's room when Lindsey got back from Mother's room. They locked eyes. Harden turned around and went back in. He didn't bother to hold the door open for Lindsey.

Inside the room, they both sat in visitor's chairs. Lindsey wasn't going to climb back in bed with Harden there. When Harden asked his question, Lindsey used the 'I got shot' line again.

Harden conceded that he knew all about that. 'What are you going to do about your job?' Harden asked.

'I want to get back to work as fast as I can.'

Harden said, 'Nope. Bad policy. Can't have you convalescing in the office. You stay home until you're ready to come back one hundred percent.'

Lindsey feigned consternation. 'But — my case load!'

'Nothing to it. KlameNet takes most of the input. Regional looks 'em over, sends 'em up to National if they look clean, National sends out the checks.'

'But — office work. Somebody has to — '

'That Ms. Wilbur of yours is a hot cookie. Don't worry about a thing, Hobart.'

'Okay. If you're sure. And I'll still be the chief area claims adjuster when I get back? You're sure Ms. Wilbur can run the office alone?'

Harden stood up and walked to the curtained window. He peered outside.

'Mr. Harden? When I get back to work?'

Harden turned around, his hands clasped behind his back. 'We can't leave that job completely vacant. I've already got a fellow to fill in for you. Good insurance head, strong background, man after my own heart.'

Lindsey agreed with that.

'Maybe you've worked with him. Local man. Name's Elmer Mueller.'

Lindsey said that he had worked with him. Harden was playing cagey about what would happen when Lindsey got back to work. He had a feeling that he was being eased out. Harden had never cared for Lindsey. He'd been particularly unhappy when Lindsey became a star by saving the company a quarter million for some stolen comic books. Harden grinned and sent his congratulations to Lindsey, especially when Ms. Johanssen at National had singled him out in a corporate bulletin, but Lindsey knew that Harden was tasting bile over the matter, and had been looking for a chance to stab Lindsey ever since.

Lindsey said, 'Well, if you're sure.'

'I'm sure. There's something else, Lindsey. Maybe I should let this wait until you're back at work, but I think you're entitled to know about it now.' He turned around and glared at Lindsey. 'We got a lawyer letter.'

Harden reached inside his jacket and

handed him a letter. It was printed on beautiful watermarked paper with a letterhead embossed in two colors. He recognized the law firm in San Francisco, with its discreetly noted branches in Los Angeles, Sacramento, and Washington. He read the letter once quickly, once more carefully, folded it and handed it back to Harden.

As he slipped the letter back inside his pocket, Harden said, 'Well? What do you have to say for yourself?'

'Are we going to pay it?'

'I think we have to. You went on a picnic with these people? A goddamned picnic? On company time?'

'I was trying to develop a lead. I was trying to save the company money.'

'Right. Just like you did in Reno.'

'You turned that down, didn't you?'

'You can bet your backside I turned it down. Fourteen hundred dollars to hire some grease monkey and fly him to Reno to look at a car museum?'

'I guess it didn't work out too well. You have to try, Mr. Harden. You're going to miss now and then, but you have to try.'

'And you went on a picnic with these van Arndt people, and they say you've given up on that Duesenberg. Their lawyer says if we don't pay right now they're going to sue us for the value of the policy plus interest plus their lawyer's expenses plus half a dozen other little things.'

Lindsey nodded. 'Have you run that past Legal? They might have some ideas. I don't think International Surety should just cave in. Besides, I thought the van Arndts were more reasonable than that. And it isn't their personal car anyhow. It belongs — '

Harden got red in the face. 'Don't you tell me how to run this region! You got lucky on one case, Lindsey, and you think you know more than an up-from-the-ranks insurance man. Of course I ran it past Legal, and they said we're up to our ears in hot water. We're a modest company, we have limited resources. You blew it on this one, buster. Next time you walk past the barn, take a look at whose hide is hanging there. It'll be yours.'

Harden pulled out a pair of rimless

glasses, hung the wire bows over his ears, unfolded the letter again and read it to himself. Then he looked up from the letter and glared at Lindsey. 'And you took a cop along? You took a cop on this picnic? The auto theft guy working on the case?'

'No. Lt. High is from homicide.' Lindsey tried to explain that without getting hopelessly tangled. The more he tried, the more involved it got.

Harden looked at his watch and barked, 'I can't waste any more time on your personal problems or on the homicide rate in this lousy burg. Crazy old geezers, lunatics of every kind. Just go home and rest up. Phone in every couple of days.'

'All right.'

Harden stood in the open doorway. 'And when you feel better, you might want to think about career opportunities with some of our competitors.' Then he left.

19

'Jesus, man, you don't look so great.' Eric Coffman helped Lindsey into the front seat of his Mercury station wagon. Mother was already settled in the back.

Lindsey said, 'Well, thanks anyhow for coming all the way in here for us.'

Lindsey couldn't turn to the left without provoking major pain from his shoulder. The wound had been clean, the bones weren't shattered, and with a cast and a sling in place Lindsey had been discharged. He'd had to sign Mother out as well as himself, but even by telephone Ms. Hernandez and Joanie Schorr had been more than willing to help out with her.

Lindsey had received one last visitor before leaving Kaiser — Jayjay Smith. She strode into his room wearing a black shirt and jeans, medium-high heels, red lipstick and earrings that looked like onyx hubcaps. It was a mourning outfit, of sorts.

'Bart?' Jayjay stood hesitantly in the

303

doorway. Lindsey, sitting up in his hospital bed, gestured with his good hand and she crossed the room. A split second of hesitation, then she took his hand. 'I just heard. Are you okay?'

'I'll be out of here today, I think.'

'What happened? I mean, it was on the TV and the *Trib* ran a couple of stories, but . . . ' She shook her head. She released his hand and pulled up visitor's chair.

Lindsey said, 'It was a case of mistaken identity. The gunman wanted to shoot a man in a white hat, and I was wearing the hat. It was all a terrible mistake.'

'Do you know who he was after?'

'It was Joe Roberts.'

'Joe!' she almost screamed.

'Jayjay, I don't know how much I can say about this. I just think that Roberts and this Jackson fellow were mixed up in something and Jackson figured that Roberts had double-crossed him. He was hopped up on everything you think of, and he just went after Roberts. He must have known that Roberts was going to be at that particular show, may even have known that Roberts would wear that white hat and where his reserved seat was. I don't know how, but I have a guess or two. Anyway, Roberts couldn't get to the show so he gave me his tickets and the hat — it was part of a promo kit — and when Jackson saw me in the white hat, in what should have been Roberts's seat, he thought I was Roberts.'

Lindsey didn't want to talk about getting shot anymore. He said, 'Tell me about old Mr. Kleiner. Dr. Mukerji was in; she told me that he died.'

Jayjay nodded. 'I found a little model Duesenberg for him, a real collector's item. Authentic paint job, polished metal.'

'Ormolu?'

That got a small smile from her. 'No, just cast iron and stainless steel. But nice.' She paused. 'He was dozing, Hobart. He was so thin and pale; he was almost transparent, lying there. I put it in his hands. He opened his eyes and looked at it and he held it to his chest like a little child. Then he closed his eyes again.' She fell silent.

Lindsey said, 'Thanks for telling me, Jayjay. Thanks for coming here. Uh

— about us — I mean, about that night and us.'

She said, 'Yes?'

'Well — I'm not sure. I don't want you to think that . . . ' He didn't know what to say, except that he felt miserable.

'You telling me it was just a one-night stand, Hobart? Listen, you didn't ruin an innocent flower.'

'It's just that it ought to mean something. Don't you think so? I mean — and I . . . ' He gave it up.

She said, 'Hobart, you don't owe me anything. I'm looking for a husband. Listen, I've had a couple of those, and I really like men, but I really don't want to be attached to one. I don't mean to hurt your feelings.'

He felt confused and he said nothing. Jayjay patted his hand and said, 'Be careful and call me when you feel like it.' And she left.

* * *

Coffman helped Lindsey and Mother into the house. Mrs. Hernandez was there to greet them. After Coffman left, Mrs. Hernandez helped Lindsey settle Mother down. A while later she left, promising to be back in the morning.

Marvia Plum called. She'd been thinking about Lindsey's idea. If it was all right, she and her brother Tyrone would drive out to Walnut Creek and bring some food over to Lindsey's house.

By the time they got there, Mother was happily reading an ancient copy of *Look* magazine. There was a photo feature on Mamie Eisenhower in the White House.

When Tyrone Plum's battered Checker pulled into the driveway, Lindsey met Tyrone and Marvia at the front doorway. They entered bearing pizza. Lindsey gave Marvia a chaste kiss and they carried the cardboard boxes into the kitchen.

Mother hardly seemed to notice until they brought the pies back out and began distributing slices. Then she peered at Marvia and at Tyrone, looking puzzled. 'Are you children Hobo's schoolmates?' she asked.

Tyrone — evidently briefed by Marvia — smiled and offered his hand. 'We're friends of Hobart's. I'm Tyrone Plum. This is my sister, Marvia.'

Mother stared at Tyrone's hand, then took it. Gingerly.

Marvia said, 'We've met before, Mrs. Lindsey.'

Mother frowned and said, 'Hobart, isn't that Mr. Plum your football coach? He's such a nice man. Do you think your friends might be related to him?'

Marvia volunteered, 'He's our father.'

Mother smiled and picked up a wedge of pizza. She'd set aside her magazine. She'd got things sorted out, in her own way.

After they'd eaten, Mother settled down to watch an old sitcom rerun. Marvia and Tyrone and Lindsey settled in the room that Lindsey used for a home office.

'Okay,' Marvia said, when they were all seated. 'It took some swapping shifts, and I'm going to owe some people, but I got time off.'

Lindsey asked, 'Did you have to tell them where you're going — or why?'

'I had to talk it over with Dorothy

Yamura. I only told her that I was going to LA for a few days. I told her it was personal and she accepted that. I think she's smells a rat, but she said okay.'

'How soon can you get away?'

'Wednesday next week — Tuesday night, if you want. Then I'll have to work Saturday and Sunday; that was the only way I could clear my shifts.'

'That's great. Thanks. Leaving next week gives me more recuperation time. And I can get Mother back on her routine.'

Marvia leaned forward and put her arm on his desk. She said, 'There's one more thing . . . I want Tyrone along.'

Lindsey said, 'Why?' He had nothing against Tyrone, and it was hardly a romantic interlude that he had in mind. But he was puzzled.

'I'm not going down there as a cop, else I'd have to clear it with Dorothy, maybe even higher up in Berkeley. And with Oakland and LAPD too. And frankly I don't think either Berkeley or Oakland would go for it, even if LA did.'

Lindsey nodded. 'I see that. But why Tyrone?'

'It won't hurt to have him along on general principles, just in case we do locate the missing car you think is down there. If you're right, Tyrone is the one who knows about cars.'

Tyrone grinned. 'I won't say I ever boosted a car, Hobart, but I work as a repo man once in a while.'

'Okay,' Lindsey conceded. 'We'll fly down. I'll call that agency you like in Berkeley, Tyrone.'

Tyrone said, 'Who's paying for this expedition? That was your personal check for my fee last time.'

Lindsey hadn't told them about Harden's turning down his expense request for the Reno trip. He didn't want to get into that right now. 'It's all part of the job. We're still trying to get that car back. We'll take care of it.'

Marvia flashed Lindsey a look. 'Okay, then. There are plenty of flights between here and LA; you set it up and let me know, all right?'

Lindsey agreed.

★   ★   ★

The Southwest Airbus dropped over the last row of hills into the ugly brown smoke that hangs over the Los Angeles basin, and made its approach to Hollywood-Burbank.

They rented a Lincoln Town Car. Tyrone would have no other. He got a second set of keys, just in case. Lindsey complained. Tyrone said, 'It's on your company, isn't it? Spend a few dollars more. It'll save your knees.' Lindsey didn't challenge that. Injured as he was, the roomy car was a godsend.

They checked into the Hollywood Holiday Inn. A suite: two bedrooms and a sitting room. It was a quarter of twelve. Tyrone phoned room service for lunch and signed the tab.

Lindsey had brought his briefcase and notebook. He spread his papers on a low table before the couch, pulled over a telephone and went to work, looking for Joseph Roberts.

Lindsey phoned the Writers' Guild. Most screenwriters belonged, and most movie and TV producers had contracts with the guild. They would have an address and a phone number for Roberts.

They did. And they would be happy to forward any mail for Mr. Roberts if Lindsey wanted to write to him in care of the guild. Yes, the secretary understood that it was urgent. Yes, she realized that this was important to Mr. Roberts. But the rules were absolutely binding; she could lose her job if she gave out a home address. But she could provide Mr. Roberts's office address and number in Oakland . . .

Lindsey gave up on that and checked his notebook. He'd made a list of Roberts's screenwriting credits, based on the posters he'd seen in the Clorox Building office and Roberts's own boasting. And the TV shows that he'd written for. He'd even jotted down the production companies for the feature films, thank heaven for that. And he knew which network had run each series.

He shuffled his papers and flipped one-handed through his pocket organizer. Trouble was, each lead represented half a dozen conversations with switchboard operators, receptionists, secretaries, personnel managers. Lindsey found himself struggling fruitlessly with one particularly maddening personnel manager, and he slammed the receiver onto its cradle.

Marvia said, 'Why don't you put your feet up for a little while, Bart. Have a drink and a sandwich. I'll try a few of these.'

Lindsey grumbled, but she was right. He turned his notes over to her and did as she'd suggested.

Afterwards he took a quiet tour of the suite, hearing Marvia's calm voice as she followed up more leads.

In the second bedroom he saw Tyrone Plum, eyes closed and legs stretched out on the bed, snoring softly.

He crossed the room and sat on the couch beside Marvia.

Marvia held the phone to her ear, smiling at him. She muttered, 'No, thanks just the same,' and hung up. To Lindsey she said, 'That's the last one. I'm sorry, Bart.'

He suddenly thought of something. '*Jazz Babies*. No! *Luv Beads*!'

Lindsey scrambled for his pocket organizer. Roberts had said that *Jazz*

Babies was sold to the network. Then he'd said that the network wanted it changed into *Luv Beads*. But — had he ever mentioned which network?

One-handed, he riffled pages in his pocket organizer, then shuffled sheets of notepaper. Yes, there it was! Lindsey picked up the telephone directory, found a listing for the network and drew a circle around it.

Lindsey picked up the telephone receiver, propped it against his ear and punched in the network's number. He finally reached the programming department and found someone willing to talk to him about *Luv Beads*.

The someone was a woman who described herself as the administrative aide to the assistant co-executive producer. She was cold and cagey. She wanted to know where Lindsey had learned about *Luv Beads*. He told her he was a friend of Joseph Roberts from northern California; that he was working with Roberts on the research part of his job, and he'd found himself in LA on short notice and wanted to get in touch with Roberts.

She said that unannounced developmental projects were strictly confidential. If Lindsey wanted to talk about it he should call the network legal department. Better yet, he could write to them. Their address was as listed in the telephone directory. Thank you for your interest.

Lindsey hung up and sighed. 'Close,' he told Marvia, 'close.'

Yawning and stretching, Tyrone Plum wandered in from the bedroom. He rubbed his eyes. 'You two love birds getting anywhere?' he asked.

Lindsey and Marvia Plum shook their heads.

Marvia said, 'We've been trying the studios and networks that Roberts worked with. Nobody'll give out his home info.'

Tyrone picked up the phone and punched for the bell captain. He muttered a few words into the mouthpiece, then hung up. He said, 'I figure if we don't do any good we'll be headed for home tomorrow, right? Right. So let's see if we can find anything amusing to occupy us tonight.'

When the knock at the door came, Tyrone stood up and leaned over Lindsey.

'Need a ten, my man.'

Lindsey produced it.

Tyrone took what the bellman had brought, handed him the ten and sent him away. He came back to Marvia and Lindsey and tossed a *Los Angeles Times*, a *Daily Variety*, and a *Hollywood Reporter* on the table. 'Pick one, little buddies. Might as well poke around and see if we can find anything.'

It was a long shot, but it was there — little article on page eleven of the *Hollywood Reporter*. The Hollywood Association for the Restoration and Preservation of Underappreciated Culture was holding a retrospective program called *Sleaze through the Ages*. Tonight's show was scheduled for a long-closed theater on Melrose near Los Angeles City College. The features, to be introduced by noted film historian Arthur Foster, were the late Edward Wood's cult classic *Glen or Glenda*, and *Wyoming Roundup*, written and directed by Joseph Roberts.

Lindsey whooped: 'Tyrone, you're a genius.' He leaned over and gave Tyrone a kiss on the cheek. Then he turned and did the same to Marvia.

Tyrone wiped his cheek with the back of his hand. 'Let's not get carried away. So we go down there and see a couple of incredibly rotten movies. So what?'

'I think he'll be there. I know he isn't in Oakland. I tried his office, I tried his home, just got a machine at each. I'm sure he's in LA — and if he is, there's no way he'd miss this screening. You don't know his ego!'

* * *

Their Lincoln Town Car glided through heavy traffic, fitting in with the Mercedes and Rolls and Jaguars. Lindsey could see the glitter types, most of them mortgaged to the eyeballs, dressed to the nines and driving leased glitz cars to keep up their facades.

The Lincoln got a quick response from the parking valet at the restaurant, and Lindsey's credit card took care of their meal and a couple of jugs of saki — one for Lindsey, one for Tyrone. 'I'm the driver,' Marvia insisted. 'No alcohol.'

The theater where the films were to be screened had never been grand, and by now it was thoroughly decrepit. The ancient box office had been reopened, and Lindsey paid for three admissions. Inside the theater, paintings that had once covered stucco walls were flaking and all but unrecognizable. The seats in the auditorium had been worn threadbare by generations of rumps and gave off a musty odor. The house lights were low when they arrived, and the floor felt as if the last few decades of spilled soft drinks had been allowed to dry.

They found seats in an audience composed of City College student types, film students talking intensely of equipment and technique, old-timers as ancient and decrepit as the theater, and a scattering of Hollywood crazies and wannabes. There was no sign of Joe Roberts.

There was a smattering of applause and a dim spotlight silhouetted Arthur Foster against a dusty velvet curtain. Foster was a white-haired individual of indeterminate age. He started talking about the history of Hollywood, Poverty Row, the underrated productions of Monogram, Mascot, Republic, and Allied Artists. Somehow he got off on the subject of Arthur Foster and waxed enthusiastic, if boring.

Finally Foster left the stage, to an even thinner round of applause. The curtains drew back and the projectionist rolled *Glen or Glenda*. It ran for just 61 minutes — Foster had emphasized that in his introduction — but even the presence of a feeble, dying Bela Lugosi couldn't make it bearable. Lindsey headed for the lobby. He studied the ancient paintings, until he saw a figure cross from the restroom to the auditorium.

Was it Joe Roberts?

Lindsey hurried after him, but the man had found his seat before Lindsey reached the auditorium. In the darkness, sitting with a hundred others, Roberts was invisible. Lindsey found Marvia and Tyrone, slipped into his seat, and whispered eagerly to the others.

When *Glen or Glenda* ended, the house lights came up again and Arthur Foster reappeared on the stage. Lindsey ran up one aisle, down the next. The audience had filled only a fraction of the seats. Lindsey peered at one face after another.

At length he grabbed Marvia and Tyrone, pulling them after him into the lobby. 'I saw Roberts,' he said. 'I was right. He couldn't stay away. But he must have spotted me too, and he's gone.'

'You sure he left the theater?'

'I think so. I'm not sure of that either.'

Lindsey ran back down the aisle. Arthur Foster was just finishing his introduction to *Wyoming Roundup*. Lindsey caught his eye, grasped him by the elbow with his one usable hand, and steered him back to the lobby, to Marvia and Tyrone.

Talking as fast as he could, Lindsey explained that it was urgent for him to get to Roberts. He said he'd seen him in the lobby during *Glen or Glenda*.

Foster couldn't help.

Then what about stopping *Wyoming Roundup* and turning on the lights?

Sacrilege! Foster wouldn't hear of it.

They waited for the end of the show,

hoping to spot Roberts on the way out — hoping he hadn't already left the theater — but it was no good.

Lindsey felt as if he was grasping at straws. He asked Foster about the association; if Roberts was on the association's mailing list.

Foster said the association had no formal membership. Lectures and screenings were announced through the trade press. Expenses were paid by admission fees. There was no general mailing list.

They left Foster there. Marvia drove. They dropped Tyrone at a comedy club on Sunset. Then Marvia and Lindsey headed back to the Holiday Inn.

20

Lindsey had removed the sling from his arm when he and Marvia went to bed. Standing barefoot on the thick carpeting the next morning, he supported his injured left arm with his sound right arm. He struggled into the sling. Using only his right hand, acutely conscious of the left and taking care not to bang it, the arm or the shoulder against any object, he managed to pull on his shorts and then his trousers.

The door to their suite rattled, despite their having put out the *Do Not Disturb* sign the night before. The bedroom door opened and Tyrone Plum's head appeared in the opening. 'Everybody decent?' Without waiting for an answer, he strolled into the room. He was still wearing last night's clothes.

Marvia said, 'You just sit down, Tyrone. Facing the other way!'

Tyrone complied.

Marvia climbed from the bed. She kissed Lindsey on the cheek before picking up her clothing and closing herself in the bathroom.

Tyrone said, 'Guess I can turn around now.' He did.

Lindsey said, 'Tyrone, did you just get in?'

Tyrone grinned. 'In a manner of speaking.'

When Marvia emerged from the bathroom they ordered breakfast from room service. Tyrone went to the other room to shower and change. Lindsey managed a clumsy sponge bath and a shave. Marvia helped him, then she helped him struggle into one of his mutilated shirts.

A little later their breakfast arrived, and they convened a council over the white linen-covered rolling table.

Marvia said, 'That film society almost did it.'

Tyrone said, 'But you can bet Roberts will stay away from any more shows like that one. Can't you do something, Marvia? The police, I mean?'

Marvia shook her head. 'Not the Berkeley police; we've been over that. Oakland might. You'd have to convince one of your pals, High or Gutierrez. Then they'd go for a warrant, and try and bust his office or his condo. But still, what would they find? What are they looking for? I don't think they could convince a judge to issue a warrant. I think Roberts is home free, Bart. I'm really sorry, but there it is.' She put her hand on his good wrist.

'I still don't think that's so. He's connected to Alvin Jackson. You know what Jackson said to the CHP officer. That's on record now. Dying statement, right? Even though it's hearsay, they can use it, right?'

Marvia said, 'That's true, but what does it prove?'

Tyrone said, 'Who's Alvin Jackson, and what dying statement was that?'

Lindsey filled him in on the information he'd got from Lt. High when High came to see him at Kaiser. At Tyrone's insistence, Lindsey duplicated Jackson's statement almost word for word.

Tyrone laughed. 'Mr. Eloquence, hey?'

'I don't think he had any education. And he was on drugs — and dying.'

Marvia put down her glass of orange juice before her mouth. 'Wait a minute, Bart! You said he had no education, he was on drugs and he was dying. Education! What about Joseph Roberts's education? Where did he go to college? Did he go to film school down here? UCLA, USC, City College where we were last night?'

'No. I remember him telling me that he never went to college or to film school. He went straight from Hollywood High to the studios. He got a job in the mail room and he worked his way up. He learned everything on the job.'

'Then maybe you could get something out of Hollywood High.'

An hour later they had checked out of the Holiday Inn. Lindsey's credit card statement was going to look like the federal deficit this month, but he was too far into this to quit now.

It was only a short drive to Hollywood High School. The spring semester was in full swing, and the school parking lot and the streets around it were full of shiny, sporty-looking cars. The sons and daughters of the rich and famous lived as well as their parents, and with fewer responsibilities.

Tyrone waited in the Lincoln while Marvia accompanied Lindsey into the school. Carrying an attaché case with his papers in it, Lindsey looked as respectable as he could, with his arm in the shape it was.

They were referred to the school personnel office and from there to the student records office, trying to find a home address for Joseph Roberts. Lindsey showed his International Surety credentials and explained that this was strictly an insurance matter. He was a claims adjuster and this involved payment on a claim for a stolen automobile. He did not bother to say that Roberts was neither the owner of the car nor the beneficiary on the policy.

Not that it did any good. The school was legally obligated to respect the right of privacy of present and former students.

If Lindsey wanted to write to Roberts, in care of Hollywood High, they would forward his letter to the last address they had for him. Otherwise, unless he had a court order . . .

As they headed for the front door, Marvia said, 'Wait! What about the yearbook?'

Lindsey stopped in his tracks. 'The yearbook! Every high school has one. The school library, or the yearbook office.'

They headed back to the place where they'd started, the general office of the school. A teenage girl done up in the latest Hollywood chic listened to Lindsey's questions. Finally she said, 'Oh, the yearbook. Yeah, I remember that. We used to have a yearbook. With pictures and stuff, right? Mostly we use videotape now, but I think we still have a yearbook.'

She went away and conferred with a colleague. They looked over their shoulders at Lindsey and at Marvia Plum, and conferred some more. Then she returned to face Lindsey across the counter. 'It's called *Visage*. They have an office upstairs. You go out of this office and then you turn left, and you walk over to the stairs there . . . '

Lindsey and Marvia actually found the office. The room was half-full of computer terminals, boys and girls staring into them.

After a couple of minutes, a boy wearing jeans and a Lakers T-shirt asked Lindsey and Marvia if he could help them. Lindsey said, 'Do you have a file of back issues of the yearbook?'

The boy pointed to a bookcase. 'You an alum? Looking up old classmates? They come in all the time. Want to know if they really went to school with someone who was famous later.'

Lindsey said, 'Something like that.'

'Help yourself. But we can't loan 'em out.'

Lindsey said, 'Right here will be fine.'

The boy made a gesture and Lindsey and Marvia started for the bookcase. Lindsey said, 'Roberts never told me what year he graduated. But he said he was thirty-three years old. He was proud of how far he'd got by that age, so he told me his age.'

Marvia frowned. 'Typical high school grad is about eighteen, give or take a year. If he's 33 now he was eighteen in '74. Let's try that.'

Marvia pulled the 1974 edition from the shelf. They went through the book. No luck. 'Let's try '73 and '75,' she said.

Roberts wasn't there. He wasn't in the '72 or '76 either.

Marvia said, 'How sure are you of that age?'

'Just what he told me.'

'I just have a feeling,' Marvia said. 'If Roberts is such an egotist, and if he's so proud of his youthful achievement, maybe he lies about his age! Let's give it a try.'

She stood up and carried the yearbooks for 1971 through 1976 back to the case. She pulled the books for 1965 through 1970.

When she put them on the table, Lindsey said, 'We could go faster if we each do half.'

Minutes later Lindsey grasped Marvia by the wrist. 'Here he is! Class of 1968.'

'So he's closer to forty now.' Marvia grinned.

Lindsey shoved the book toward Marvia. 'Take a peek.'

'Joseph Roberts. That the guy?'

Lindsey nodded. 'No question about it. He's wearing glasses — guess he's got himself contacts now. This is definitely the guy.'

'Okay. What does it say about him? No home address. Damn.'

Lindsey said, 'What else is there? They have some quotation about each senior. Look at these — Shakespeare, Einstein. Roberts has a quotation from somebody named McLandburgh Wilson, whoever the heck that was.'

'Read it.'

'It's a poem. 'Twixt the optimist and the pessimist / the difference is droll / the optimist sees the doughnut / but the pessimist sees the hole.' Huh! Nice piece of pop philosophy. I don't get the point.'

Marvia shook her head. 'Neither do I. What else does it say?'

'The usual credits. Drama club, literary society, whatever. And a few little jokes. Jelly doesn't go off half-fried. Sprinkles us with joy. His eyes are clear, not glazed.'

They looked at each other blankly, then: 'Now I get it!' Lindsey was exultant. 'They're all donut jokes. Sprinkles, glazed, jelly. And that quote from that poem.'

Marvia said, 'So what?'

'It's a pun. You know how kids make puns on each other's names.'

'Tell me about it. Can you guess what it's like going through life named Plum?'

'Right. Sure.' He shoved all the yearbooks away except the one with Joe Roberts's picture in it. 'Donut isn't a pun on Joseph Roberts,' he explained. 'It's a pun on Dönitz. Admiral Dönitz. The guy who succeeded Hitler in 1945. Morton Karl Kleiner had a shrine to Hitler and to Admiral Dönitz in his home, up in Petaluma.'

'And you think Joseph Roberts is connected to Admiral Dönitz in some way? You think Roberts is a Nazi? He's connected to Morton Kleiner's Petaluma group?'

'Somehow Kleiner and Roberts and Admiral Dönitz are connected. And I think the Duesenberg is connected, too.

331

And the missing Kleiner fortune.' He struggled to his feet and picked up the 1968 *Visage*, carrying it to the boy who'd helped them. 'You have a photocopy machine here? I'd like to copy one page.'

The boy said, 'Sure thing, sir. Right over there.'

Lindsey copied the page. Marvia returned the books to the shelf. They thanked the boy and left Hollywood High School.

21

Tyrone chauffeured them to the public library. Marvia and Lindsey went through valley phone books. There were a wealth of Robertses, too many by far to be useful without a task force that they didn't have.

But they found a listing for Joachim K. Dönitz in Van Nuys. Lindsey said, 'Well, well. I'll bet that K stands for Karl! Okay, let's beard the lion in his den.'

They cut through the Hollywood Hills, leaving the smoggy Los Angeles Basin in favor of the smoggy San Fernando Valley. Tyrone Plum drove. The rain seemed to have no effect on the pollution that saturated the atmosphere.

Tyrone piloted the Lincoln through columns of cars crowded bumper to bumper as they sped through the San Fernando Valley at 65 miles per hour.

The heavy traffic at least meant they had time to plan their strategy. If the Dönitz they were looking for was the right

Dönitz — a lead to Joseph Roberts — they would have to be ready to move.

Marvia Plum sat in the passenger seat beside her brother; Lindsey sat behind them leaning forward so they could converse.

Tyrone said, 'Tell me again, now, who was this duck?'

'Admiral Karl Dönitz was the führer of Nazi Germany after Hitler killed himself,' answered Lindsey. 'Morton Karl Kleiner had a shrine to him in his home in Petaluma. The Hollywood High School yearbook entry for Joe Roberts is all full of donut puns. Donuts — Dönitz. My guess is that Roberts's real name is Joseph Robert Dönitz. He dropped the Dönitz but somehow the other kids found out about it and they wouldn't let go. Typical kid behavior.'

'And you think this Admiral Dönitz was Joe Roberts's grandpa?'

'Something like that. The Kleiners were from Germany. Old Otto Kleiner's younger sister, Brunhilde, went back to Germany in 1931, two years before Hitler came to power. She never turned up again. Otto had a few letters from her, then nothing. According to Iskowitz, a researcher who interviewed Otto Kleiner, Brunhilde was a great beauty. And she didn't look particularly Jewish.'

Tyrone cursed as a huge Bentley swooped past the Lincoln.

Lindsey continued his story. 'Dönitz wasn't much of a Nazi; he was a career navy man. He might well have been on leave when he met Brunhilde Kleiner. Maybe they had a love affair. Of course he never married Brunhilde; he had an official family. But if there was a child — a son — he might have been Joachim Dönitz. Our boy in Van Nuys.'

'I thought the Nazis were crazy to kill all the Jews. The ones they didn't kill wound up in concentration camps, and they only survived because the war ended before the Nazis could kill them all.'

'Not so. You ought to talk to my friend Eric Coffman some time. He's read up on the subject. Says he has to teach his children so they'll know their history. The Nazis gave some Jews special treatment. People with valuable talent, scientists and a few doctors, the Nazis were willing to use them. And an admiral could certainly get his mistress onto the special treatment list. Or maybe Brunhilde managed to pass as Aryan. I don't know. That's what I want to find out.'

'So what's the connection between all of these folks and the stolen car and a murder? I think you watch too much TV, Hobart!'

'There was a fortune missing since the 1930s. And old Otto Kleiner was distraught about the stolen Duesenberg. Maybe the fortune was hidden in it. Old bank books or stock certificates hidden in the upholstery, or diamonds or gold, something like that. I think that was why the car was stolen, not for its value as a car.'

'And Roberts knew about this, and nobody else did?'

'My guess is that Otto hid the money and told his sister about it. When she went back to Germany, that would leave only Otto knowing where the fortune was hidden.'

Over his shoulder, Tyrone said, 'Okay, I'm with you so far.'

Lindsey went on, 'Say Brunhilde did have a son by Admiral Dönitz. Brunhilde lived long enough to pass on the secret of the Kleiner fortune to her son. Somewhere along the line, Brunhilde disappears from the story. Probably dead. But her son knows about the money. He immigrates to America. Even though Admiral Dönitz never married his mother, the son takes the name Dönitz.'

Tyrone hit the brakes to avoid rear-ending a Citroën. 'We're not up to Joe yet, are we?'

'Not Joseph. His father, Joachim. He settles in Hollywood. Maybe he went to the army after the war and convinced them that his mother was American and he had a claim on American citizenship. He wound up in Hollywood. Married, had a son, Joseph Robert Dönitz. Young Joe didn't want to carry around a name with Nazi associations, especially not with ambitions in the film industry. So he dropped the Dönitz.'

'Wait a minute,' Marvia interrupted. 'You're telling me that this guy Joachim came to America, to Hollywood of all places, and used the name Dönitz? What was he doing, looking for a necktie party?'

A motorcyclist roared past the Lincoln. The driver was wearing a replica Nazi battle helmet.

'There were thousands of refugees flooding into the country,' Lindsey resumed. 'And maybe Dönitz wasn't such a distinctive name. I'd guess that Joachim went around telling people that he'd fled the Nazis; that he was one of the good Dönitzes, not those horrible Nazi Dönitzes. And all the while he was laughing inside.'

Marvia said, 'It sounds weird, but I guess it could be. But where does Joe Roberts come into this?'

'Somehow Joachim convinced the army in Germany that his mother was American, whatever. He marries — either in Germany and brings his bride with him, or someone he meets in America, whichever. There's a son, Joseph Robert Dönitz. But Joe doesn't go for this secret Nazi stuff, or maybe he doesn't even know about it. But he's living in Hollywood, and there are tons of Jewish kids in his school. He doesn't want to get tarred with the Nazi brush, with his ambitions to get into the movie industry. So: exit Joseph Robert Dönitz, enter Joe Roberts, all-American kid!'

Marvia shook her head. 'But he was just a high school kid. Changing records, changing his name — and his father didn't know about it?'

'Maybe he did know.' Lindsey shrugged. 'Maybe the kid pulled the wool over his old man's eyes. Or maybe he let him in on what he was doing — fooling those stupid Americans, climbing to the top in a town full of Jews; wouldn't that be a rich one?'

'But those donut jokes prove that the kids knew Joseph's real name.'

'Yes. And they went along with it, too. Maybe he gave them the good Dönitz/bad Dönitz story too.'

Marvia said, 'Okay. That's no nuttier than anything else in this case. But in the meantime, what about the car?'

'Well, Joe learned about this legendary Duesenberg and the missing fortune from his dad. He made it his business to move up north, near the old Kleiner homestead. He got into the mansion and got his shot at the car by joining the Smart Set.'

Tyrone said, 'What about the murder?'

'Morton Karl Kleiner was Otto's grandson. That makes him Joe Roberts's second cousin or something like that. Anyhow, Morton Karl Kleiner learned about the Dönitz connection, ran into some rednecks up around Petaluma, and got into a Nazi gang. He probably never knew about the missing fortune and the money hidden in the Duesenberg because he never made any fuss about it that I know of. But . . . ' Lindsey pressed his good hand against his eyes. 'Oh, my gosh!'

Marvia turned in her seat. 'Bart, what is it?'

'Joe Roberts knew about the fortune. Morton Karl Kleiner didn't know about the fortune. But Joe didn't know that Morton didn't know! Do you see what that means?'

'What?'

'Joe Roberts killed Morton Karl Kleiner! He thought Morton knew about the money in the car; he was afraid if the fortune turned up Morton would get it away from

340

him because he was a direct descendent of Otto. It was Joe Roberts who clouted Morton over the head and threw him in Lake Merritt.'

Marvia said, 'Wow, it fits. Oh, my gosh. We'd better get back to Oakland and have a talk with Lt. High.'

Tyrone said, 'Gonna scrub our visit to Joe's daddy?'

'No way!' Lindsey was adamant. My job is still to get that car back, and this is my chance to do that.'

Tyrone pulled the Lincoln to the curb in front of the Dönitz house. It was a miniature ranch house, the kind that sprang up by the tens of thousands in the years after World War II.

Tyrone offered to scout around on his own whilst Lindsey and Marvia walked up the path to the house. Lindsey sounded the doorbell. There was a pause, then a voice, then another voice. The sounds of a scuffle. Three voices altogether, two of men and one of a woman.

Finally the door swung open. A tall white-haired man stared at Lindsey and Marvia. He wore a white turtleneck shirt, a dark blue blazer with brass buttons, and sharply creased slacks. He had a yachting cap on his head. Standard Nazi U-boat captain gear. Lindsey had seen it in a hundred old movies. No Nazi regalia here, but white-hair had the look. He definitely had the look.

Lindsey said, 'Mr. Dönitz?'

'*Ja?*'

'I'm looking for Joseph Roberts. He's your son, isn't he?'

From behind the white-haired man a woman of the same age said, 'Tell him nothing, Joachim. Nothing!'

Joachim Dönitz said, 'I will tell him what I choose. Who are these people? Look! This cripple, probably a Jew. And an African. Hah!' To Lindsey: 'What do you want?'

'I told you, sir.' Lindsey tried to see past the couple, into the room. He had almost expected a duplicate of the Nazi den in Petaluma, but there was nothing here. The furniture and fittings were ordinary. An archway led from the living room into a buff-colored hall. 'I'm looking for Joseph Roberts, the television writer. I believe this is his home.'

He heard a stirring from deeper in the house. He wished that Marvia were in uniform and that she had a gun on her hip.

'Why do you ask me for this Roberts? How did you know me? Why did you come here?'

'I know your son. Mrs. Dönitz — ' He appealed to the gray-haired woman. She had emerged from behind her husband.

She said, 'He is our son. He doesn't want them to know who he is. The Jews run that film business. You run America, don't you? The Jews and the Africans. But that will change.' She turned to her husband. 'Show them! Get rid of them!'

She started to slam the door on them, but Lindsey stuck his foot in the way, then shouldered the door open, praying that he wouldn't injure his one good arm.

He'd heard three voices. There was a flash of shadow in the archway.

The elderly Dönitz ran for the archway, surprisingly agile for a man his age.

Lindsey ran after him.

Dönitz ducked through another doorway, Lindsey in hot pursuit. And here it was — the Nazi den. Red and black swastika flags on the walls. Portraits of Hitler and Admiral Dönitz and other bigwigs. Displays of military regalia.

Dönitz threw something at Lindsey. It bounced off the cast on his shoulder. A wave of pain shot through him. He saw what Dönitz had thrown — a hand grenade! Lindsey launched himself backward through the doorway he'd entered. He collided with Marvia Plum, shouted something at her and got her headed back toward the front of the house. The older woman — Mrs. Dönitz — ran ahead of her.

Lindsey waited for the explosion. It never came. Finally he started back.

Joachim Dönitz pounced on Lindsey. He held a bayonet in his hand, held it upraised for a moment, then plunged it into Lindsey's chest.

Nothing happened.

Dönitz staggered backward, then slid to a sitting position against the wall. His wife pushed past Marvia and past

Lindsey, took the rubber bayonet from her husband and helped him to his feet. She picked up the toy hand grenade and returned the grenade and the bayonet to their places on display.

Mrs. Dönitz turned to Lindsey and Marvia. 'Jews! Africans! Communists! We'll show you yet. Now, get out. Leave the old man to his dreams. Leave us in peace. Get out of my house this minute.' She put her arms around Joachim Dönitz and began to murmur to him in German.

There was a roar from the alley that ran past the house to a single-car garage. Lindsey and Marvia ran to the front door and stood watching as a 1928 Duesenberg SJ Phaeton rolled past the house. Lindsey could see Tyrone Plum's dark face leaning over the wheel. Joseph Roberts ran after the car.

The car turned west on the street in front of the Dönitz house and started to pick up speed. In its wake, Joe Roberts ran and shouted, waving his arms like a Keystone Kop.

Lindsey grabbed Marvia. 'Quick! You have the other keys.' He shoved her toward the Lincoln, ran to the passenger door while she unlocked the car, and climbed behind the wheel. They headed down the street, putting distance between themselves and the Duesenberg, Tyrone, and Joseph Roberts.

★ ★ ★

After nightfall the sky cleared. Marvia pulled the Lincoln off 101 south of San Luis Obispo and headed westward on highway 1 to Morro Bay. It was off-season. They had no trouble getting a motel room with a balcony overlooking the bay itself and the huge rocks that rose like titanic eggs a hundred yards offshore.

They washed and changed and walked to a seafood restaurant for dinner. Lindsey didn't know whether he'd been through a drama or a farce.

After they had ordered, Marvia said, 'It's always fun when you invite me on a trip, I'll say that, Bart! But I didn't figure on meeting a crazed Nazi!'

Lindsey smiled. 'So much for my theory about Joachim passing for an anti-Nazi refugee.'

'I don't know about that.' Marvia mused. 'That was forty, forty-five years ago. Maybe he lived that double life for most of those years. He's retired now. Maybe he's going back to his youth, to the 1940s.'

'Like my mother.'

'Well, sort of. You saw — he still kept up the pretense. That yachting outfit, the plain room. He still kept the Nazi stuff hidden. Of course, his wife was as bad as he was. But I still can't see the Kleiners, Jews, becoming Nazis. First Morton Karl Kleiner, now Joachim Dönitz.'

'Yeah. I asked Dr. Bernstein about that when I found out about Morton Kleiner. Another one of my professor friends, another Smart Set person. She has some kind of theory about reaction formations and oppressed people identifying with their oppressors rather than their own kind. It kind of makes sense. Say, don't some light-skinned blacks pass for whites?'

Marvia hesitated before she replied. 'Not as many as used to. Black pride, all of that. But it still happens.'

347

'And do they ever turn on other blacks? Join the Klan, that kind of thing?'

'Yes. And you think these Kleiners, with their Dönitz connections, totally denied their Jewishness and became anti-Semites?'

'Something like that.'

Their food came, and after their meal they went to bed.

★ ★ ★

During the night, Lindsey asked Marvia to marry him.

He could feel her shake her head. 'No.'

'Is it — the things we talked about before? Your ex-husband?'

'It's Jamie.'

'Jamie's a fine boy. I'll do my best for him.'

'I know you will.' He felt her mouth on his chest, warm. Maybe morning would never come; maybe this night would last forever. 'It isn't your fault, Bart. But — he's confused enough. He knows he has a father somewhere. A black father. He knows I'm his mother. He has a good home with my parents, a good role model.'

'Marcus is wonderful.'

'I don't want to change that. I don't want to upset him.'

'But . . . ' He didn't know what else to say.

'Just leave it, Bart. Please. I can't marry you. You know your situation. I know mine. We can't. It wouldn't work.'

'Marvia!'

'Let's just leave it, okay?'

He ran his good hand through her hair. She pressed closer to him.

They had a good breakfast and resumed their journey. Just south of Salinas, the cellular phone burbled. Lindsey picked it up. It was Tyrone Plum.

'How you two doing, Hobart? You better be nice to my little sister there, or you'll be one sorry dude.'

'Where are you? What happened?'

'I just drove back to Oakland. Been here for hours. Of course, I'm not a lover bird. What you two do, stop over at some hot palace?'

Lindsey smiled. 'Something like that. Listen — you drove all night, you drove all the way to Oakland and nobody stopped you? Didn't Roberts phone in a report?'

'You're talking to an old repo man, Hobart. I knew he wouldn't phone in any report. He had a stolen car. I just repo'd it from him. What's to report?'

'Where's the car now?'

'Well, I took it over to the Kleiner Mansion. Your friend Ms. Smith called OPD, got a Sergeant Gutierrez. He came over, looked at the car, said they really ought to impound it, but he didn't want to put it in the 'pounding lot. So he put a police seal on the garage. Car's right here where it belongs.'

Lindsey said, 'Tyrone, you are a wonder. Okay, we'll be back in a couple more hours. Where will you be?'

'I think I'll go over to Mom and Dad's on Bonar. Marvia knows the number. Give her my love, Hobart. And you be good to her.'

Marvia smiled at Lindsey. 'I heard enough of that. We have some business with Gutierrez, okay. But we have business with Lt. High, too!'

22

Marvia pulled the Lincoln into the driveway at the Kleiner Mansion. They got out and went to the front door. There was a hand-lettered sign in the doorway: 'Closed today. The Kleiner Mansion will be open for regular hours tomorrow'.

Lindsey knocked on the door. After a while he saw two faces through the glass — Tyrone Plum's and Jayjay Smith's.

Jayjay opened the door. She grinned at Lindsey, started a move toward him, then stopped when she saw Marvia. 'You did it,' she said. 'You got the car back. You and Tyrone and — you must be Marvia.'

The two women shook hands.

They went inside and settled in Jayjay's private quarters. Tyrone said, 'I'm supposed to call OPD now. Get Gutierrez over here.'

Marvia said, 'Let me call. We'll need more than Gutierrez.' She punched in the number and talked with High. She hung up and said, 'He'll take care of Gutierrez.

They're both coming over here.'

Lindsey said, 'Tyrone, Jayjay, can we look at the Duesenberg now?'

'The garage is sealed. Gutierrez put an OPD seal on it. Said not to dare touch it or I'd have to stand in the corner.'

Lindsey walked to a tall Victorian window and peered toward the Alameda County Courthouse. Inside the mansion it could have been the age of Teddy Roosevelt. A hundred yards away teen-aged crack dealers were on trial for blowing away business rivals with Uzis. Suddenly the age of Teddy Roosevelt seemed immensely attractive.

There was a sharp rapping at the front door and they all went to meet High and Gutierrez. They talked for a minute, then they headed around the side of the house to the garage.

Gutierrez inspected the seal he had put on the doors earlier. 'You've been a good boy, Tyrone. I half-expected to find this broken.'

'I'm a law-abiding citizen. My sister's an officer in your neighboring community.'

Gutierrez removed the seal and they entered the garage.

The Duesenberg stood in the center of the big work room looking like an exhibit in a museum of modern technology.

'This the correct vehicle?' Gutierrez asked Lindsey.

'I'll have to check the serial numbers.' Lindsey reached for his pocket organizer. 'But I think it is.' To Tyrone Plum he said, 'Can you imagine, if we repo'd the wrong car?'

Gutierrez said, 'Very funny, Mr. Lindsey. You folks are going to have some fancy explaining to do anyhow.'

Lindsey jotted the numbers and handed them to Gutierrez. 'Don't you already have these — in the theft reports?'

'Doesn't hurt to double check.' Gutierrez moved toward the car but stopped, his hand outstretched, a few inches from the beautiful metal. He turned toward Marvia. 'You're Sergeant Plum, right? From Berkeley Homicide?'

Marvia nodded.

Lieutenant High turned to Lindsey. 'You've been a big help already on this case, Mr. Lindsey. You can help me with the Morton Kleiner killing, is that correct? You know who did it?' High smiled diffidently, then fumbled in his pocket and took out a pocket notebook of his own. A man after Lindsey's heart, that Lt. High.

Lindsey gave him the theory he'd worked out with Marvia on the way back from LA. Then he gave High a rundown on the information he'd got from Iskowitz's dissertation.

High said, 'You can put me in touch with this Iskowitz fellow?'

'He's dead, according to Martha Bernstein. You can check that with her. But the dissertation itself is at UC.'

High nodded. 'I'll want that. Probably the DA will want it, eventually.'

Out of the corner of his eye, Lindsey could see Gutierrez and Tyrone Plum working over the Duesenberg. They were talking loudly enough for Lindsey to hear their conversation. Gutierrez said, 'You drove this all the way back from Van Nuys? Up I-5 and across? Where'd you get the key?'

'No key.'

Jayjay Smith said, 'There's a spare set in Mr. Kleiner's room, in the mansion.'

Gutierrez grunted.

Lindsey resumed explaining his ideas to High. High scribbled. When Lindsey got to the part about Joe Roberts — Joseph Robert Dönitz — murdering his cousin Morton Karl Kleiner, High put up his hand.

'We'll have to work on that. It's all very neat. But we'll need more than your theory. About his parents. Joachim, you said the father's name is?'

'Joachim K. Dönitz. I'll bet you a good dinner his middle name is Karl.'

'No bet, but I'll buy you one if this case wraps up the way you say it should. You didn't call the local police down there?'

Marvia said, 'About what crime? Being Nazis? Having World War II souvenirs? Attacking Bart with a plastic hand grenade and a rubber bayonet?'

Lindsey nodded. 'Good point.'

Lt. High added, 'Apparently they didn't report you folks for anything, either — including car theft. Which suggests that they knew the car wasn't their son's. Not legitimately, anyway.'

Marvia said, 'You ever get anything further on Morton and his Petaluma connections? Anything on a murder weapon?'

'In fact, just a little more. Coroner studied the impact wound that was the cause of death. Very nice indentation, apparently made with a cylindrical object — a bottle.'

Marvia said, 'We get a lot of those. Getting to be a weapon of choice. Usually doesn't break off on impact; they're pretty strong. But if it does, so what? This one didn't break, though, did it?'

'No. We'd have seen some cutting, probably glass fragments imbedded if it had.'

'Any label in the wound?'

High smiled beatifically. 'Sergeant Plum, if you ever want to get out of Berkeley and come work for me . . . There *was* a little bit of label. Looks like something off a very unusual bottle. You ever hear of Frankenstein vermouth?'

'No,' she admitted.

'Little winery started making the stuff

years ago. Studio laid a trip on them, said they were violating their copyright. So they changed the brand name. Anybody has any of the old Frankenstein stuff, it's a collector's item.' He smiled faintly. 'I got this from a friend of mine who runs a bottle shop — you never know who's going to help you with a case. As I was saying to Mr. Lindsey, here. Mr. Lindsey, do you think, by any chance, that Mr. Roberts drinks Frankenstein vermouth?'

Astounded, Lindsey said, 'I saw it at his condo. I wouldn't normally care, but I noticed the label.'

High smiled. 'We'll check on that. If it's such a great collector's item, he may still have the very bottle — with part of the label missing.'

Gutierrez and Tyrone had finished their examination of the Duesenberg. Gutierrez walked back to High and said, 'That's the right car, okay. So it was a proper repo. Van Nuys might be a little bent over the way these guys did it. Especially Sergeant Plum here.'

High said, 'I want you to get back to the car, get on the horn and send somebody to Roberts's condo. Here, Mr. Lindsey can give you the address. Get cracking on a warrant in case Roberts is difficult, but tell them to send a couple of officers and see if he'll consent. If he will, look for a bottle of Frankenstein vermouth.'

Gutierrez started for the garage door. He almost bounced off Joseph Roberts coming in.

Roberts looked around the room. 'The car,' he said. 'The Dusie's back.'

Lindsey said, 'Of course it is. You took it, we took it back. But you've got — '

Lt. High interrupted him. 'I'll handle this, Mr. Lindsey.' He looked at Roberts. 'Maybe you can help me, Mr. Roberts. I'm Lt. High. Could you tell me what brand of vermouth you drink?'

'Uh — I don't remember. I'm not much of a drinker. Whatever they have at the store. I'm just so — just so relieved. I mean, that's a wonderful car.' He'd managed to slip sideways in the middle of his answer. 'I was going to go for a ride in it, see if I could get old Mr. Kleiner to take me for a ride in it. As research for the

TV series I'm working on about the 1920s. *Jazz Babies*.'

He'd dropped the part about *Jazz Babies* being scrapped in favor of *Luv Beads*. Small matter.

'Anyway, I'm really glad that you fellows got the car back. You're from the auto theft squad, right?'

High said, 'Well, in fact, Sgt. Gutierrez is from auto theft. I'm from homicide, myself. Morton Kleiner was killed with a bottle of Frankenstein vermouth. You're sure that isn't your brand?'

'No, I — '

Lindsey snapped, 'Oh, come off it, Roberts. Donuts. Jelly.'

'Donuts! Who told you about that? Is that how you found my house?'

Marvia said, 'We looked up your old yearbook. You lie about your age, too.'

Lindsey said, 'What were you after? You hired the Jackson brothers to steal the car, didn't you? You thought the treasure was hidden in it, and you flew down to LA and looked for it and you couldn't find it anywhere in the car. So you burned them for their fee and they tried to murder you to get even. Did you set me up to take that bullet? How did you know they were going to do it at the revival show? Did Buddy Barton warn you?'

'No! I didn't even know Buddy knew them. That was all an accident. I — ' He stopped. 'God damn it!'

From where he stood next to Marvia Plum, Lindsey could see High and Gutierrez both reach.

But Roberts was faster. He was wearing a jacket cut so loosely that a little revolver in a shoulder holster wasn't obvious.

Roberts's revolver came out as High's and Gutierrez's did, but Roberts had a fraction of a second's head start.

Lindsey and Marvia Plum launched themselves at Roberts simultaneously. Roberts tried to get his shot off at High. Marvia and Lindsey hit him. Lindsey felt a transcendent shock as pain lanced through his body when his injured shoulder thudded into Joe Roberts.

Roberts's revolver went off.

Lindsey was rolling on the floor, waves of pain washing over him. Then Marvia and Jayjay Smith were helping him up. The waves of pain were receding slowly. Somewhere in the distance he could hear the drone of Gutierrez's voice. He recognized the Miranda routine from a thousand movies and TV shows, and from that dreadful moment in Lt. High's office at Oakland Police Headquarters.

His eyes were coming back into focus. Somebody — High or Gutierrez — had cuffed Roberts's hands behind his back. He was vaguely aware of Tyrone Plum's excited voice. Leaning on Marvia, Lindsey turned gingerly around. He saw Tyrone standing beyond the Duesenberg. He walked slowly toward him.

'Look at this,' Tyrone said. Something — probably Roberts's bullet — had ripped the canvas tarp that covered the spare Duesenberg engine and transmission. Tyrone was holding the edges of the tear. He grunted with effort as he ripped the tarp. 'Look at this,' he repeated.

Lindsey tried to see what Tyrone was so excited about. Through the torn canvas he could see that the bullet had cut a path through the creosote, gouged the metal of the spare Duesenberg engine block, and ricocheted away.

'Look at that,' Tyrone said. 'That's not cast iron!'

Where the bullet had gouged the engine block a streak of shiny metal was visible.

'Then what is it?' Lindsey asked.

'I think it's silver. Why would anybody make an engine out of silver? That's crazy!'

'Not so crazy. Wait a minute.' Lindsey's eyes were gleaming. 'That's the missing fortune! It wasn't in the car; it was in the spare engine and transmission. How much did you say they would weigh?'

'Carter out at Harrah's told me, six hundred pounds.'

'Okay. If Otto Lilienthal Kleiner turned the missing money into silver back in 1930 or '31, when the Depression was starting to get really serious and frightening, he could have taken it to the Kleiner Foundry in Emeryville. He could have cast it into an engine block and transmission. Six hundred pounds of silver.'

'No,' Jayjay Smith said. 'I know my metals. Silver is pretty heavy stuff. Almost twice as heavy as iron.'

Lindsey said, 'Okay. Twelve hundred pounds, then?'

Jayjay said, 'They used silver dollars back then. A silver dollar contained an ounce of silver. That's where the value came from. One ounce of silver, one silver dollar. So that would be — ' She broke off, frowning in concentration. 'Wait a minute. Precious metals are valued in troy ounces. A troy ounce is a little heavier than a regular ounce. Avoirdupois. But there are only twelve ounces to a troy pound. It comes out to . . . give me a minute to work this out . . . At 1931 prices it would be about eighteen thousand troy ounces. Eighteen thousand dollars.'

'And today?'

'Something like six dollars an ounce — about $108,000. That's a little more like it, isn't it?'

'No.' Lindsey shook his head. 'Why would old Mr. Kleiner bother to have an engine cast of silver, to hide away a mere eighteen thousand? It doesn't work.' He peered at the silvery metal. 'Anybody know what platinum looks like?'

Jayjay Smith said, 'It looks a lot like silver, but whiter and heavier. And more valuable. It's worth more than gold.'

'What would be the equivalent of six hundred pounds of iron — in platinum?'

Jayjay Smith did some more mental figuring. 'What was platinum worth in 1931?'

Lindsey shrugged. 'I remember from my high school history books that gold was either thirty-five or thirty-six dollars back in the Depression. What about platinum?'

Jayjay said, 'I think that's pretty consistently run maybe a third more than gold. Maybe fifty percent more at the most. Call it fifty dollars an ounce in 1931. Okay. Thirty-six thousand ounces of platinum at fifty dollars an ounce is worth . . . hmm . . . about $1,800,000. There's your missing Kleiner fortune. Not many millions, but a million-eight. In 1931 dollars, when you could buy a meal for a dime. A worker who earned twenty-five dollars a week lived comfortably. And Otto sent half a ton of platinum down to the Kleiner Foundry and had it cast into a Duesenberg engine and transmission.'

Lindsey said, 'And Brunhilde knew about it. Otto's son Georg didn't, so Morton didn't either. That's why he only wanted insurance money. But Brunhilde knew, and she told Joachim, and he told Joseph. That's why he wanted the car. He didn't know the platinum was in the spare engine; he thought it was in the car itself. And that's also why he wanted his cousin out of the way. Even though Morton didn't know about the platinum, Joseph did know that Morton didn't know. Does that make sense?'

Joe Roberts swore luridly.

Lindsey said, 'And what's that platinum worth today? I saw something on a business report the other night. It was somewhere around $550 an ounce.'

'All right. At $550 a troy ounce that would be — ' Concentration lines appeared and disappeared on Jayjay's face. 'Something like $19,800,000.'

Tyrone Plum whistled. 'Twenty million dollars!'

Jayjay Smith said, 'Who gets the money?'

They all looked blankly at one another.

Lindsey said, 'I wish Eric Coffman were here. He'd know. But I'd guess that Joachim Dönitz will have a pretty strong claim on it.'

Lt. High said, 'If I know the City of Oakland, they'll put in a claim. They own the mansion, right?'

'But not the car,' Jayjay Smith said. 'The Smart Set owns the car.'

Marvia said, 'But who owns the tools and spare parts?'

'They usually belong to the mechanic,' Tyrone said. Unless Mr. Kleiner specifically sold them to the city or to the Smart Set, they're still his. He would have kept them, wouldn't he, if that's where the money is. So the engine would still be his.'

'Or his estate's,' Lindsey said.

'Okay,' High said, 'let's get everybody out of here. Gutierrez, you make another try at calling in, will you? We'll still need that warrant, to see if Roberts has a bottle of Frankenstein vermouth with part of the label missing.'

'Have them check his videotape collection,' Lindsey suggested. 'See if he has a copy of *U-Boats Westward*. Starring Grandpa Admiral Dönitz.'

Roberts shot a murderous look at Lindsey. 'It's there, God damn you! Pudgy little nosey insurance bastard, I should have hit you with that bottle, not Cousin Mort.'

Jayjay was shaking. She asked Roberts, 'How did you get Morton back to your place to kill him? And then why did you dump him here? Why did you do that to me? Why did you do that?'

But Gutierrez and High had started away, Roberts still between them. High turned back at the doorway. 'We'll have to get all of you folks out of here and seal this place up. Crime scene tapes, you know the drill. For now, let's all just clear out of here and lock it up.'

They began to move. Lindsey was feeling light-headed between elation at the solution to the mystery and the pain in his shoulder.

Lt. High turned toward Lindsey once more. 'Thank you again, Mr. Lindsey. We really do need citizens to help us.'

23

'So why did Roberts — Dönitz — use that vermouth bottle to kill his cousin Mort? You'd think he'd have a better weapon than that. And why did he dump the body at the mansion when he could just have thrown it in the Oakland Estuary? And transporting a dead body in a Porsche was risky business.'

Lindsey shrugged. 'You're the homicide cop, Marvia. You tell me.'

Lindsey had invited Jayjay Smith and Tyrone to join them in the Silver Dollar, but both had declined. The room was dark and nearly empty. The kitchen was closed but at Marvia's request the chef had rustled up a couple of sandwiches for them, and they sat at the bar eating them. Marvia's friend Robert was tending bar, ministering to a few late drinkers.

The juke box was playing and Billie Holiday was singing something very sad and very beautiful.

'I don't think he intended to kill Morton,' Marvia said slowly. 'He must have found out about him through Jayjay, and invited him to his condo to find out how much Morton knew, and what he planned to do. Roberts was after that fortune, and he didn't want his long-lost, newly rediscovered cousin horning in on it. And of course Morton didn't know anything about the fortune, but he was apparently such an obnoxious creep, and so greedy, that Roberts got really spooked.'

The record ended and Billie Holiday's voice was replaced by that of Ella Fitzgerald.

'So,' Marvia went on, 'Roberts saw his fortune suddenly going up in smoke. All his dreams to maybe start an independent production company. Anyway, he just grabbed the first handy object.'

Lindsey said, 'Why did he keep the bottle, then?'

'Dumb. Confused. Not thinking straight. One minute he's freaking out over maybe losing the fortune that he doesn't even have but thinks he's going to get, then the next he's got a corpse in his living room and the murder weapon in his hand. So he carefully cleans off the bottle and puts it back in his liquor cabinet. They're like that, Bart. The cold-blooded, logical killer is one in a thousand. The rest of 'em . . . ' She shook her head.

Lindsey said, 'Roberts really had the hots for Jayjay, and she didn't want any part of him.'

'That's probably why he gave her the corpse. As a love-hate offering. Jesus, Bart, this is really getting sick. Can we talk about something else?'

The bartender had finally got rid of the last lost souls and drifted down to Lindsey and Marvia's end of the bar. He lifted a coffee pot from the hotplate and refilled their cups. 'You guys play a lot of those records, don't you?'

Marvia said, 'I like the disk jockey who stocks your juke box.'

The bartender laughed. 'Yeah. Say, you hear about that disk jockey got arrested today? Just came over the car radio. I was driving to work.'

'No. What was that?'

'Guy named Buddy Barton. I thought

you'd know him, plays a lot of oldies.'

Lindsey said, 'Buddy Barton? Arrested for what?'

'San Francisco cops and the feds, they went right into the radio station and pulled him off the air. They said he was mixed up in some really heavy dealing. I think they all use stuff in that business, you know. I guess you can never tell.' He took a swipe at the mahogany with his bar mop. 'You guys about done? Can I take those plates away?'

Lindsey dropped some money on the bar.

Marvia said, 'Who do you really think will get that money?'

'My guess is Joachim Karl Kleiner.'

'The Nazi son of a bitch?'

'It was Otto's money. I think the old fox kept it back from the City of Oakland and from the New California Smart Set, although I'm sure they'll have their lawyers in there with torts at the ready. But if the money went into old Otto's estate, think about this. Morton was killed before Otto died. The only other Kleiners that we know of are Dönitzes

— Joachim, Mrs. Joachim, and Joe Roberts. Unless a will turns up — pretty doubtful — the money goes to Otto's surviving relatives.'

Marvia said, 'That's justice for you.'

Lindsey drained the last of his coffee. Half the lights were out, and Robert was hovering behind the bar, ready to take Lindsey's and Marvia's empty cups. Lindsey muttered, 'I'd rather see Andy Hammersmith get the money.'

Marvia said, 'Who's that?'

Lindsey shook his head. 'An old soldier. Fellow I met over in San Francisco. Served in Europe after the war, helped the refugees get out. For all I know he helped Joachim get to America. That's justice, you're right.'

Standing in the parking lot beside Marvia's classic Mustang, their breath visible in the night air, Marvia said, 'But I can't figure out why Roberts came back to Oakland. I mean, he was still after the Kleiner fortune, that's obvious. But he must have known the jig was up.'

Lindsey shrugged with his one good shoulder. 'Arrogance. Thought he was smarter than anybody else, thought he could get away with anything. Invincible greed and unlimited arrogance. And curiosity. He still hadn't found the treasure and he had to keep trying. Well, at least he got his answer to that. For all the good it will do him now.'

They climbed into the car and Marvia started back toward Oxford Street.

Outside her house she said, 'You can stay over, Bart. Unless you want me to give you a ride back to Walnut Creek.'

'I want to stay over.'

A few minutes later, in Marvia's apartment, he managed to put his one good hand on one of hers. She clasped it with her other. He said, 'I want to marry you, Marvia. Please.'

She said, 'I just can't. I wish you'd stop asking me.'

'Then I suppose it's International Surety and life with Mother forever after.'

Marvia said, 'You'll do what you have to about your job. After your latest exploits that should be pretty safe. But as for your mother . . . I can't tell you what to do, Bart.'

He nodded. 'I know. But I think about just dumping her in some rest home. I can't do that.' He looked at Marvia. She laced her fingers through the fingers of his good hand. 'And I think about what my life is like. And I think about what it would be like to live with you. Marvia — can that ever be?'

That drew a smile. 'Not now, and not any time soon.'

'But you didn't say 'never'.'

She said, 'No.'

We do hope that you have enjoyed reading this large print book.

Did you know that all of our titles are available for purchase?

We publish a wide range of high quality large print books including:
Romances, Mysteries, Classics
General Fiction
Non Fiction and Westerns

Special interest titles available in large print are:
The Little Oxford Dictionary
Music Book, Song Book
Hymn Book, Service Book

Also available from us courtesy of Oxford University Press:
Young Readers' Dictionary
(large print edition)
Young Readers' Thesaurus
(large print edition)

For further information or a free brochure, please contact us at:
Ulverscroft Large Print Books Ltd.,
The Green, Bradgate Road, Anstey,
Leicester, LE7 7FU, England.
Tel: (00 44) **0116 236 4325**
Fax: (00 44) **0116 234 0205**

Other titles in the
Linford Mystery Library:

HOLLYWOOD HEAT

Arlette Lees

1950s Los Angeles: When six-year-old Daisy Adler vanishes from her upscale Hollywood Hills home, Detective Rusty Hallinan enters a case with more dangerous twists and turns than Mulholland Drive. Hallinan's life hits a bump or two of its own when he's dumped by his wife and falls for an enchanting young murder suspect half his age. But what's the connection between her murdered husband and a dying bar-room stripper? How does Hallinan's informant, exotic and endangered female impersonator Tyrisse Covington, fit into the puzzle? And where has little Daisy gone?

THE WITCHES' MOON

Gerald Verner

Mr. Dench left his house on a wet September night to post a letter at a nearby pillar-box — and disappeared. A fortnight later his dead body was found in a tunnel a few miles away. He had been brutally murdered. Called in to investigate, Superintendent Robert Budd soon realizes that Dench hadn't planned to disappear. But it's not until he finds the secret of the fireman's helmet, the poetic pickpocket, and the Witches' Moon that he discovers why Mr. Dench — and several other people — have been murdered . . .

TILL THE DAY I DIE

V. J. Banis

Shot at point-blank range while trying to prevent the kidnapping of her daughter Becky, book editor Catherine Desmond has a mysterious near-death experience. When she recovers, she learns that Becky has been murdered by a gang of child abusers, who are still active and being hunted by the police. To her dismay, she finds herself linked psychically with Becky's killer — and he begins shadowing her as well. An ethereal cat-and-mouse game ensues, with life — and death — hanging in the balance . . .